I0710048

Bretts Mountain *Book 1*

Copyright © [2024] by **Sandra K Lee**

Bretts Mountain
Book 1

Author: Sandra K Lee

To obtain something you never had
You have to do something you never did

To hold onto something you will cherish forever
You must give something in return

To walk holding hands with someone you love
You must show love

To stay with someone through life forever
You have found your soul mate

Author: Sandra K Lee

INTRODUCTION

Benson Carver made his plans to destroy Dominguez Tally—the man who killed his brother in a fit of rage and jealousy.

There are more ways than one to destroy a man. Watching your child suffer in pain, knowing there is nothing a father can do about it, will drive a man insane. I will cause much pain and grief for Catherine, his daughter. More pain than Dominguez ever thought possible, and he will watch!

After all the hurt and humiliation Catherine can endure without dying, then I will torture Dominguez until his death.

~

A murder on Lovers Lane had the authorities puzzled—no clues, except for the woman who disappeared into the cold winter night. They must find her to unravel the mystery of the horrific crime.

Little Matthew

Spur Lacy, Oklahoma: There were three murders committed On Lovers Lane.

Matt's big sister, fourteen-year-old Creitta, kept an eye on him while their mother worked at 'The Fine Arts Museum.' Six-year-old Matt wasn't supposed to be outside while his mom was away, but Creitta was washing her hair, getting all gussied up for her boyfriend, so he decided to ride his bike up the lane from his house.

Although Matt knew to avoid strange cars and strangers, when he saw the beautiful little car, he had to investigate. He peeped inside, and what he saw caused him to almost fall off his bike.

He had to tell the police and right now!

He knew this was an emergency and had to tell someone fast! He peddled his bike as quickly as possible.

Matt headed to town, although it was three miles to the police station.

His face was ashen when he reached the police station.

What he saw was unbelievable, just too horrifying for his age.

"Help me, someone, please!" his voice was just above a whisper.

Lieutenant Markham shuffled his papers. "Hold on there, young fellow. Sit down there on the bench until I finish these reports. It's been a long day, so please be patient, okay?"

"I can't hold on, Sir. The man looks dead. He's all bloody and stuff. There's blood on the windshield all over the place. You just gotta see. It's really bad!"

"What's your name, son?" the lieutenant asked.

Matt was crying and looked scared. "My name is Matt, Sir, Matthew Drake," his voice trembling.

"Let's go over what you saw again. You sure there's a dead man?" The lieutenant asked, looking irritated. Matt knew he must make him understand that what he saw was real.

"I was riding my bike up the lane and found a car with a man in it. The car smelled like a dead rabbit. I looked inside, and this man was bloody and stuff. I hurried here to tell you."

Lieutenant Markham didn't believe Matt; he figured it was just another kid wanting attention, but he grinned. "Well, I guess I better have a look. Where do you live, Matthew?"

The lieutenant treated him as his dad had when he didn't believe him. Matt frowned and shrank down in his chair.

In a demanding voice, the lieutenant said. "Young man, I must have your father and mother's name."

Matt sat up straight and paid attention.

"My father was Colonel Charles Drake, Sir. My mom is Celine Drake. I live at 205 Mountain View Estates."

"You're Colonel Drake's son? He was a highly decorated soldier. We owe him a lot. Where is your mother?"

Matt replied. "She's at work, but my sister's at home."

Then Matt, getting aggravated, said. "Sir, the man needs you. I can show you where he is."

The lieutenant grinned, still unsure that he believed Matt's story, so he went along to make young Matt feel important, just like his dad.

"Okay, let's go. You show me this car, then we call your mother."

Matt sat straight in the police cruiser and thought; *the lieutenant would believe me when he saw the car, that's for sure, and I'd be famous just like my dad!*

When the lieutenant saw the car, he felt like his hair crawled. "Wow, what a mess, Matthew. You stay in the car. Don't get out."

The lieutenant was well aware; Matthew was no ordinary six-year-old. He was brilliant, just like his father. He knew to report the man in the car and did it.

"This is Lieutenant Markham. Send the Coroner and an ambulance to Lovers' Lane, just past Mountain View Estates. Also, send the homicide detective. Then see if you can locate Mrs. Celine Drake at the Fine Arts Museum." he told the dispatcher.

I'm going to be here for quite some time. I wonder just how much the kid saw. After her husband's death, Mrs. Drake does very well for herself; she owns and operates 'The Fine Arts Museum,' but raising two children alone must be challenging, the lieutenant pondered.

The lieutenant leaned over the unfortunate man in the BMW. *I never adjust to seeing death stare me in the face. I want to close his eyes to the scenario. Why would someone kill a man in this manner,* he wondered. *Someone sliced the man's face and battered his body as if beaten by a ball bat. It looks like an animal attack on his body, too.*

Detective Robbie Rommeria was meticulous not to disturb any evidence but was like the lieutenant; it sure looked like an animal had been in the car.

"Lieutenant, someone gouged him with a knife. I don't believe that is animal bites. We have one weird killer on our hands. This murder is the worst I've witnessed, and I've been on the force for over thirty years. I'll say one thing: this will be hard to solve," the detective said.

The detective began gagging and headed for the bushes away from the scene.

"Lieutenant, I think we need to scour this area. "It doesn't look like the victim got out of his car; there aren't any footprints because the ground is frozen solid.

Robbie went back to the cruiser to speak with Matthew. Son, when you first came here, did you see another automobile? Think hard, son. It is very important."

"No, Sir. I didn't see anything else. I was scared. I was afraid they might kill me, too. I thought they might be Iraqis. They killed my daddy. I thought they might be coming for me too."

Detective Robbie regretted asking the boy. He opened the car door and held the frightened child. "Son, listen to me. There are no Iraqis here in America that would harm you. Colonel Drake would be very proud of you if he were here. Bravely, you went for help when you knew you couldn't do anything for the man. That was a good thing. You're a trouper, Matthew." Robbie felt the child begin to calm down.

"I want to be a detective, just like you, when I grow up. Do you think my daddy would mind if I don't become a military man?"

"No, Matthew, I don't believe he would mind. It takes a lot of us good guys over here, too. I don't think your daddy would mind at all, and who knows," Robbie laughed. "You might make a better detective than me."

Matthew stood tall, proud, as he answered. "You think so? I have to tell my mom about this. She won't believe it. She thinks I'm just a kid."

The mutilated dead man had no identification, and there were no clues. The Detective sent for Police dogs to search for other victims.

Lieutenant Markham commented. "The killers were interrupted before they finished."

"I believe you are right. Hey, let's see what clues we can find before the Feds get here," the detective stated.

"Hey guys, here is another woman, but she's alive!" One policeman yelled.

"Stay beside the cruiser, ma'am; we will get you to a hospital." Detective Rommeria spoke softly.

The police searched diligently for clues as the lady disappeared into the underbrush.

"A crime scene like this is hard to work, but it's near impossible in the dark. Let's take what clues we have back to the station and come back tomorrow," the detective said.

"I don't understand why that lady left, but maybe she has amnesia or is scared," the detective stated.

"That woman won't get very far tonight. Have you seen her before?" Lieutenant Markham asked the detective.

"No, but I knew the other two women we found dead."

"She must be visiting with someone here. She isn't from this area. I know everyone in this town," the detective stated.

"Lieutenant, did you notice the size of the woman? I bet she didn't weigh one hundred pounds soaking wet."

"Yes, I did. She won't live very long if she doesn't find shelter."

"Tomorrow is a new day, Lieutenant. She won't be hard to locate." The detective exhaled.

The lieutenant became more anxious as the moments ticked away.

It was nearly dark when Lieutenant Markham heard that Mrs. Celine Drake was missing.

The dispatcher informed the lieutenant. "I spoke with Crietta, Matthew's sister, who informed us that her mother and friend, Anita Bowman, left the Fine Arts Museum four hours ago. Crietta began to worry even before I contacted her. She said her mother was always home after jogging for about an hour. Also, she asked if she could take her brother home."

The exhausted lieutenant muttered to the dispatcher when he became aware of Mrs. Drake. "Just my luck, another kid coming up here. Okay, send him home with her. We found some particles of women's clothing just down the embankment from the car."

Crietta came on the scene to get her brother, she said. "Come on, Mattie, you don't need to be here."

When she saw the article Markham held, she gasped.

"That's my mom's shawl! She wore it to work this morning." She turned ghostly and leaned against the cruiser.

"Hold on, little lady, while I get some help up here." The lieutenant caught her as she fell.

"Dispatcher, send child services up here, stat! We have a huge problem."

"Stay here with your brother; we don't know who is out there!" The lieutenant told Crietta as he helped her inside the police cruiser.

The lieutenant stayed with the children until Mrs. Pennegraph arrived.

I'm thankful child services are here, and she brought sister Mary. I will need a nun before this night is over, Markham thought.

Sister Mary, please take these children to St Joseph's. Keep them away from here. Their mother may somehow be involved."

The Lieutenant heard Robbie swear under his breath.

"What have you found down there, Robbie?"

"You might want to look. The dogs have discovered two mutilated bodies and found more bits of clothing. It looks like a massacre!" Robbie answered.

What had happened in the quiet afternoon of the little mountain town, Spur Lacy?

Police Officers could hardly work the scene, for being sick and taken aback at such a horrific murder.

"Everybody spread out, comb this area like you were looking for a diamond on your lawn. I will get more people to help find things we may have overlooked." Markham shouted.

"Lieutenant, wait," Robbie said. "More people would destroy evidence. What do you say, we wait until morning for that?" The detective suggested.

"I see what you mean. We must be careful, but hurry, or the feds will arrive before we finish our investigation," Markham stated.

"Have you noticed those deer tracks? Look how they go in circles. That's odd. I'm no hunter, but they stayed for some time." The lieutenant suggested.

"True, but I believe the deer were just nosy. For some reason, they go toward sounds and car lights," Markham pondered.

"Maybe Matthew came up, scared off the killer, and the deer came in after the boy left for the station,"

"Yeah, maybe. It's getting dark, and it is difficult to find anything else." Markham stated.

"Here. Lieutenant, I have two flashlights and other officers are getting theirs from their cruisers. It will help us see the trail. We don't want the site to get cold until we collect what is needed. It may take longer, but it could prove productive." The officer suggested.

"Watch your footing; the undergrowth is slippery, and the grade sloped. I don't want to lose you in here."

The detective snickered.

"You're trying to say I'm getting old, huh? Well, let me tell you something, Robbie Rommeria. The day you have to babysit me is when I quit and move to that retirement village down on the Ivory Coast."

They both laughed heartedly.

They were doing everything they could to break the monotony of the horrible scene. "What will we find around the next tree branch? This scene is simply barbarism," the lieutenant exhaled.

Both men were shaking; both had their guns drawn. They didn't know who may be lurking in the underbrush.

Wildcats and bears are in these woods; they follow the scent of blood, and there is plenty of that.

Dogs yelped farther down the draw. Slowly, the men eased on down the lane. Robbie went to the right of a brush pile while the lieutenant went left.

Both men whispered a little prayer that they wouldn't find anything else tonight.

Maybe the killer, now that would be great! They both would like to put a big hole right between his eyes.

The Mountain Man

Everything seemed ghastly—when the lady realized she was lost and in unfamiliar surroundings.

The highway is close, she thought.

She found it impossible to know where she entered the forest because of its density.

What happened to me? She thought.

The tree branches screeched. "I heard trees could talk if you'd listen. What are you saying to me? Trees, why can't you tell me where I am? I'm scared, hungry, and dirty," she shouted, then giggled to think such a preposterous thing.

Her fingers were cold from the icy wind.

She spent one night in these woods, and it looked like she would again tonight.

Why am I running in the woods? Oh, I remember, that cop had handcuffs. I can't remember my name. Now, that is something to worry about! She thought.

It was nearly dark as she made her a bed of leaves.

What's that sound? Something is grunting like a pig. She thought.

-- That's no pig -- it's a bear – Egad – and it's coming up the hill toward me. She thought *if I stood still, maybe it would leave!*

Animals can smell fear from a person. Well, it's not Clive Christians #1 that he smells that on me.

She closed her eyes to the scenario of being eaten by a bear.

The undergrowth crunched loudly, not far from where she stood.

As she opened her eyes to run, something grabbed her from behind.

She started to scream, but a large hand clamped her mouth shut.

-- She fainted --

It was dark in the room when she awoke.

A massive fireplace burned brightly, and she was warm.

An ewer of water sat on a table near the door, and a towel hung on a rack above it.

Near the walk-in closet, there was a chamber pot.

"Where in blue blazes am I?" she whispered. "I wonder who found me? Being here frightens me almost as much as being in the woods."

The lady swung her legs off the bed and stood.

Now, I need to get my thoughts straight before whoever brought me here returns. The lady thought, *I remember people were demanding my name, where I was from, and who was the dead man in the car. Everything was so loud. The people were obnoxious and spoke cruelly."*

When she ran her fingers through her hair, her scalp felt sore. She had a big lump on her head, and her nose felt broken. Her body hurt all over. Her eyes were swollen, and she could hardly see.

"Something else, why was I in the woods to start with? I don't remember anything about my past after someone hit me with a gun butt," she said aloud and then shivered.

She could only squinch her eyes open.

I remember that someone lifted me from a deep hole. I must have amnesia! The unfortunate lady thought.

The drapes in the room were floor-length, curving gracefully at the bottom. *How beautiful!* She thought *they are gold, trimmed with green, a gorgeous color combination, with green ropes to hold them open for the sunlight.*

It began to snow, and the wind howled. *I am fortunate someone found me.*

The lady walked to the large window and looked outside. *I see a smaller building in the back, made of brick and logs. It appears like another part of this house, but not connected. Maybe it's for the ranch hands, a shed, or could be a meat locker.*

An album lay on the desk near the window. Being curious, the lady opened it. There was a picture of a man, a woman, and two children.

The woman was light-skinned, blond, and very beautiful. The man had dark skin, dark hair, and green eyes, a handsome couple. The children were small, with the same blond hair as the woman's but copper-toned skin. The names on the back of the pictures were Brett and Margo. The photo of a boy and girl had an inscription on the back that read, 'Laura and Larry,' On their eighth birthday.

There were many pictures in the mauve-colored family album: grandmothers, grandfathers, aunts and uncles. Some had dark skin of Indian descent; others were light-skinned, possibly Caucasian. It looked like many family connections with different backgrounds and ethics.

She pondered, *I'm in a house where a family lives, so I am safe.*

Knock, knock, "Are you decent? May I come in?" the lady pulled the coverlet up under her chin and waited.

"Yes, I'm decent, come in."

She realized that she wore a long tee shirt and giant sweatpants. I wonder where my clothes are?

"My name is Brett Canterfield. I found you in the woods, nearly frozen to death. Are you okay?"

The lady nodded as he sat in the chair next to the bed.

"My cook is bringing you some warm soup. She washed your clothes; they should be dry soon. She said you have many bruises. She will doctor them for you if you wish."

This man is the husband in the album, she pondered.

"Your eye is black. Maria will bring you an ice pack to help with the swelling. How did you get out this far? It's miles to the nearest road, and you could have died on a day like this."

He grinned as he eyed her closely, seemingly more concerned for her welfare than who she was.

"I was walking in the woods and didn't realize how far I had walked. Then, there was this massive bear. I thought he would eat me alive! I suppose I panicked!"

He roared with laughter. "I don't think you are on Charlie's menu today. He had already eaten, and you're too small for a mouthful anyway."

The lady felt out of her league and didn't know how to react, so she said, "Okay, he's your bear?"

With a twisted grin, he said, "Charlie is nobody's bear. I found him as a cub. Hunters killed his mother, and I found no other cubs, so I brought him home. I bought the land as far as the eye can see so there won't be hunters within miles of Charlie. I let people hunt for food, but not for trophies. I will speak with you after you have rested and eaten."

Without another word, Brett walked out the door.

He didn't ask my name, which is good. What will I say when he starts asking questions? I don't know if I am a murderer, a housewife, or a runaway! I could never take someone's life, but why did the police want to arrest me? The lady pondered.

When Maria opened the door, the lady jumped, ready to run.

"I didn't mean to startle you. May I come in? I brought you some soup and a sandwich."

"Yes, do come in."

The lady sat beside the bed. The food smelled delicious, and a long-stem yellow rose lay on the tray to compliment it.

Maria grinned, "I will bring you some clothes shortly. The ones you wore are in bad condition. I found some things of Margo's that look your size. When you have rested, I will tend to your bruises if you like. That eye will be black for some time."

"If I had some clothes, I could come to the kitchen for food. I don't want to be a bother," the lady stated.

Maria gave her a stern, frightening look and stated sharply. "Mr. Canterfield would never allow a guest in your condition to climb stairs. He would be angry with me for even suggesting something like that! Now, eat your food before it gets cold. I'll be back later."

The lady stared as Maria closed the door. Click, she locked the door!

The bewildered, lost lady considered her surroundings. The bedroom is massive. The ceiling is made of beautiful logs, honed out just right to fit precisely together and polished to the max. That painting above the fireplace is exceptionally gorgeous! The lady posing in a dark green silk velvet dress is beautiful. She's the lady in the album. With the fedora she's wearing, she looks like she stepped out of Vogue magazine. The fireplace is magnificent and massive; the logs are gas, not natural wood. The carved rock made the mantle exquisite, with stones reaching the twenty-foot ceiling.

The lady looked out the window and believed the house to be a three-story, and this was the top floor. *I'd love to see the rest of the house. How can Brett Canterfield afford a home like this? It would be my luck that he's some notorious gangster. I might never be allowed to leave. I had better stop these thoughts, or I would be more scared than I am already. I wonder if I am poor. Oh well, I will find out in the future.* The lady thought as sleep overcame her.

Somewhere in her dream, she was running and running. I have to get away! Before he puts me in jail, I can't remember who I am, so whom shall I call? Everyone is a stranger. I can't run any faster; he's catching up to me. There's that bear, I hope he eats that cop, and then he can't arrest me. I need somebody to please help me! Somewhere, she could hear someone screaming.

Brett was beside her bed in a flash.

"What's wrong, little one? Did you hear something, or was it a nightmare?" he held her tightly.

"I heard someone screaming. I must have been dreaming, but it seemed so real, I …

"Well, you are okay now," Brett interrupted. "I will sit by the fire until you go back to sleep. Try to get some sleep. Rest is what heals the body and mind."

"Thank you, you are very kind," the lady whispers in a yawn.

"I put you in this room because it has a spectacular view. My room is just two doors down on the left," Brett reflected. "My mother did the decor in here when she visited me."

She wanted to ask who was in the portrait but didn't want him to think her too inquisitive.

"Mother enjoyed it here, and this is her room. A person can see the slope from the window, and the stream below is a fantastic scene in the summertime."

Fascinated by the acknowledgment of his mother, the lady could envision him being kind and loving. A man who speaks well of his mother is a man who would care for his family immensely. His mother raised him well.

"Don't be frightened if you awake and find me here. I will protect you while you sleep."

That was a strange thing to say; he probably thinks I'm still scared because of the bear. Good 'old Charlie the bear. She couldn't help but giggle softly.

How could harm come to anyone in a big house with all the security? The heavy doors have locks. It's like a sanctuary. I hope the snow gets so deep tomorrow that the police from Spur Lacy can't come up the Mountain. I need to obtain information about myself before they take me to jail. Well, I'm sweating again; that happens every time I think of being incarcerated.

Gently, Brett said. "Goodnight, Lady, go to sleep. I need my rest, too, and tomorrow is a new day."

The lady was alone when she awoke. Sometime in the night, Brett had left the room.

The Discussion

"**M**aria, do you see the lady as a threat? I find it strange for someone to be on this mountain. She had a terrible ordeal in the woods; even so, I don't like a total stranger wandering around in my home. When you took her breakfast, did you lock the door? Last night, she had a nightmare, so I slept by the fireplace. I heard someone scream. I don't know if it belonged to that lady or if it came from outside. It was dark when I brought her here, so I don't believe anyone saw me. That would be dangerous." Brett stated.

Maria recognized the agony on Bretts' face.

"I absolutely locked the door. Please don't get involved until you find out more." Maria warned.

I hope he doesn't let another woman become a part of his life too soon. Maria shuffled her feet as she left the room, a habit when disturbed.

A blue-eyed blond, also a beauty, was the apple of Bretts' eye. He loved her deeply, but why did she break his heart and spirit with her angry retaliation? He hadn't bought the BMW when she said, 'I want it right away!' He was on a cattle drive that week and couldn't take time away from the herd. Whatever Margo wanted, she had to have instantly. I don't understand why she did those horrible things. Margo was selfish and denied me the joy of hearing my grandchildren's laughter or spending time with them. My daughter couldn't control her temper.

It had been ten years since Maria slept soundly. She was always aware of eerie sounds, like the wind rustling leaves or a coyote yelp.

It is not known if she's out there somewhere.

The next day, the mysterious lady dressed in the clothes Maria had brought her. They fit perfectly, and she wondered if they belonged to Margo. The skirt was red satin with sequels, and the blouse was a darker red with puff sleeves. She wears the finest of clothes and lives in this extravagant home.

Mr. Canterfield's wife is exceedingly pampered. I wonder where she and the children are. Maybe Maria will tell me, the lady thought.

"Good morning. I hope you slept well," Brett grinned. He was clean-shaven, and his hair well-groomed.

"Oh, yes, quite well, sir." she stammered; looking into his gorgeous green eyes, she tried to speak but stuttered. "I, I wi will leave as soon as I ca can get down the mountain."

He laughed, "Well, it will be weeks before the road is passable, and by then, we may be old friends."

She swallowed, backed away, and turned to the window. "Have you fed Charlie yet? I was hoping I could help you feed him."

"Stay away from Charlie. He is a wild animal; one never knows when an animal may turn ugly.

With that, he asked her if she was ready for breakfast.

"I am famished, but I didn't want to be a bother to you."

"I will send Maria up," he answered, glancing at her as he exited the room.

She stood, ready to leave, but click-the door locked again.

What is going on here? I wonder if I can find an escape route if I need to.

The window -- how far to the ground? There's a roof just below that could be my way out. With that thought, she shoved hard against the window to raise it, but to no avail.

Maria climbed the stairs, her back hurt from an injury, when she saved Brett from being killed by Charlie.

I don't know what we would have done without Latte, our friend and private investigator who helped me and Brett, she pondered.

Brett asked her to come for a few weeks. The change in Margo, his wife, seemed uncanny, so he turned to her mother for help. That week, everything turned nasty.

"So here I am," Maria grunted.

____ Here on Margo's Mountain! ____ Maria shivered.

"Here is your breakfast, Missy."

Maria sat the food tray down, which sported another newly cut rose.

"Why the rose every time you bring a tray? The lady asked.

Not even a grin. This woman makes my skin crawl with her rigid attitude. The lady thought.

"The master of this house says to start the day with a beautiful setting, which makes the day more appreciative. Something new and alive is something very striking."

Then, with piercing eyes, she asked, "Don't you agree?"

"I suppose. It is a lovely rose, but where does he get roses in the dead of winter?"

Come on, Maria, talk to me! The lady thought.

"He has a garden in the basement. He raises flowers and vegetables year-round. It's his hobby. He doesn't go out with the herds until spring. The hired hands take care of the cattle. When the weather breaks, he's back in the fields, the lifestyle he loves. His father, before him, kept the ranch in excellent shape, but he didn't raise range cattle. Since his father's death, Brett expanded it considerably."

Then Maria shivered; something caused her to be afraid, cold, and distant.

"The Master has only lovely things around him," she commented.

__ *creepy* __ the lady thought. *Really creepy!*

Maria left before the lady could ask why the door must stay locked.

The lady wondered what Brett and Maria were afraid of.

Having the day to herself, the little lady decided to make the best of it. She found a pen and paper and began to post things she remembered.

There was a huge knot on her head. She had bruises everywhere. Her body was sore and stiff, and she had a black eye. "Well, it looks a little green," she giggled aloud.

She got hit by a gun butt, but she couldn't remember who did it.

The man was in a BMW—a fast car. I don't know that man or where this occurred. There was a hole. Was it dug for a grave? My grave? It was deep, muddy, cold, and she was in it.

The man was Bloody and those cuts! It was an awful, gruesome death for any man.

Frustrated, she threw down the pad.

I must leave here and find out who I am. I don't know where to start! The police wanted to arrest me, so I could not go to them. Maybe someone is searching for me, friends, or a husband or children -- Oh, God, What if I have children? After posting these things, she felt helpless.

It felt stuffy, enclosed in the room, and hard to breathe, or was it her scrambled nerves? She wasn't sure of anything anymore.

"Mr. Canterfield!" she yelled, banging on the thick wood door. "I need out of here, please! Just let me come down to the living area, please! I mean, you no harm. Mr. Canterfield!" She began sobbing uncontrollably.

Maria entered quickly. "No more of that yelling or crying, do you hear me? No more!" her face was distorted, and she seemed angry.

"What is going on? Why am I locked up? I can't go anywhere." Maria looked strangely at her, trying to control her emotions.

"Look, you must stay in here. There are things you don't know, so, for your sake, stay in this room."

The lady ran past Maria and hurried down the stairs, paying no attention to where she ran. She just wanted to escape Maria's proximity.

She scampered into the great room and ran impetuously into Brett.

"What are you doing down here? Didn't Maria tell you to stay in your room? I am not ready to explain why, but you are in danger." He snarled.

Big blubbery tears began to fall, and she sank to the floor. Brett placed his arm around her shoulder, making her cry harder.

He held her close as she tried to control her tears.

"Lady, you must understand this is my home, and you are an uninvited guest. We need to talk about why you were on my mountain, and soon. You must stay in your room without I'm beside you. I will not explain, but you will honor my wishes -- Do I make myself clear?"

"Yes, I understand. I am sorry for intruding on you. I will leave soon, but please, don't lock me in that room!"

Then he said the strangest thing. "I am not locking you in to be cruel. I am locking danger away from you."

The lady hoped he would understand without her telling him that someone buried her alive! That's what happened, and someone had found her. Oh my God! She remembered and began to tremble.

As Brett peered into her eyes, he felt he could see into the depths of her soul.

"Since you're already down here, come into the kitchen while I make coffee. What do you drink, coffee, soda, juice, or something else?"

The big hand on her arm felt firm but comforting as he led her to the island in the kitchen.

"Coffee would be nice. I haven't had any today. When Maria brought my meals, she always brought milk and juice, but never coffee." *Now, why did I say that? I don't know if I like coffee or not,* she thought.

Trying to make the conversation uncomplicated, he began messing around with the coffee pot.

She slid off her stool and took the pot from him. "How much water do you use?" she asked.

"That's okay, just sit and relax," he replied, showing straight white teeth.

His fingers brushed her hand softly. They stared into each other's eyes, feeling like a lightning bolt had shot through them. He cleared his throat and said. "Lady, you could be dangerous to me."

While they enjoyed their coffee, he turned on the TV to hear the local evening news.

The lady hoped the news was over, but there was a 'news break.'

"We just received news of a bizarre death four days ago. Mr. Max Robertos, CEO of a major corporation, was found dead on Lovers' Lane. His brutally battered body was still inside his car. We are here now with Chief of Police Perry Davis.

"It's an ongoing investigation. There isn't much we can say until we finish putting the pieces together," the chief stated.

"Has his wife been notified? I didn't hear you say anything about his family." The reporter asked.

"We haven't located his wife. We think she may be out of town. We will keep you updated," the chief stated.

News reporter Arlene Gray wasn't ready to cut him loose, not just yet.

"Are you looking at her as a suspect?"

The chief looked at the camera and declared. "There are no suspects yet. Please excuse me. I have work to do."

The news lady summed it up. "Well, this is all we have right now. We will keep you updated as news of this murder develops."

Brett commented. "Never know what's going to happen anymore. Poor guy probably didn't know what hit him."

The little lady grinned. Thankful he didn't connect her to the dead man. What was she thinking? Maybe she is that man's wife. – Maybe she killed him. – Oh, my!

"I will walk you back to your room now. It's time to get some shut-eye. Pay no attention to any out-of-the-ordinary noises, okay? "Don't leave your room to investigate, understand, not inside the house or outside," Brett stated.

The lady looked up at the handsome man and said. "Have a nice evening, sir."

He bowed, saying. "You also, my lady."

There must be a phone in this house, although I didn't see one while downstairs. If I can convince Mr. Canterfield to let me lock the bedroom door while he and Maria are away, I will gain entrance to other parts of the house. Maria is going to the store tomorrow, and Brett will be out with Charlie; that's when I will take my chances, the lost lady schemed.

The next morning, Maria unlocked the door.

The lady grinned and then said in the most likable voice. "Good morning, Maria; getting to the store today will be a task. The snow is still coming down by the buckets."

"Not today. I would get stuck out there somewhere and freeze to death. The horses can't even get through in this kind of weather. There's five feet of snow, and the drifts are deeper."

"Maria, would you please send Mr. Canterfield to my room? The lady asked. "I need to speak with him."

"Absolutely not! Stay away from him!" she snapped.

"Maria, where is his family? I saw their pictures, but where are his wife and kids?"

Tension was extremely high in the room.

"That's no concern of yours. Please do yourself a favor. Mr. Canterfield's family is on vacation. Please don't ask him about them, either, or you will be most regretful," Maria lowered her head as tears fell down her cheeks. "I will ask him to come up, but you stay quiet about his family, Missy."

Brett entered her room shortly after dinner.

"Mr. Canterfield, may I please have the key to my room? I have this fear of being burned alive! I would feel much safer. I will stay in my room and keep the door locked. Honest Indian," she said, crossing her heart with her finger.

Brett went straight to the point: "I don't know anything about you, and I don't want to be awakened by a stranger in the middle of the night and scared half to death. By the way, what is your name, and where did you come from?".

She felt cornered. "Okay, let's see if this makes sense to you. I don't know."

"You don't know what?" a blank stare now on his face.

"Well, I had a nasty fall, and I lost my memory. That's why you found me in your woods. I don't know how I got there or where I came from."

"You can't be serious!" he jested.

"Oh, but I am very serious."

He almost laughed. "This is ridiculous."

The unfortunate woman lowered her head and shrugged her shoulders.

"Sometimes, I'm not sure when, but I was buried alive. I vaguely remember hands pulling me from a deep pit, and you know the rest: you found me." She answered as tears fell down her cheeks.

He wiped the tears away, then let out a whistle. "What are you planning to do?"

I just want to fall in those strong arms and let you protect me. The lady thought but shivered instead.

"Well, I thought about calling that news reporter to see if there was a missing person, then I would ask for the description of the absent wife. Maybe I'm the missing wife."

Brett paced the floor. "Hold on there, Sherlock, if what you say is accurate, someone wants you dead in the worst way. You have no idea about your enemies. You have nothing to go on at all. It sounds like a fairy tale, but in real life, you best pay attention and try to remember any detail, no matter how small. I will help you in any way possible. Before you begin to dig and let people know you're alive, let my private investigator check into all this. Never take chances when your life is at stake. Don't get hasty. Latte knows all the angles; that's his job, and I pay him well. Will this be agreeable?"

"Oh yes, it's very agreeable. Will I meet with Mr. Lattermar today?"

Brett asked. "Do you know any part of your name?"

"I don't have a clue. It's all a blank," the lady said.

"Well, yes. Right now, you need rest, and sleep will do wonders. You have nothing to fear here as long as your door stays locked. Understand?"

"Yes, I understand! Maria told me not to ask you anything, and I know she wants to protect you from something, but there are some things I'd like to know. May I ask a few sensitive, or maybe private, questions? If they offend you, I'm sorry."

The look on his face suggested she choose her questions carefully.

"What do you want to discuss?"

"First of all, what is so dangerous in this house? Why am I locked in, and why is Maria so protective of you? You are a grown man, and I would think very capable of caring for yourself."

--- Whew, just look at those ripples --- geez --- the lady became highly excited by his physique, making it hard to concentrate.

He straightened his necktie, then turned his back to her.

"Lady, whoever you are, you have no right asking questions about my household and none whatsoever why Maria is so protective, but I will tell you why Maria is so protective; she's my wife's mother, and I give her that right. On several occasions, she put her life on the line for me. Sometime in the future, when I know you can handle the answers, I will tell you about the dark secrets of my home, but until then, do not bring this matter up to me again!"

Brett was stern; she could tell he was not a man to negotiate.

The next day, Brett dialed Ramond Lattermar's office.

"I need to speak with Romond Lattermar, please." My name is Brett Canterfield.

The receptionist replied. "He's not in at the moment. I'll have him call you when he returns."

"Thank you." Brett was in a hurry to speak with Latte without delay, but he remembered what Latte always said. 'Never hurry, or you'll miss the most important article.'

The receptionist replied. "Hold on a moment. I believe he just came in."

Brett was anxious; by the time Latte answered, he was sweating.

"Brett, me boy! What can I do fer ya?"

"I need something done, but very discretely, without any questions. I have a lady staying in my home. She cannot remember her name or where she came from. She's a mess right now. I can't go into detail on the telephone, but if you could drop by, I will make it worthwhile."

"Me, man! You can count on me, but I don't think the roads will be open for another two or three weeks. Will you still be interested?"

"Absolutely! I won't let her out of my sight. I will be interested, should it take all winter," Brett stressed. "I will visit the city when the road is passable. It's time I did a little roaming, if you know what I mean," Brett chuckled.

"You old rascal, I can't believe you will come off that mountain, even for party time! If you can't, I can go up there. Tell Maria I loved those cookies she made. They were the best."

Latte remembered the last time he visited Bretts Mountain. Maria had made cookies that day. He held her in his arms as she cried her eyes out.

He would ask her to be his wife if she would have him. Now, that would make Brett a happy man. *How long has it been since I was on the mountain, nine, maybe ten years? It has been a long time since that horrible tragedy,* Latte thought.

Brett and Maria are such good people. Where did he meet this strange lady? Brett is interested in a woman, ha! It has to be something more than affection, but what? He adored his wife; this is interesting.

Now, I can concentrate on something other than the case I've been working on. The one I know I can't possibly win and hope I don't. The man has money, and I tried to explain that he was taking a considerable risk, taking his ex-wife to court, but he wouldn't listen. The judge doesn't give custody of the three minor children to a heel like him.

The man left his wife for another woman, and he wasn't good to her or their kids. He was always a worthless piece of dung. Oh well, but that's another case.

I'm tired. I need to rest. If Maria took me as her husband, I would take an extended vacation with her on my arm, sipping on a Mai Tai or martini; That would be heavenly!

I don't believe she would leave Brett for that length of time. She adores him, and he loves her dearly. It's a good relationship, an unbelievable one at best. He is very attached to his mother-in-law.

Dratz, though! That leaves me out in the cold, he thought, snickering.

Thinking about Maria, Latte decided to call Brett.

"Brett, how much snow do you have on your mountain? I have a case pending, but if I could get over the Mountain pass, I could start on the quest you asked."

"Listen, Lattermar, there's too much snow. It's impassable, and I don't want you to start up the Mountain and get stuck in the drifts. Then I would have to be out in this crazy weather to rescue you. What I need can wait until the weather breaks. It's important but not drastic enough to put you in harm's way."

"Okay, Brett, but to ease my curiosity, where did you meet the woman in question, and furthermore, why are you so interested in her? I haven't heard you speak of a woman since that terrible episode at your ranch. By the way, don't you think Maria and I would make a good couple?" Latte questioned.

"Lattermar, I don't think so. Without Maria, I couldn't survive, and besides, she wouldn't want to look at your old ugly face every day," Brett laughed.

"Just what I thought you'd say. I'll be there soon."

"Maria, I've been in this room for nearly two weeks. Don't you think I could go outside for a while? The snow has let up, and the sun is melting the ice. I would be safe with you, wouldn't I?" The lady pled.

"I can't do that without Brett's okay." She grunted. "Besides, I have to clean up the house out back. I've let it go too long as it is. That takes all day and sometimes two."

Well, shoot me! That didn't work again! The lady thought.

"I could help you clean. It wouldn't take long with two people working on it." She said.

Maria stood frozen. "Never go near that cabin at any time, you hear me, girl? That is off-limits to anyone but me. Brett doesn't go there either. Not anymore."

The lady thought that Maria looked angry, or was that a hurt feeling I had captured? It seems she can intermingle her looks from anger to grief almost at the same time,

What is it with that small cottage in the back where no one ever goes? Why must she clean it?? That cabin activates my curiosity, the lost lady ponders.

What's with this big old log home? I wonder if they have ghosts or a sasquatch hidden away. It's just too mystic, but Mr. Canterfield told me he would explain when the time was right.

I must be patient and wait, but for how long? Things here are weird.

I have enough to worry about without thinking of ghosts or the notorious Yati. She shivered with that thought.

Oh, my word! Ghosts!

Back On Lovers Lane

Celine Drake was a very respected and wealthy woman, the sole owner of 'The Fine Arts Museum,' she was in her early forties and beautiful, but now she was unrecognizable. With her face slashed and her body cut all over. What had happened to her?

Anita Bowman and Celine Drake became best friends over the years. Anita is beautiful, rich, and also a widow. Where you saw one, the other was near. Anita had no children. She enjoyed the love of Celine's children. She considered Celine to be her sister.

The man in the car was Mister Max Robertos. It wasn't a robbery because his money was still in his wallet, and his expensive Rolex was still on his wrist. The car was a new BMW. The car's location was a mile up the lane in the dense woods. No one could have seen anything from the street.

Lieutenant Markham remarked: "I'm hoping we can keep the news media away for a time; we don't need them or the public tromping around right now. They destroy too much evidence. I want this area secured; I don't want anyone inside the perimeter. I want a man posted, twenty-four-seven until further notice. Those children lost their father and now their mother, too. I need to get to St. Joseph and see if I can help them. What a tragedy."

When Lieutenant Markham walked into the church, he saw the children on the kneelers praying to Mother Mary. His heart broke. Oh God, what can I say to these children?

Matthew and Creitta saw Lieutenant Markham at the same time and ran to him. When Matthew saw the lieutenant's eyes, he stared at the floor and straightened his back, trying to be strong for his sister.

"Did you find anyone else? Did you find my mom?" Creitta sobbed.

"I'm not sure. I want you both to stay here with Sister Mary tonight. I'll return in the morning; we should know something by then. Sister Mary, may I please speak with you for a moment?"

The Lieutenant led the Nun to the front of the church. He then turned to Sister Mary and asked, "Did you know Mrs. Drake well?"

"I knew the family well, yes. Why do you ask?" She lowered her head.

"I must locate some of the family for the children," he said with tears in his eyes.

Sister Mary told him that she knew Mrs. Drake had a sister, and she would contact her. The Nun realized they found Celine Drake. She gave a blessing, a silent prayer, and then looked into the lieutenant's face.

Markham nodded and walked away.

Sister Mary returned inside to the table and lit three candles. She would call the Aunt and notify Father Ryan to come to the children.

Name The Lost Lady

The unfortunate lady stopped counting the nights and days; fear constantly surrounded her.

Brett sat in the chair near the window. He studied the lady sitting beside him on the window edge.

"Lady, please call me Brett. It makes me feel old when you call me Mr. Canterfield." He laughed.

She grinned. "Okay, if you wish. What will you call me, hey you? Can you give me a nice name until I know my real one?"

At some point, I must win this lady's trust. Maybe that will help her remember her past. She feels insecure and alone among strangers. It's hard to believe what she's been through.

Had she read my warning sign, Beware Of A Grizzly— No Trespassing: Private Property. I wonder if she would have entered the woods. Brett thought.

"Hmm, I have been thinking about that. I will call you my mother's name. She is called by Little Dove in the Cherokee Indian village. Somehow, you remind me of her. I shall call you Little Dove Two."

"That's a pretty name. It will suit me just fine."

"Little Dove Two it is, then." She looked at him, thinking. *He doesn't look old, maybe a little weather-worn from brutal winters, but old, Nada. There's nothing old about this fine-looking man. There I go again; I must not think about how handsome and refined he looks.*

"How old are you, Brett? I don't think you're much older than I, if any. I hope to find out my age before long." Little Dove Two stated.

"I will be forty-two next month. How old do I look?"

"Oh, about that age, she grinned."

"Well, it's late, and it's time to rest. Oh, by the way, Lattermar will be here in the morning. The roads are passable now, and he wants to start your case before it gets too cold."

"Goodnight, Brett. I will see you in the morning. Sleep well."
He nodded to her and left the room.

He didn't lock the door! Maybe I can sneak out while they sleep and check out this gorgeous place. What would he do should he catch me, throw me out? Little Dove Two snickered.

That's not going to happen. Brett wouldn't throw me out in this weather.

I may as well be brave and challenge my fears. Little Dove two giggled.

Little Dove Two slipped through the door into the large hall when she thought it was safe.

She remembered the location of the kitchen and hurried down the long, winding stairs.

Nightlights glowed on the staircase, down the hall, and in every room.

What on God's green earth was that eerie scream? Where is that scratching coming from? That's a woman. No, that can't be; there's only Maria and myself here. It came from outside. I bet it's a bobcat or some wild animal.

This house has many sounds at night. I think I will go back to my room! -- Right Now! --

Little Dove Two ran back up the stairs, closing her door quickly.

Maybe I don't want to know about this house after all! She propped a chair under the doorknob. *I know that won't stop whatever it is. Okay, now I'm scared. I hear something outside my door, and that knocking. What is that?* She thought, shivering.

Egad! I wish it would go away! Whatever it is, it just hollered. Okay, I'm hiding under my covers.

"Brett! Brett! Somebody, help!" she screamed.

"Are you okay?" Brett asked, touching her shoulder. She screamed at the top of her lungs. He then pulled a shaking, trembling Little Dove Two from under the covers and held her tightly in his arms. "Are you okay?" I think you had a bad dream."

Is he crazy? He must have heard that. I will ask the private investigator tomorrow to take me to a shelter. I don't want to stay here anymore. I've been through enough! Little Dove Two thought.

Lattermar Arrived

"Greetings, lovely lady," he said.

"Hello," Little Dove Two answered.

Lattermar raised his eyebrows, questioning Brett's look of disbelief. "Well, I had to call her something, and it sounded good."

"We call her Little Dove Two," Brett said a little too sharp.

"That is your mother's name, Brett, but call her whatever you please; I need to speak with you, Little Dove Two. Let's see what we can make out of what you remember."

Lattermar had a kind face, a little gray showing around the temples. Not young but still attractive, Little Dove Two reflected.

"Okay, but I don't remember much," she stated.

"Someone pulled me from a hole. I was buried alive, or almost. I don't know how I got here. I don't remember my name or where I came from. That's all I remember."

"Hmm, not much to go on, but I'll give it a shot," Lattermar said, looking stunned.

Brett grinned. "Well, do your best. I can't ask more than that of you."

Lattermar stood to leave, and then he turned to Maria. "Hey, there's my best gal? I haven't forgotten your cookies."

Maria blushed, then grinned. "Come in the kitchen; I might accidentally have a batch stashed away somewhere and maybe a glass of milk to go with them."

"Hmm, Maria, I would ask you to marry me if I weren't afraid that you would say no."

He's serious! Maria thought.

"Why don't you try me, or are you afraid I might say yes." They both laughed like it was some old joke.

They cared deeply for each other.

Everyone gathered in the kitchen to treat themselves to a piece of Maria's famous cookies.

Suddenly, Little Dove Two said. "Mr. Lattermar, could you drop me off at a shelter in town? I've stayed here too long on these folks. It's time for me to move on."

Everyone stopped eating and looked at her as if she had lost her mind. "You are the most unpredictable woman I have ever met. Why would you want to stay in a shelter? There's plenty of room here, and until we know who you are, you are safer here with Maria and me than in a shelter. Whoever tried to bury you could succeed if you're out there in the eye of the public." Brett stated.

"I don't want to be a burden."

Mr. Lattermar slapped the counter as he stood to leave, "Those cookies were delicious as always, Maria, and I thank you, but now I best be on my way. I have lots of paperwork to finish."

Little Dove Two looked at Brett and asked, "Are you sure it's okay for me to stay here? You sure neither of you would mind?"

Please, say leave! After last night, I don't want to stay here. They have been so good to me, took me in like a lost sheep, and gave me shelter, food, and a bed, but I feel something eerie is happening in this house! The lady thought.

Brett made it sound easy. "We don't need to speak of this until we find out where you came from."

But I'm scared! I must conquer my fears again tonight, and that's nearly impossible.

Little Dove Two watched Mr. Lattermar conquer the massive steps that led to his carriage drawn by four horses. She hoped he got off the mountain before dark. She felt there was something dangerous lurking out there in the dark.

Marie flittered around in the kitchen while Brett sat near the window. Little Dove Two felt they were waiting for her to retire.

Well, they will be waiting for a long time. I'm definitely not in a hurry, Little Dove Two thought.

"I like a good Cuban cigar after supper. If you don't need me in the kitchen, Maria, I'll be in the sunroom," Brett grinned.

Maria shook her head. "Take all the time you need."

"May I walk out with you, Brett? I could use some fresh air, and it's too early to retire. The night air might help calm my nerves. Believe me, I'm a little more than anxious."

Brett thought for a few moments. "Yes, you may go to the sunroom as long as I'm with you. Care for a smoke?" He grinned.

"Eu-fooy, that's the grossest thing ever!" she said.

He let out a deep, bellowing laugh.

Brett took her arm and said, "I've had all the cool air I can handle for one night."

Little Dove Two didn't argue because she felt someone was watching.

"Maria, may I speak to you before we retire?" Little Dove Two asked.

"Sure, what is it?" she thought. *She's nice while Brett's around.*

"Did you hear something strange the other night? Sounds of a woman screaming, or maybe a cat of some kind?

Maria gave her a thoughtful look, "No, and you need to get your fears under control. It makes me jumpy when you say you hear strange screams. Old houses make cracking noises like I do sometimes when I bend over too far," she laughed.

The Police Station

"**A** private investigator is now asking questions. It's been four weeks, and I still don't have any clues. What is your opinion, Robbie?" Lieutenant Markham asked, standing by the window looking at the street below.

"Something doesn't feel right. Please send Mr. Lattermar in so I can get on with my day. I can't get anything done with a P.I. hounding me. I know he won't leave until he hammered the answers out of me.

"Mr. Lattermar, the lieutenant will see you now."

Robbie closed the door but remained outside just in case the lieutenant needed him to remove the private investigator bodily. *That would be sweet*, he laughed.

Maybe Lattermar knows something that we don't, Robbie thought.

"Sit down, Mr. Lattermar; how about a cup of coffee? We still have doughnuts from this morning if you'd like some." The lieutenant offered.

"No, thank you, Lieutenant. I'm fine."

"What brings you here? Let me guess. It's about the murders on Lovers' Lane, correct?" Markham stated.

Lattermar hoped the lieutenant would mention the missing lady without him asking.

"Oh, I was just in the neighborhood and heard a triple homicide had occurred. Naturally, as I'm in the limelight, I thought it interesting, and curiosity got the best of me." Latte fished.

"Well, we don't have much to go on. The man in the car is Max Robertos, C.E.O. of Landerberry Computers. Detective Robbie believes when Max left his workplace, he was accosted and made to drive by some unknown assailant to the lane where we found his body. Maybe someone wanted his BMW as a getaway car, and the two women joggers caught the killer or killers by surprise, and perhaps they knew them, which was unfortunate. Anything is possible.

"Who were the women, or do you know?" Latte asked.

Markham answered. "One woman is Celine Drake, a wealthy art dealer. She still had on her diamond earrings. Mrs. Anita Bowman worked for Celine Drake. They were wearing tennis shoes and jogging clothes. That's all I can tell you."

"That's not much to go on, is it, Lieutenant? I heard something about some graves found at the site. Anything about that?" Latte waited for the lieutenant's reaction.

The lieutenant snapped. "That wasn't released; where did you hear that? If you know anything Lattermar, you better tell it! You might get charged as an accessory after the fact."

"Easy there, Lieutenant, don't get worked up. Arteries have enough punishment from daily activity; I don't want you going into cardiac arrest. I don't believe I could do CPR on you." Latte chuckled.

"We found open holes that looked like grave sites. We need to work together on this, Lattermar!" the lieutenant snapped.

Latte realized the lieutenant almost spilled it, and he would if he kept up the pressure.

"I know my rights, Lieutenant, and free speech is legal," Lattermar stated.

"Listen, Lattermar. I have three dead people and no lead. I need anything that could put some light on what happened, anything at all."

"Okay, Lieutenant. I heard there was another person."

Wow, Markham thought! He knows something! But I'll have a hard time getting him to talk.

The flabbergasted lieutenant said. "Look, let's just say there was another person, but we don't know who she is or where she came from. How would you reveal the identity of an unknown person?"

Aha! He slipped. "So, there was another woman?" Lattermar grinned.

"I didn't say that. I said what if!" the lieutenant stuttered.

"No, Lieutenant. You said, she. Now, do you want to work together? If so, first of all, check for missing persons, let's say, in another county or state. What about the CEO's wife? Have you located her yet?" Latte asked.

"Yeah, we located her. She was visiting relatives in California, but she didn't seem surprised. I don't think she cared that Max was in the morgue. She said, 'I guess one of his lady friends finally did him in, and it was about time,' then she laughed."

Sharp twist … geez … Maybe Little Dove Two is the girlfriend.

"No missing women from around here lately, and I have already checked with the adjoining states, and there are no missing reports anywhere in the tri-state."

"Not much to go on, huh, Lieutenant? Latte said.

The lieutenant said sarcastically. "Hold on, I can't remember what that woman looked like. She was one muddy duckling with stringy hair. I saw a dark color when the policewoman dried off the mud. When the lady policewoman rubbed the woman's hands, they were also dark, a medium brown, reminding you of Indian people or their culture. I was going to question her, but then she ran away. She was nearly buried alive. We figure her to be the girlfriend."

"Lieutenant, I know you're busy; how about I check the missing person files? Maybe I can track some of them down."

"Sounds good," the lieutenant agreed.

"In the meantime, I'm leaving early to spend time with my wife. You never know when it might be the last time you see each other. Every time there's a murder, I think more about retiring." The lieutenant said.

Lattermar borrowed photos of all the missing women from the police department and left. He would do whatever it took to help

Brett Canterfield. As Latte drove home, he pondered what he knew about Brett Canterfield.

He is a wealthy man who owns ten thousand acres of the best cattle grazing land in the state, with enough cattle to feed the army for a year—the log home where he lives costs probably twenty million dollars. Brett was also a brigadier general who served his country to the max. He retired with many honors. His family is also handsomely well-off, and he is the only heir; best of all, he is my friend.

Then there is Margo, his wife. She almost ruined him, not financially, but mentally. Her family was also wealthy. He couldn't buy her enough, and when he did, it didn't please her. She gave him a real hard time, and now, another woman?

Enough thoughts. I need to find out about Little Dove Two.

There are so many pictures of missing women. Hopefully, there is a picture of her in the bunch.

Lattermar continued looking through the pictures most of the night, but none held his attention.

He looked at a photo that resembled her several times to ensure there wasn't some tiny detail he missed.

I'll tell Brett I haven't had much luck. I'll show Little Dove Two the pictures and see if any ring a bell.

"Brett, I'm bringing pictures of missing women from the Department of Records. I'm stumped at finding out who the little lady is, but I want her to look at the pictures too."

"Okay. This afternoon sometime will be fine. I'll watch for your arrival on the mountain."

Brett met Lattermar at the Hillcrest. Good 'ol Charlie is absent, and Brett wasn't about to take the chance of the Grizz eating his best friend.

When Lattermar arrived, he and Brett searched the faces in the pictures.

Little Dove Two watched intently as the men studied each photo, and then she began to cry. "I just have to know my name. I am somebody!"

Brett put his arm around her and said softly. "Don't cry. You are someone. It's not the end of the world. We will find out who you are. It may take longer than we assumed, but eventually, we will know; this I promise."

Where do I go from here, Latte thought?

"Well, I'm heading back to the valley before dark. My horses want to spook every time they hear a twig snap. I will keep looking. Maybe tomorrow I'll learn more. I need time to rest and get re-organized. I'm sure something will turn up," Lattermar said.

The next day, Lattermar visited the Police Station. He confronted the dispatcher. "I need to speak with Lieutenant Markham again, please."

She sneered, then answered gruffly. "I'll see if the lieutenant is available."

Latte shook his head. "I don't understand why people can't be happy. Everyone either has a frown or a smart-alecky attitude. Really! That needs to stop."

"Mr. Lattermar, please, come in," the lieutenant said with a forced grin. *Now, he thinks he may need me. What a laugh. I have nothing.*

"Lieutenant, have you noticed any strangers in town that don't quite fit the look of hometown folks? You know the kind, wrong type of clothing or carrying a knapsack?" Latte asked.

"No, I haven't seen anyone, but we hauled in an abandoned car by the lake. I ran the tags, and they're stolen. Ballistics ran lab tests on the fiber and fingerprints, but the report isn't back yet. It came from the Florida Keys. We found a woman's compact and lipstick but no identification or money. We found lots of blood inside and out. What have you found?" Markham asked.

Latte shook his head. "Have you checked the motels and hotels to see if anyone has checked in from Florida? You do realize that they may still be in the city. They must use their license plate number to check in, right?"

The lieutenant hadn't considered that, so he called Robbie.

Lattermar is getting way out of line with his suggestions. Murder is a police matter, not something a private investigator needs to tinker with, but I guess the lieutenant knows what he's doing. Robbie thought.

"Robbie, have you heard anything else about the stolen car?" Markham asked.

"No, but I notified the State police in Florida that we have the stolen car in storage. I don't know if the owner will come here to pick it up or not. Florida is many miles away. What are you getting at? That maybe there's a connection with the murders?" Robbie questioned.

"Let's check it out. It's quite a way from the lake to lovers' lane, but we don't have much to go on, and anything is possible." Markham replied.

"I have a few other things to check out, so I'll see you later. Keep in touch. Lieutenant Markham and I will do the same. I guess we will have to work together after all," Latte chuckled.

"That man is going to give me ulcers, Robbie. He knows about that missing girl but is too tenacious to realize we can help each other. It won't be good for me if he solves this case before the next election. I'm running for Chief of Police next term. Darn—see what you can find out. I'll see what I can shake out of the motel clerk. Who is Lattermar working for, do you know?" Markham asked worriedly.

"I'm waiting on D.N.A. ballistics to come back from the lipstick. It may tell us who the female was in the car with that man. Do you want to drop by the greasy pig for lunch? I'm buying." Robbie asked.

Markham shook his head as he popped a few Tums in his mouth. "No, I'll take a rain check. This case has left me with the jitters."

Robbie studied the lieutenant and wondered if he looked that washed out. "Not. I can't look that bad," he chuckled.

The lieutenant rang the bell at the local motel in town.

"Hello in there."

A fellow wiped his hands on a towel.

I wonder what he wants, the clerk thought.

He will find some way to harass me.

"What can I do you for lieutenant?" he said, half grinning.

"I'm looking for someone that checked in on or about November 3rd. one man alone, or maybe with a woman, possibly a stranger."

"Not that I can think of." He didn't like talking to the police.

"Better check your books, man." The lieutenant wasn't in the best of moods.

"Okay, okay, let me see here. I had an arrival on the first of November, but I don't know where they were from. I don't see any other new ones.

The elk hunters keep me booked up, mostly all year. You know, for the season?"

The lieutenant grabbed the book from the clerk. "This is important, man. Think back, what did they look like? What were they driving? Do you remember anything that would stand out? Tattoos? A scar? Anything?"

Startled, the man backed away. "I don't remember anything, nothing; they were just here and then gone. I can't help you, Lieutenant!"

I'm afraid to tell him about the man in room fifteen. The clerk thought the lieutenant couldn't protect his family from the intolerable man. He said he would kill my family and me if I spoke with the police.

I saw what he did to that poor girl. He said she was his wife --Ha!-- No man treats his wife like that. He shoved her to the ground just because she was hungry.

"I think you might be scared, but let me warn you; either you talk to me now, or I will run you in for questioning. Understand?"

He's covering up something; he's just too fidgety. I have to know what it is, Markham thought.

"I don't know anything. Take me to the station, but I can't help you, Lieutenant. Please, I must return to my kitchen."

The clerk was pale as a sheet. If he takes me down to the station, that guy will kill my wife and both the children before I return. He'd believe I talked.

"Alright, I may be back. if I return, I will run you in for withholding evidence." The lieutenant realized something was wrong, but for now, he decided to watch who came and went to the motel.

The police are in the office. That old coot better not talk, or he and his family won't be worth a plug nickel; when that cop leaves, I will pay a visit to that old codger and make sure he doesn't forget. The man snickered *people will do many things when their family is in danger.*

Clouds were rolling in. More snow was imminent.

Brett finished lunch and retired to the sunroom for his smoke.

Little Dove Two asked, "May I join you out here while you're enjoying your Cuban cigar?" she grinned.

Brett nodded and motioned her to sit.

"It's much better to come in the kitchen and dine with you and Maria. I appreciate everything you have done for me. I will always be grateful. Hopefully, someday, I can repay you for all your kindness." Little Dove Two said. "I believe I was a kind person in my other unknown life. I wish I could remember."

Brett didn't want to admit it, but he hoped she never found out about herself. He had taken her in like a bird with a broken wing, and in return, she had shown him there was more to life than what he was living. She put an almost forgotten smile on his face. *I wish I could take care of her for the rest of her life,* he thought.

"A penny for your thoughts, Brett, and if they're good, I'll give you a dime?" *That is, if I had one,* she thought.

"You don't want to know my thoughts," Brett answered in a mellow tone.

"Try me, and let me decide," she admonished. "I might surprise you."

Brett caught his breath. "Maybe later, I will tell you my inner thoughts, but not yet."

Little Dove Two wasn't about to give up. "This is a beautiful night. I love watching the clouds drift by. Do you think it will snow again? Maybe in drifts like the last time?"

"I hope not. It took my men almost a week to shovel the cattle out from snow drifts and longer than that to get it cleared to the highway. That was a lot of work. We're still using the team to get to and from town." Brett expressed his disapproval of more snow.

Little Dove Two gave Brett a grin that made his heart flutter. "Latte really likes Maria, doesn't he? He always has a grin for her."

Brett laughed. "Yes, I believe he does,"

"There's a masquerade party at St. Joseph Catholic Church, in Spur Lacy, around Christmas time. Maria will find you a nice dress if you want to attend."

Little Dove Two froze. "I haven't considered going out in public. Do you think it would be safe?"

"__Hmm__ well, let's see. I think I can handle myself well enough should the time arise. Isn't that what you thought the other day? I'm not much older now." He laughed.

Little Dove Two loved Bretts' laugh and trusted him, but she trusted no one when push came to shove.

"I will think about it. I need to go in now. I'm chilled," Little Dove Two exclaimed. "Brett, I have an uncanny feeling that someone is watching me. Is there someone out there?"

Little Dove Two was shocked to the core at what Brett professed.

"Yes, there probably is, and she can be very dangerous. Now I must tell you. My wife roams these premises all the time. We cannot see her, but we know when she's here. She leaves little clues behind. She screams like a banshee and makes the noises of a wildcat. She has lost her sanity and lives with my mother in the Indian camp."

Little Dove Two thought he had to be kidding. She stood with her mouth open in disbelief.

"Brett, you are kidding. There is no way she could live in this weather out here." she gasped.

"You saw the little house out back? Well, that's where Margo stays when she comes here. I ensure there's food and water, and I keep it heated. When she gets angry, she destroys the inside. That's why Maria cleans it for me. She always hopes that she might get a glimpse of her daughter."

"Brett, you can't be serious!" Little Dove Two exclaimed.

"Oh, but I am serious. I noticed a terrible change in Margo's attitude a month before the tragedy. I called Maria and asked her to come because I needed help with her.

She needed a psychiatrist, but she wouldn't hear of it. I tried to get her to the doctor many times, but she changed the subject, saying, 'I'm fine.' That's when Maria came here to live." Brett lowered his head, unable to look Little Dove Two in the eyes as tears filled his eyes.

"When the twins were eight years old, Margo wanted a BMW. I tried to tell her it was during the cattle round-up that I couldn't possibly get into town until the next week, and she threw a fit.

I went to the tack room to saddle my horse, and she went berserk. She took my 30.06 Remington rifle off the rack and told Maria she was going to shoot my precious Charlie, that I loved him more than her, and that she would get even.

Maria tried to stop her, but she pointed the gun at her and said she best stay out of her way. Maria backed off. She thought it better to shoot the bear than her.

The twins were crying and tried to stop their mother, but she was enraged. Margo ran toward the cliff with the twins right on her heels.

Charlie never liked Margo, so he became offensive when he saw her and smelled gunpowder." Brett's voice broke.

"The twins ran behind Margo and fell sixty feet down the cliff. She was so enraged she didn't even know they had fallen until she heard Maria scream."

"Margo shot at Charlie, and he attacked her." Tears ran down Bretts' face as he continued.

"I heard the commotion and came running, just in time to see Charlie attack Margo. I screamed to draw his attention. When he charged me, I ran toward the shed, giving Margo time to escape Charlie's proximity. Charlie was going to kill me. I kept a loaded dart gun with enough medicine to knock Charlie unconscious in case I needed to move him to another location, so Maria grabbed the dart gun off the rack and ran outside. She ran between me and the charging bear. Maria had no way of knowing where to shoot the bear, so she shot him in the shoulder. He dropped just three feet from me.

I went down the cliff, retrieved my dead children, and buried them in the family graveyard. There is a cemetery a few yards from the porch. I miss them so much. I can still visualize them laughing and running across the lawn in the summertime. It still hurts badly.

Margo kept screaming and screaming. My mother was here that day. She told me she would take care of her, so she took Margo and returned to her original home in the village over the mountain.

I contacted the police department and told them about the accident. I never mentioned Margo. They don't know about any of this." Now, it was all Brett could do to talk from crying.

I called Lattermar and asked him to come here. When I told him what happened, he said there wasn't any need for the public to know anything other than a horrible accident had occurred. That's the way it has been for ten years.

I fixed Charlie's shoulder while he was unconscious and talked to him while he was awakening. He hasn't liked me very much for a long time. I had to carry the dart gun with me for a long time. I have only been able to be near him for the last few years.

That's why I clamped your mouth shut when I found you. Charlie would have attacked you. No strangers have been near him since that day.

He stays in the forest. I go out there to feed him. He doesn't come to the house anymore."

"Oh, my God, Brett. Are you afraid of Margo? Do you think she would harm you? Or Maria? What about me? She might come after me if she knows I'm here. Now I am scared!"

Brett answered. "Yes, I believe she is dangerous. So far, she only comes into the house while we sleep. We lock all our bedroom doors at night. After what she did, I could not look at her.

I think she was a child that never grew up. Bad things happen to children sometimes when they are young, but they get over it. I always thought she would eventually come to grips with her younger years and become a loving wife and mother. It didn't happen. She didn't even come to the twin's funeral.

Little Dove has sent word that Margo roams the woods day and night. She carries a crossbow, which she means to kill Charlie, but she's capable of shooting a person.

If she saw me with another woman, she would shoot us both. You never know about someone like that. Her tracks in the woods suggest that she goes to Spur Lacy."

"Don't you think you should notify the sheriff about this? My God, Brett, she may kill anyone that comes up this mountain!"

"That's why I didn't tell you about this before. The tribe watches Margo. She is the daughter of Little Dove in the eyes of the village people. My little sister died when she was twelve. That's why Mother loved Margo so much. They realize she is mental, but not how severe. She tells them she is unmarried and barren. I am the only heir to my mother and father's estate. Mother could never bear children after my sister."

"Then why does she come to your house when you are asleep? She may hide and attack you or someone else at any given time. The house is so large she could hide anywhere. You don't believe she could be faking it? The mental illness, I mean?" Little Dove Two asked.

"No, she isn't faking anything. She came up as a child. We played together when we were youngsters. My father was very wealthy. Well, filthy rich. I am his only child. I inherited all this when I reached the age of eighteen. He died just before I came of age. I was seventeen.

My mother wanted nothing to do with all this. She only wanted my father. When he died, she went back to her village. She said that was all she wanted. She wanted nothing to do with a ranch.

No matter how much I protested, she put all my father's assets in my name. She kept saying I was his only son and his wealth was my birthright.

I keep the bedroom vacant for her, but she doesn't want to return. I hope she changes her mind. I miss my mother.

My father built a swing made from an old tire for Margo and me. We each had one tied to that big tree in the front yard. Margo used to say. 'When we grow up, I'm going to marry you.' I always thought of her as a sister, but when she would go home in the afternoon, I was so lonely that I would go to my room and stay there until Mother called me to dinner.

Then, as we got older, Margo stopped coming so much. She was always doing one project or another. She loved to do things that would make people notice her. Later, I discovered that her parents wanted as little to do with her as possible, especially her father.

Then, one summer, she didn't come here at all. When school started that fall, she didn't enroll. I went to see her parents. They told me that she was at an all-girls school and wouldn't be back here until after graduation, and then she had to attend finishing school. That was our last year. I invited her to my senior prom, and she came.

At my senior prom, I asked her to marry me. Her father wouldn't consent, but there wasn't much he could do because we were almost eighteen.

After my father died, we married the following week. I promised I'd never let her want for anything, but she went too far. I suppose that I spoiled her too much.

I found out later that Margo's dad was rough on her. He often slapped her and her mother. He thought Maria should do whatever he said and not ask questions. Her mother adored her, but she couldn't show affection because it made her father angry, and he would hit them more.

Maria came to this country as a migrant worker, met Margo's father, and married him. He always held it over her head that she wasn't an American-born citizen.

He told her she obeyed him or he would have her deported, and he was mean enough to do it.

He was a big-time Colorado lawyer. He had money and the means to do whatever he pleased.

Margo held it against her mother for not defending her against him when he slapped her; of course, it wasn't Maria's fault. It was his.

I believe Margo comes in here to feel the comfort of home. I don't think she remembers us. That's just my guess. I don't think anyone can help her anymore. Now, you know the demons of my life, if only we can find yours," he finished by kissing the top of Little Dove Two's head.

Brett took her hand and led her into the house.

"Brett, I cannot sleep soundly at night, and I'm afraid Maria may see her daughter as the one unduly harmed in a way. She may think I'm trying to take her place.

If Margo is out there, it's just a matter of time until she tries to get into my room. I would have a heart attack should I awaken with her standing over me. She wouldn't have to shoot me with the crossbow." Little Dove Two told Brett.

"Maria would never feel bad at you, and she wouldn't think you were hurting Margo in any way.

If your door stays locked, there is no way Margo could get in. Did you know you didn't have the lock on when I entered your room the other night?

The scream you heard, well, it was her screaming like a banshee. She calls herself Sheba, the cat. She also has grown fingernails like a wildcat's. She could do some damage with those claws."

Little Dove Two dropped her head when she answered, "Brett, I wouldn't be so afraid if I knew you would be near when the screaming starts."

"Sweet lady, I will not be far from you at any time, so try not to be afraid, okay?" Brett pulled her into his arms and held her trembling body close. "I will protect you."

They Kept Searching

Someone must have seen something, maybe leaving the car garage when Max, the CEO, was abducted. Latte thought.

"Good morning. May I help you, sir?" The receptionist asked.

"Yes, ma'am. My name is Ramond Lattermar, P.I. I work with Lieutenant Markham on Max Roberto's case. I need a list of the employees who park on the upper deck of the parking garage, please."

"Sir, I must check with my boss before I can give out information."

"Just a moment, please," the lady was back in a flash. "My boss told me to cooperate with you to the fullest. Okay, what do you need?"

Great, he thought, and she's cute. Down boy! Back to the business at hand.

"Just the names of the ones that park on the upper level of the parking garage, and what time they clock out? It is important."

Lattermar thought. *There are thirty-three names to check out, but that's the name of the game. It only gets tougher from here on. I hope Markham is having better luck than I am.*

Lieutenant Markham asked his stakeout team if they saw any movement at the motel or if anyone left their rooms that looked out of place for this area, like different types of clothing or acting peculiar.

No one had seen anything suspicious, and they had watched closely ever since the lieutenant put the motel under surveillance.

The nasty man in room fifteen decided to revisit the motel clerk!

"Hey, old man, what did that filthy cop want? I told you not to talk to a cop, or there would be consequences to pay. Now, I'm going to give you a taste of what will happen if you call that cop back," He snapped.

The wicked man held a small blackjack inside a sack. Whop, whop, whop, he struck the clerk.

"Do you want me to use this on your family? If not, you better keep your trap shut. I will hurt them in the worst way possible, then kill them slowly. You got my drift, man?"

"Okay, yes, yes, okay. I never told the cop anything. Just leave us alone. I have a business to run. I don't have time to play a game of cops and robbers. Whatever you did doesn't concern me or my family." He stressed.

This fellow is a dangerous man. I wonder what happened to the lady he had with him. He may have killed her already. She was too tiny to protect herself from a man of his size. The clerk thought.

"Hey, old man, I heard about a masquerade party. Where are they going to have it, and when?" The cruel man demanded.

"St. Joseph Catholic Church is where they usually have it. Can I get back to my kitchen?" the clerk snapped.

"Yeah, but you better not forget what I told you, or I will make you one sorry man." The appalling man snickered.

The clerk was tempted to call Lieutenant Markham and tell him, but he thought it best not to make waves.

When the clerk returned to the kitchen, he wrote down every detail he saw or remembered about this shameful man. He has on dark blue slacks and a light blue shirt. There's a rattlesnake design on the lapel. He has a small scar on his cheek under his right eye. Medium completion. A tattoo on his right hand that reads, *De-man*. He weighs approximately 190 pounds—about five foot eleven, or six foot tall. His hair is sandy brown, and he has green eyes. He carries himself like a policeman. He spoke with broken English, but I think it's a put-on. He has one gold stud earring in his left ear that looks like a natural diamond, and he wears a Rolex. He paid in cash, which bought him the room, and his threats gave him silence.

The clerk then put the paper into an envelope, sealed and addressed it to his lawyer, then dropped it in the outgoing mail.

The Masquerade Party

Come one, come all! The letter read.

The masquerade party has been a success for the last several years, and we want to extend our thanks to all the merchants who participated in making this year's ball even more successful than any other we have had to date.

On the eve of December 23rd, starting at 7:00 P.M., the best-dressed person will receive an all-paid vacation to the Vatican City in Rome, Italy. Also, the winner shall receive two thousand dollars of spending money in their vacation package.

There will be refreshments, a breakfast banquet served in the cafeteria of St. Joseph Catholic Church, and delicious foods of many kinds for lunch and dinner, prepared by the ladies of the church. Come and enjoy the fellowship!

There will be a stayover until Christmas morning for those who decide to stay for sunrise services. Everyone, please bring a dish as is custom.

Please remember the costumes must be of a Christmas nature. Thank you all; we hope to see you there!

God Bless All,

Fr. Ryan

Maria read the invitation. She couldn't get in the Christmas spirit. She knew Brett had always donated quite handsomely to this cause, but her Christmas spirit wasn't the same as Margo's, and the twins were gone.

She knew it was impossible to visit them at Christmas, so Maria sent the children a card and a gift. She often wondered if Margo let them have what she had sent.

Brett and the children signed a Christmas card and sent it to her every year. Brett always sent a present, too, without Margo knowing about it.

Maria thought about the past. *Margo never forgave me for not standing up for her against her father. Oh well, I did the best I could. I had many beatings she never knew about, with me defying him immensely when he wanted to put Margo up for adoption.*

All mothers are appalling, and the guilty ones when things go eerie.

I blamed my mother for things, too, but she probably did her best with what knowledge she had.

I need to think of something else so that I won't become too depressed. The thoughts of Margo make me want to cry my heart out. I loved my daughter so much. She just never accepted my love.

I will put the invitation on the table by the back door so Brett will see it when he gets home.

Bretts' Hired Hands

Brett's workers were discussing plans for the following year; he listened quietly because his hired men kept the ranch running smoothly. One worker speaking out captured Brett's attention.

"Carl? Did you say we're losing cattle from wildcats?"

"I'm not certain, but we're losing one steer weekly. What would you have me to do? Someone must watch the cattle constantly to catch the varmint, but it's too cold to set up a camp." Carl explained.

"Brett said, "That's exactly what I want. Put four men on watch every night. It is frigid, so build a lean-to onto the chuck wagon with a wood stove. I want two men on watch at all times. Exchange the drovers every two hours; this must stop. Carl is the foreman. He will be your boss for the rest of the winter."

The ranch hands had free range of Brett's ranch; they were the backbone of operations.

"Stay on top of this, Carl. We can't afford to lose one a week. It would put me out of business and you guys out of a job."

The wind picked up, and the afternoon sun was nearly covered with clouds threatening more imminent snow.

"Carl, wildcats can't get to the cattle with the snow so deep, right?" Brett asked.

Carl said. "Boss, I need to tell you something. There's more going on than meets the eye. Someone cleared a path to drag cattle from the south fork mesa to the cave. Hides are curing inside the cave. We're not dealing with just a wildcat."

"Tell the men to shoot anyone if their lives are in danger," Brett snarled.

"Yes, Sir, I will remind them to be extremely careful."

Now that the boss knows about this, I won't feel so bad when I kill it. Good old Charlie may bite the dust, but I'm confident we are also dealing with poachers, Carl thought.

Brett entered the house after working in the tack room.

He picked up the mail and entered the kitchen. After reading it, he laid it on the island. It was nothing big, a letter from Latte and news of what the hunters had killed that week. *I hope they use it for food. I hate to see any animal killed for sport,* he thought.

Oh, and there's a loose leaflet about the masquerade party at the church. Little Dove Two will enjoy this, he thought. *I can hardly wait to see how Maria dresses her. I hope she dresses as well as Margo did.*

He marveled that Margo was beautiful, but Little Dove Two was also lovely. He didn't know how to take her to the social without everyone knowing there was a new face in town, but that's three weeks away.

Brett reflected on the past. The first masquerade party I went to was with Margo. It was fantastic. She wore that long dark green silk velvet dress with matching green slippers. She curled her hair on top of her head.

She was so beautiful she took my breath away and turned every head in the church. I wish she could have adjusted to life better. She should have gone to the doctor like I asked, but she always refused. Had I dragged her there, she might still be in her right mind. I will always love her, but I can't change the past.

Margo shouldn't have held so much against Maria. Her mother is an extraordinary person. She always thinks of others before herself.

I need to move on with my life, but it's hard to let go and start over. But when I do, I will hire a lawyer to arrange our divorce.

Where is Maria? She is always in the kitchen at this time of day, Brett thought.

"Maria, are you in the parlor? Where are you?" *Something isn't right.* Brett began searching the house and calling for Maria, but she didn't answer.

He had a strange feeling again. The hair crawled on his neck. Going up the third flight of steps, he called, "Maria, are you up here?"

Brett opened the last door to the upstairs room and found Maria holding a dress against her body – Margo's green silk velvet dress!

"Maria, are you okay?" he asked, draping his arm around her shoulder; her eyes were puffy from crying, and she was shaking from head to toe. He held her and let her cry until she controlled her anxiety.

"I read the invitation about the masquerade party, so I came up here to see what I could repair for Little Dove Two to wear. Finally, I've accepted the inevitable. Margo isn't coming back, is she, Brett?" she asked.

Margo was selfish; she wouldn't let Maria get close to her or the children because she held her responsible for her pain, but her mother couldn't stop her father from inflicting pain upon her. She wasn't strong enough.

"No, she won't come back. Maria, we did all we could. I tried to make her happy with all my heart and soul, and I thought she was content. Margo will only come here at night; then, she roams the halls like we did when we were kids, playing hide and seek. She doesn't know us anymore."

Brett didn't realize, but he was also crying.

Maria wiped away Brett's tears, and in a gentle whisper, she said. "Brett, we should remove all of Margo's clothes. Either box them up for the poor or burn them."

Her heart was broken, not just for herself but also for her son-in-law. He was the son she never had, and she loved him dearly.

Maria said, "Brett, come to the kitchen while I put on some tea. There's something we need to discuss."

"Brett, why don't you buy her a new dress for the masquerade party? She needs other clothing, too." It was hard to speak about Little Dove Two's situation.

"Maria, my thoughts exactly," he laughed.

"Brett, you or I will have to buy for her. All we need to know is what color she likes best," Maria beamed.

A deep blue silk velvet would make her skin tone creamy and smooth. I think she would be pleased, Maria grinned.

"Okay, that will be the color for her," Brett said. "She will look more Indian than white. I'm certain she is of Indian descent. We will pick out many beautiful things for her."

That's what I was afraid of, Maria thought. *He'd been lonely too long and fallen for her too quickly.*

"Brett, I want to speak my mind. I love you like a son, and I will speak to you as one," she said.

"Well, of course, Maria, you are my second mother. I always want your advice." Brett grinned.

"I know you are fascinated with this young woman, but I think you should wait awhile. I'm saying what I feel because I don't want to see you go through heartbreak and pain again. She may or may not be married. She may have a family!"

"I understand, Maria. I have feelings for her, but I'm only helping her now. When she arrived, she was afraid of us and Charlie, and we couldn't blame her; we kept her locked in her room. She felt sympathy for us when I told her about Margo but no longer feared the locked door. She is concerned that Margo might come in and harm one of us, and she's also afraid for herself." Brett explained.

Maria grinned. "Tomorrow, I will find the perfect outfit for her to wear to the party. Later, we can buy the other things she needs. You will stay at the house until I return, right? I'll take the buckboard. It will be easier than driving your caddy. I would get stuck, and with my luck, you wouldn't get it home until summer."

"If you leave, I will undoubtedly stay here all day. It isn't safe to leave Little Dove Two here alone."

Brett knew Margo would kill her if she found the lady in 'her house.'

"Maria, ask Little Dove Two what she thinks about the idea." He suggested.

"Thank you, Mr. Canterfield. I sure can use a few things." Little Dove Two grinned as she overheard him tell Maria to buy her some clothes."

"What kind of clothes will she get me?" Little Dove Two asked.

"Anything you wish, ma'am," he bowed to her, using a hand jester as though he wore a hat.

Little Dove Two blushed. The red on her face showed a beautiful glow.

"Maria, if you could come up with a gown to match the color in her cheeks, the dress would be absolutely magnificent. I think maybe a deep red silk velvet. What do you think?" he laughed.

Maria grinned. "Yes, you're right. Deep red or deep blue is the color for her complexion."

"Oh, Brett, you make me feel special." Little Dove Two grinned, blushing a deeper red.

Brett's heart raced when Little Dove Two said, "Whatever color you believe good, that's what it shall be. I do love silk velvet. Oh my God. I can't remember anything about me, but I remember silk velvet. Maybe there is a connection somewhere between silk and me!"

Brett answered slowly. "You may be right. One day we will know for certain."

He suspected she came from wealth. I could quickly love this lady so easily. I pray she loves me before we find out! Maria asked Brett to beware, but it had been long since he had loved a woman or a woman had loved him. It took Brett a long time to adjust to losing Margo, but it was time to move on.

Should Margo reappear, I will take care of her, but I could never love her. Her blue eyes haunt me in my sleep, but I think that will pass in time. I sure hope it does. Brett was deep in thought.

"Brett, did you hear me? What's wrong?" Little Dove Two stared at him in wonder.

"I'm sorry, I was thinking about what you need now," he fibbed. "Maria will sign for me, as she has done many times, and no one will know who the clothes are for. Buy anything you desire. There is no limit."

Oh my God. Is Mr. Canterfield that rich? Little Dove Two thought. "Okay, you can buy the things I need for now, and Maria can pick me out a dress. Later, I will buy clothes for myself when Lattermar finds out who I am," she grinned. "Is that agreeable?"

Little Dove Two knew Maria would buy her a gorgeous dress. Margo's clothing was simply stunning.

I can hardly wait to have clothes! Oh, what am I thinking? These clothes won't belong to me, well not exactly. I will repay Brett after I find out who the heck I am, Little Dove Two thought. *Right now, I only want to marvel that Brett is so incredibly kind to me. I hope to make him proud of me when we go to the masquerade party. I realize it's a religious ceremony, but having a ball to get people to attend church to worship is incredible. That's something I always did when I was home. Now, where the heck did that come from? Maybe I remember some of my past! Wouldn't that be hunky dory to remember when I am so excited to go to St. Joseph Church? I must have been religious or wouldn't have wanted to go there so badly.*

Little Dove Two worried about her past, whether she was married or had children. If married, did she say her vows in the church? Or maybe as a child, was she christened. She hoped she didn't have children, or they would think she was a lousy mommy not coming home. She didn't feel like she had children. When I get to town, I shall ask a physician very discretely.

Maria was busy looking at beautiful garments, not paying attention to someone watching her.

There is the dress for Little Dove Two, she thought. Silk, red shimmering with blue and green with the laciest high top. *Wow! It is perfect. Now I must find shoes to match.*

Deep in thought, Maria was surprised when Lieutenant Markham bumped into her. "What a beautiful gown. Margo will look simply beautiful in that this year."

Maria said, "Oh, yes, it is stunning."

Really! The lieutenant thought. *She's so rich; she could wear that to a hog killing, and no one would notice the difference. She's always dressed fit to kill every time I see her. I love my wife, but I can't help but remember the good times that Margo and I had just before she married Brett Canterfield. She still has a place in my heart.*

"Will she be wearing this gown this year? I want to say hello to her while we're there. I haven't seen her for some time." he grinned.

Maria almost fainted. "I haven't heard her say. Margo changes her mind on a dime. I must excuse myself, Lieutenant. Good day, sir."

Maria was shaking from head to toe; she thought, *I hope he doesn't ask me any more questions.*

"Oh, Maria, would you tell Brett I must speak with him sometime after Christmas? I need to visit him at the ranch. There are things we seriously need to discuss."

"Lieutenant, you will see him at the Christmas party. Can't it be discussed there? Being on Bretts Mountain with the Grizzly running at large is not wise. He might not know the color of your uniform and eat you." She snickered.

"I remember what Robbie told me about that Grizzly. Brett still has him, huh?" he wished he could put that grizzly bear down.

The lieutenant's face said it all. He was afraid to come up on Brett Mountain. Maria wanted to giggle; she didn't care for Lieutenant Markham. She remembered how he kept trying to date Margo just before she and Brett exchanged their wedding vows.

"Oh yes. That bear will be there until the day he dies." She laughed as she walked away.

Now what will we do about the party dress? We can't put Little Dove Two in the lieutenant's spotlight. He would definitely know she wasn't Margo. Then, he would ask some serious questions.

With Maria in town, Little Dove Two and Brett were alone in the big house.

"Brett, would you show me the house? We have nothing to do, and I don't feel safe with you in one part of the house and me in the other. Maria even takes me into the kitchen while she prepares the meals."

Little Dove Two looked at Brett with shining dark brown eyes.

Brett thought, *my God, she's beautiful;* unexpectedly, he took her into his arms. She stiffened. "I'm sorry, Little Dove Two, please forgive me. I never meant for that to happen. You are so breathtakingly beautiful. It won't happen again, I promise. Please don't be afraid of me. I will not harm you."

Tears rolled down Little Dove Two's cheeks. "Brett, I'm not afraid you will hurt me. I'm worried that I may hurt you. You've just accepted that your wife may never return, and I'm possibly married. You might find yourself in turmoil between two loves. That would be devastating. We need to keep our distance until we know where we stand. I couldn't tolerate losing you if I ever let you get close to my heart. I do care and maybe love you. But we must put a damper on this right now!"

Brett wiped the tears from her eyes and held her momentarily. "Yes, you are correct. I love you. I will keep my distance but won't stay away from you. Agreed?" he held out his hand, taking hers in his.

"Agreed," she said.

Maria barged through the door with bags and bundles.

She spoke with urgency. "I dropped some packages in the yard. I was so nervous that I nearly went into the ravine when I started up the grade. I must talk to both of you now!"

"**D**etective Rommeria, a fax just came in from statistics, and it is interesting." The desk clerk said.

"Thank you, Holly. Hold my calls. I need to review these, which will take some time. I could use a cup of that good eye-opening coffee you make if you please."

Holly grinned. "Coming right up, sir."

"Lieutenant, you might want to see this. It's extraordinary. The ballistic report just faxed about that stolen car we found by the lake. I can't believe what I'm reading. It's just too surreal!"

"What clues do we have here? Okay, it says there was blood on the outside and inside of the car, but it doesn't match any of the victims. The items found don't have D.N.A. from the victims either. Nothing matches." The detective scratched his head.

"I ran the fingerprints on the car, and guess what? It must have been the first time this person was ever in trouble. There is no record of that person ever being arrested anywhere," Lieutenant Markham said.

"We have zip. Someone or something was inside that car, bleeding profusely. Blood splatters were on the seat, and the door handle inside and out." Robbie told the lieutenant.

"Robbie, it looks as if we may have a serial killer on the loose right here in Spur Lacy! Do you realize that the car by the lake was actually on Bretts' Mountain? We need to notify Brett Canterfield and find out if there's anything suspicious up there because he may have some odd phenomenon going on there, too. Do you think that Grizzly could be what killed the people in the car at the lake?" the lieutenant asked.

"I wouldn't advise anyone to attempt a visit on that mountain until we notify Brett. That Grizzly still runs loose." Robbie stated.

Robbie could still remember the growl from that Grizzly the day he went there to ask permission to hunt. He climbed a large tree until Brett found him. That bear held his complete admiration.

"Lieutenant, no bear can open car doors. Why don't you call Brett and ask him to come to the station? I hope you reconsider going on Bretts' Mountain," Robbie grinned.

Robbie laughed because he knew the lieutenant was afraid of Charlie, too.

"Well, it's almost Christmas Eve, and I don't want to work on the 23rd. The wife and I want to be at St. Joseph's to purchase a ticket for a chance to go to Rome, so what do you say about us doing this after the holidays?" Markham suggested.

Robbie thought *this investigation had better not cause Jeri, the Lieutenant's wife, to miss her favorite holiday. He doesn't realize Jerrica would flog both of us should she miss out on the party.*

"Robbie, that sounds like a plan. I'll see you around the twenty-seventh if we don't get snowed in," Lieutenant Markham grinned. "I better get to the ladies' apparel shop before they close the doors and buy my wife a nice present before I go home. Jerrica expects a Santa's gift under the tree on Christmas morning. She looks forward to her surprise when she awakes, all sleepy-eyed, and checks under the tree. Have you finished your shopping? You better not forget that cute little wife of yours either; she will shave off what little hair you have left," the lieutenant chided.

"What are you talking about? She wouldn't stop with the hair. She would pull out all the chest hairs, too, and by the roots, ugh, and since when have you been checking out my cute little wife? I heard that," he chuckled.

"Just a matter of speech, my dear friend. I have all I can handle at home. I would hate to think about my Jerrica being as young as your wife and me the age I am. That would be murder!" the lieutenant remarked.

Robbie grinned. "I'm not going today, though. I might run into my wife. She is accompanying our daughter, looking for a daddy gift. Sadie would be madder than a wet hornet if I should see my surprise present."

"Okay, well, I'm out of here. I thought I better remind you of a present. You best not forget, or another Santa might visit Sadie on Christmas." Markham laughed.

Robbie threw the phone book at him as he shut the door, laughing the whole time. "I'll get even with you. The very idea!"

Robbie thought about the night he asked Sadie to marry him: Her beautiful dark eyes shone like diamonds.

She said. 'I thought you'd never ask! I've waited four years for this proposal! I have a lot to prepare, so we can't get married too quickly. I have to call all my friends, well, all the friends that still live here. I made the list out over two years ago.' She then snuggled up close to me on the couch and grinned. 'I was beginning to think I would be an old maid!'

Shaking like a leaf, I said. 'I was afraid you would say no, so I didn't dare ask.'

Then there was the birth of our daughter. This child was a blessing because the doctor said this would be Sadie's last child. She was to have an emergency hysterectomy that day. Complications from the pregnancy destroyed her uterus, and the removal was inevitable, or she would hemorrhage.

Sadie cried her eyes out; she wanted more children, at least three, but it wasn't to be, so I spoiled the child and Sadie rotten. They are the apples of my eyes.

The very idea that I would forget her Christmas present. Ha! That is preposterous. I will never forget Sadie on Christmas. Never!

When Robbie got home, he sat beside Sadie and told her his thoughts.

"Sadie, this year, I will buy two more presents, one for Crietta and one for Matthew. They need Christmas more than anyone I know," he said sadly. "Right now, they are staying temporarily with their Aunt during Christmas. I wonder what fate befalls them after their Christmas vacation from school. Sadie, I have been thinking about their welfare lately. Have you considered adopting those kids?"

The Cave

"**B**oss! Boss! Am I glad that you're home? We checked the caves, and it looked as if someone is living in there. We found hides curing and a campfire. Then we scouted around and found another cow dragged back to that cave. I'm afraid for the men to go inside. They might become trapped. What do you want me to do?" Carl exclaimed.

"Hold on, Carl. Let me get into my heavy coat and boots, and I will go with you." Brett said. "Maria, I'll be back as soon as possible."

"Was a horse saddled for me? I hoped to be back home before dark," Brett asked Carl.

"Right outside, Boss. I had your big black stallion saddled. okay?" Carl grinned.

Brett stated. "You know me well; the stallion is my favorite."

As Brett and Carl headed up the canyon toward the mesa, they heard movement in the underbrush. Both men were already spooked; they kicked their horses' flanks to pick up speed.

"What do you think that was, Brett?" Carl asked with his heel still deep in the horse's side.

"Dang, if I know, but I'm not sticking around long enough to find out either. I think maybe a cat. It moved like a mountain lion. Animals are more dangerous now; they're hungry. A man better beware, or he will find himself dinner." Brett laughed.

"Yes, or maybe a Grizzly burger." Carl shivered. He didn't trust being around Charlie. He still remembered when that grizzle chased Brett and would have killed him, too, had it not been for Maria.

Carl and the ranch hands figured the bear knew the men belonged on the ranch. Margo, well, that was something else. That bear hated her after she shot him. I think he will kill her if he gets the chance, and for sure, she will kill him.

Now I know what was wrong at the house. I was upset and didn't pay attention. Now that I think about it. That wasn't Margo! Carl thought.

"Brett, we've been friends a long time, right?" Carl picked his words. "I have a question. Who was the little lady in your kitchen?"

Brett was never a man to lie, and he wasn't about to start now. "Carl, I don't want to talk about our visitor just now, and I would appreciate it if you kept what you saw between your teeth. There is nothing illegal or bad about the lady residing at my house. I will tell you later on, okay? I have too much to worry about right now to worry about gossip."

Carl thought it strange for his boss to hold a secret from him. "That's okay, Sir. I don't have time to think about it anyway." He laughed but would watch more closely who stayed at Bretts' house. If possible, he would prevent harm from coming to this family.

It had taken most of an hour to reach the mesa.

The men were guarding the cave entrance as they arrived.

The sun hid behind a cloud. The temperature was so cold a person could freeze to death.

Brett rode closer to the entrance. "Hello in there. I don't know who you are, but you are about to be shot. The best thing you could do is come out with your hands up. I don't want to shoot you, but if you don't come out, my men will shoot you down like dogs. Do you hear me?"

Then, in the language of the village people, he repeated the same warning: no answer. What did these people think he would do? Just let them steal him blind? Not in this lifetime.

"Okay, you've had your warning. You have to pass us to leave, and we will be waiting. We have plenty of food and water and can wait for you. You may as well give yourself up," Brett advised.

No answer came from the cave.

Carl pondered. He was curious about the lady in the kitchen. Maybe Margo invited a friend or a family member to visit. How long had it been since he had seen Margo? Indeed, a very long time. Today was the first time he had been inside the house in many days. Brett clarified, 'his home was off limits to any hand.' He made that clear on the day he was hired. *I used to see her once in a while, but not anymore. My curiosity is kicking in! I will speak with Brett about this tomorrow.*

A terrible thought came to Brett's mind. *What if it was one of the village people over the mountain?*

He didn't want his men to shoot one of the braves from Little Dove's village, but they would ask for meat, not steal from him.

"Carl, I don't believe it's Indians, but be careful with the guns. I wouldn't want to shoot any of my mother's people."

"Okay, Boss, I agree. They use every piece of meat and the hides from animals. They don't waste food. Indians don't stretch hides the way these are, either. They won't be good for anything. The skins they're drying are lying on the rocks instead of hanging. Last week, Two-Toes came by and said they were hungry. I gave him a good-size-steer. That's what you would have told me to do, right, Boss?" Carl asked.

Brett nodded. "Exactly. I always give the tribe beef when they're hungry. That's why I'm positive they aren't killing the steers. They don't ask much from the white man. The white man stole their land years ago. I don't see how they can even speak to a white man."

Carl reflected. "Brett, have you forgotten you are half-Indian? It's probably different talking to you than to other men."

"Thanks, I needed that. I'm primarily around white men, but I am very proud of my heritage, and I love my Indian brothers. That's another reason I don't think they stole from me. We have always been brothers to the village people. I would lay my life on the line for any one of them at any time, as they would do the same for me. Carl, I have things to do back at the ranch. When whoever comes out, make sure you un-arm them. Then, bring them to my house. I want to question why they were stealing from me or if they were hungry; I must know. I won't tolerate anyone stealing from me. I don't like thieves, and they won't like me when I get my hands on them."

"Yes, Sir," Carl answered. He would like Brett to stay, but he was a busy man. Not only did he take care of a ranch, but he also had real estate to tend.

"Okay, Brett. It's pretty dark. There's a lot of movement on the trail from here to your house. Be careful, if you know what I mean."

"Okay, Carl, I know what you're doing, but it isn't going to work. I can't afford to be a scared cat. I will talk to you tomorrow. Wake me up if you catch that person tonight. I am anxious about this problem. By the way, I am a little leery on the trail." He snickered as he rode away.

As Brett rode down the drawl, he kept his rifle handy; he was well aware of what was happening around him.

There may be a big cat somewhere in the underbrush that could leap on him at any moment. He wasn't sure what he and Carl heard coming up the mountain, but he wasn't taking any unnecessary chances. He knew whatever it was wasn't gone.

His stallion whinnied and side-stepped. Brett's heart skipped a beat. Yes, now he was scared.

He thought about letting off a few rounds from his rifle to scare the varmint away, but he knew the men were within hearing distance and would leave the cave to rescue him.

"Okay, whatever you are in there, just show me your face!" Brett was surprised and most definitely not ready for what he saw! It was Margo, and she had a crossbow aimed at his heart!

"Margo! What on earth are you doing out here? It's so cold and dark. If you lower your bow, I will get off my horse and give you my coat. I know you must be cold."

Margo looked at Brett with a blank stare.

"Margo put down the crossbow, and I will help you." She held the crossbow tightly aimed at his heart.

The horse sidestepped again, throwing her off balance enough for Brett to slide off the saddle and grab for the weapon. The crossbow went off as he reached for her. Brett felt a burning pain in his side.

Margo jerked away from him. She slid through the snow and ice, gaining her freedom. She held tightly to the crossbow as she fled.

Brett fell to the ground and doubled up in pain. The stallion whinnied and ran away, leaving a bleeding Brett lying on the ground. "She didn't recognize me." He grunted weakly.

The last Brett remembered before he passed out was releasing three shots from his rifle. He knew his work hands would rescue him.

The Man In Room Fifteen

Benson Carver wanted money and had already chosen his next victim. He knew he must dress appropriately to attend the masquerade party at St. Joseph's Church, and Benny was a man of his word. So he lost Little Goody two shoes but knew of another target.

The banker had a cute little daughter and a healthy appetite for sports cars and fancy houses. Yes, he had an abundance of wealth.

Ha, ha, Bennie snickered under his breath. *I only want half. I could be greedy and take it all. He will pay what I ask when he sees his daughter in handcuffs and a bikini. She is his pride and joy. I'll put a leather strap and handcuffs next to the girl's sleeping body that should convince him that I mean business. No daddy wants his little darling daughter harmed in any way.*

Still laughing, the ruthless man left the motel and headed for the downtown shopping center.

Not knowing the streets, he decided to walk around and get acquainted. "Good morning, ma'am. Looks like it's gonna be a nice day," tipping his hat to the ladies he passed.

Bennie looked like a gentleman and had the speech of a politician, but what they didn't know could kill them. The small-town folks had no idea who they were dealing with.

Looking like a millionaire or bigwig, he walked into the costume shop. Bennie had millions of dollars in Cayman banks but loved taking from the wealthy.

Bennie smiled with satisfaction as he tried on a great costume. *I found the very thing for this six-foot man. Aha, it fits well and feels good.*

The lady at the counter looked at him admiringly. She grinned and said, "I haven't seen you around before. Where are you from?"

Benny answered. "Well, I'm here looking for places to hunt, and when I find the right location, I'll make the necessary arrangements for next year's hunt. Don't you believe that's wise?"

That's odd, she thought *he didn't say where he was from. Well, it takes all kinds to make a world. He may not have understood me.*

I will be the best-dressed, wise man of all time. He laughed at his choice as he left the shop. *This costume will do.*

Too bad little goody two shoes can't see me now, Bennie snarled.

"I know that carbine!" Carl declared. "The boss is in trouble. Come with me," he said, pointing to the younger man beside him. "We'll ride down the slope and see if we can find him."

Carl knew he must hurry; Brett's life depended on it. The men scampered down the hill, watching both sides of the path for some unknown animal and their boss.

They spied a crumpled form lying face down in the snow.

"Boss, can you hear me?" Carl saw Brett's eyes flicker. "We heard the shots and came running. The men have the varmint cornered in the cave. Boss, can you hear me?"

Carl couldn't leave his men to take his boss home. He did take one man with him to locate Brett. There were too many mountain lions roaming around, and then there was Charlie. It was too dangerous to go alone.

When Carl and the young cowboy reached the cave, he built the fire higher. Speaking to the men, he said, "The boss has been shot with something. It looks like a clean wound, but we must tend it. The smell of blood will draw animals, so keep the fire built up high; it will also lighten the area. There's more danger out here than what's in the cave. Keep your eyes on that wooded area over there and stay alert." Carl said.

"We haven't seen anything since you've been gone," one Dover said.

Carl scratched his head. "The Boss is out cold and still bleeding. I must somehow get him home! He needs heat and a doctor real quick."

Listening intently, Carl could hear something moving inside but didn't recognize the noise as he slowly eased up to the cave opening. He saw the shadow of a person on the wall and drew his pistol.

"Freeze, mister. Who are you, and why are you stealing the cattle?"

A swoosh sound came from somewhere in the cave! An arrow stuck in an artificial wooden brace right beside Carl's head.

Carl dropped to the ground and yelled. "Drop your weapons."

Then another swoosh! "Whose in here? Come out where I can see you."

No answer. Then another swoosh!

The man inside the cave cried out, "I've been held here for almost two months. You better leave, or you will be killed."

A figure appeared suddenly with a crossbow aimed at Carl's heart. He fired his weapon. The person fell at his feet. Carl was overwhelmed when he turned the figure over: It was Margo!

"What in God's name is she doing here looking like that? She looks like a dark blond-haired Indian!" Carl gasped.

The man stepped forth and said. "Thank God. I was about to give up, and I assumed this was to be my demise! That woman appeared out of nowhere with that wicked crossbow. She is mad, and I don't mean that as a joke, either. She is a nut case. Is she dead? Who is she?"

"Yes, she's dead," Carl stated. "I need to get the wounded man in this cave for shelter," he told the intruder. "Build the fire as hot as possible, and don't even think about leaving. The boss will want to speak with you when he regains consciousness."

"I'm not going anywhere. It's dark, and I left my four-wheeler down the Mountain. When the weather turned bad, I needed shelter and walked to this cave. I wasn't anxious to go tramping around without a light; too many wild animals were moving about," Jessie explained.

I'm surprised you didn't meet Charlie," Carl snickered.

"Who is Charlie?" The man was curious.

"He's the most ornery Grizzly in these parts. Brett raised him from a cub. He got shot with a 30.06. It just made him mad. He shook it off; it didn't seem to bother him at all." Carl stretched it a little.

Jessie felt his skin crawl up the back. "I feel lucky that I didn't run into him."

"He may have made his den in this cave, but he could be anywhere. We're unsure if he hibernated this year since he's old; the boss feeds him year-round."

Carl was having a good old time scarring Jessie; Brett began to arouse and heard most of the story the stranger told Carl, which was unlikely, but he wanted to hear it from the stranger.

"Why were you hunting on my ranch? There are signs everywhere reading no hunting. Can't you read? Someone bring me the bullwhip, now!" Brett was beyond mad. He was furious!

"Sir, I'm sorry. I hunt elk to put meat on the table for my family. I am no trophy hunter. That wild woman found me before I found any game. Hey, who is she anyway?"

Carl answered, not meeting Brett's eyes. "Her name is Margo, Brett; I am sorry. She came from nowhere and started shooting. She aimed it straight at my heart. She was going to kill me. She gave me no choice.".

"I can't imagine what I'd gotten myself into. That woman is like a wild animal!" the man exclaimed.

"Shut your mouth! I would worry more about my hide than that woman," Carl shouted through clenched teeth.

"Did she come from the Indian village?" The offered.

Carl shoved the man hard against the nearby boulder.

Why did Carl protect me from that man's questions? He knows Margo. He is a true friend who showed loyalty to me. Brett thought.

The other men in the cave didn't know who she was. They had never seen her before.

Calming down is what I need to do before I take the bullwhip to the intruder. I might accidentally kill him if I gave him the whipping he deserves. He wouldn't be standing there with his mouth agape if I could handle a whip now. That's a fact! Brett thought to himself.

"Thank you, Carl. Tomorrow morning, I will send word to Little Dove that her adopted daughter has been shot."

Carl nodded. His sorrow was for Brett, the man he felt as close to as a brother. It was a sorrowful thing that Margo died. Brett was in mourning, and there was nothing he could say to help ease the pain he endured.

"Boss, you should get some rest. We will keep the fire up all night to stay reasonably warm in the cave. You have lost a lot of blood. I patched you up as best I could, but we didn't have many rags to clean the wound. I washed out most of the debris from the canteen, but it still needs appropriate cleaning and stitching. I will wrap Margo in a blanket and care for the body until morning."

"When I'm stronger, there are things I need to tell you, Carl," Brett closed his eyes.

The village where Little Dove resided wasn't far from the cave where Margo died.

Carl looked around to see if any braves lurked in the shadows. He was satisfied there was no one else.

Brett knew the man in the cave would talk to people, so he informed him the following day. "The woman shot last night was called 'Sheba cat woman'; she lives over the mountain with one of the tribes. Her mind has been gone for many years. Last night was the first time I saw her in months. I hardly recognized her. She doesn't look very much like she did when she was younger."

Brett turned to the stranger in the cave and said, "The Indians won't take it kindly for you to say anything about her in town. They still scalp people sometimes."

The man nearly fainted; he turned pale and began stammering. "There's no way I will say anything. I don't want anything to do with those Indians!"

Carl nearly strangled on his coffee and turned his face to keep from laughing. He knew the tribe was very friendly and kind.

"Have you heard of the Indians skinning anyone lately? They used to do that, too." Carl said, making it a bit worse.

"I haven't heard anything lately, but a person never knows about that band of Indians," Brett answered, grinning into his coffee cup.

The Indians over the mountain were tamer than Brett or any of his men!

"Listen here, I saw nothing. I didn't even hear about someone getting shot. I'll be out of here as soon as possible and never be back in Oklahoma, either. I can't handle crazy Indians and loco women.

He was so pale that Brett and Carl thought the man might get sick.

They laughed heartedly, and Carl said, "Well, maybe the Indians are probably not quite that mean."

"Yeah, right! I've heard enough. May I please go now, find my four-wheeler, and get the heck out of here?" The man choked.

"Yes," Brett said. "You may leave, but let me warn you before you go. Watch for Charlie because he is definitely dangerous. If you wait, we will go with you to get your ride before we leave. We will only be up here a few more days. Then we can all leave together."

I'm sending two of my men to retrieve Detective Rommeria. They should be back by tomorrow, and then, God's willing, I will be well to get back to my home the following day. We have food and supplies that will last until then, and we can finish cooking the steer you killed." Brett stated.

"Wait a minute. Do you think I killed that steer? No, Sir. She made me help her drag it here. That she-cat killed it with that crossbow. I never killed any steer."

Brett thought; Margo shot the steers herself. She owned half the ranch and the steers. She didn't steal the cattle; they were already hers.

The men all sat around the fire, waiting for the ranch hands to get back with the detective. They found out more about the mystery man.

His name was Jessie Latham, and he had come from Illinois. He and his hunting buddy had been told by other hunters that there were lots of elk in Oklahoma, that it was open range and free to hunt on. He took the men for their word and had driven over a hundred miles to hunt elk on the mountain.

Jessie said, "Brett, I am probably listed as missing by now. Please, forgive me for hunting on your land."

As the day came to a close, Brett told Jessie. "I tell you what, Jessie, if you want to hunt here next year, I will ask one of the braves to be your scout. They will help you find elk. The animals must be thinned out yearly, but I won't allow trophy hunting."

Jessie looked at Brett and said with eyes as big as saucers, "No, sir. I thank you kindly. But I won't come back to Oklahoma. I have seen enough of this beautiful country for the rest of my life, but I must say it's the prettiest state I've ever visited." They all laughed for some time.

The detective came to the cave with the coroner to examine Margo's remains and return her body to Spur Lacy.

The detective asked Brett where he wanted her buried. "She will be buried in the family plot next to our twins. I will be home to make the arrangement as soon as I can travel without losing too much blood."

Brett left the cave for a while to let the tears flow and settle his mind. It was unfortunate that this had happened, but he was relieved at the same time. He had loved that woman with all his heart, and she had broken it into little pieces. After tomorrow, he would say his goodbyes to her forever.

The men remained in the cave another night. They were all anxious to return to the bunkhouse to rest. The horses had to stop and rest several times. Going down the mountain was treacherous, but they had to get Brett off the mesa. The horses kept slipping in the snow, ice, and underbrush.

Brett had been gone for four days. He was miserable, and in excruciating pain by the time his crew of men hauled him to the tack room in a wagon.

Whew! He thought *what a trying week I had* as the crew lifted him from the wagon.

Decorating The House

While the men were away tending to the cattle, Little Dove Two talked Maria into getting down the Christmas decorations. It would be wonderful to make this big, beautiful log home with the long, winding stairs and the newels with the square tops all Christmassy. It is such a magnificent house, Little Dove Two thought.

There were many decorations in the upstairs walk-in closets—electric lights for the inside and out. The robes were plentiful, and those large bulbs were simply out of this world!

Every ornament was so beautiful!

I wonder if I could decorate the big fir tree outside. I will mention it to Brett when he returns. It would be fantastic to put bulbs and lights on that big tree, yes, it would! Little Dove Two thought.

"Maria, I need a ladder. I can't reach the treetop to put the robes on. These ceilings are what twenty feet tall?" Little Dove Two asked.

"Yes, they are. How did you know?"

"I just guessed," Little Dove Two laughed.

"The ladders are in the shed, out by the tack room, but I don't think it safe to go out there until the men return, and we need someone around in case one of us should fall. We can decorate the stairs and put out the small things, but we best leave the larger tasks alone until later." Maria grinned.

"The chandeliers here in this house are Lussorian type, aren't they? The chandeliers light up the halls and sitting rooms exquisitely. This house is beyond beautiful, and all the furnishings are brilliant. Who designed it, Maria?" Little Dove Two asked.

"Brett's' father. He came from France and settled in America. He was a shipbuilder. He had shipyards all over the world. He met Little Dove and fell for her hook, line, and sinker. Little Dove didn't care for fancy things but loved him so much that she would have lived rich or poor. He had expensive tastes. He made sure she had the best of everything. Brett told me this," Maria said with a twinkle in her eyes.

"She was never comfortable here after he passed. When Brett reached eighteen, Little Dove returned to the village where she was raised."

Maria and Little Dove Two worked for hours on decorations, sorting out each piece and separating color coordinates.

The handrails look very Christmassy indeed! Little Dove Two mixed holly with bells and ivy, and on the newels, she put red and white poinsettias, which Maria had grown for this very occasion.

They put tinsel, robes, and ivy on the mantels. Everything looked warm and cheerful.

Little Dove Two hung mistletoe in the doorway that led into the foyer.

"That's a good way to be kissed, don't you think, Maria? Catch someone unaware. Well, how does it look? You think Latte would enjoy a kiss or two?" Little Dove Two laughed, raising an eyebrow at the older lady.

Maria swatted the little ladies behind and grinned. "Get down, young lady. It's time we had a cup of hot cocoa and maybe a bite to eat. My tummy says it's mealtime." The two laughed spontaneously and walked happily to the kitchen.

Little Dove Two giggled under her breath, knowing she did it right. Maria wanted the mistletoe as much, if not more than she did. She was anxious to see her and Latte under the mistletoe.

If I owned this big mansion, I would have so many children running around that there would never be time for sadness or worries. I might even start an orphanage.

But the thought made Little Dove Two sad. She knew that would never come to pass.

Maria began pouring the coco when she heard horses coming around the house.

Brett said, "Carl, put the horses up, and don't forget to rub them down. I don't need a sick animal."

"Maria," Brett called from the doorway as he flung his hat on the custom-made wall hanger.

"Would you please run a bath water for me? I can hardly wait to soak in the tub. I also need some patching up on my side. I fell on something sharp."

He didn't want her to know a crossbow had shot him, nearly causing his death.

Holding onto Carl, Brett said softly, "Maria, I need your help to remove my boots, coat, and muddy chaps, or I will track in snow and leaves."

Carl helped Brett into the straight-backed chair and left for the tack room.

Brett couldn't face Maria as he told her of Margo's death. They sat in the mud room and cried together.

"We will bury her tomorrow, here in the family plot. Everyone will be here. I must bring Little Dove here; she loved Margo like her daughter. We will have the funeral at noon if it's appropriate with you?" Brett asked.

Maria sobbed. "It is best. She didn't find peace in her lifetime and forgot who she was, but Brett, I loved her dearly."

A while later, tearfully, Maria asked Brett. "What happened to her?"

Brett couldn't look Maria in her eyes as he recalled the incident. "Four days ago, she tried to shoot a man with a crossbow, and the man shot her. It was self-defense. She gave him no choice." He omitted to say it was Carl.

Maria said with a heavy heart. "I need to rest now. I want to speak with Little Dove when she arrives."

Maria helped Brett remove his spurs, wet boots, coat, and chaps.

Suddenly, Maria became weak. "I will run you some bath water."

Walking by the island slowly, she handed Little Dove Two a tube of anti-biotic cream.

"Brett has been wounded and needs a clean bandage for his side. Would you please take care of it? I am exhausted."

Little Dove Two was stunned at Maria's expression. "What happened!" She said with concern. The older woman began to shake and cry uncontrollably.

"My daughter died four days ago. I understand she tried to kill a man. I can't talk about it now. Go to Brett. He can tell you what happened." Maria sadly walked away.

Little Dove Two found Brett in the mudroom. "Brett, what happened? What happened to your side? Are you still bleeding?" Little Dove Two was wide-eyed and scared when she saw the stab wound in his side. "How did this happen? Are you sure there's nothing inside that needs to come out? Maria told me Margo died. What happened to her?" Little Dove Two asked, her face drained of color and not slowing down for a breath of air between sentences.

She loved the older woman who was grief-stricken and hated to see her hurting.

"Little Dove Two, I don't think I can tell you everything just now, but yes, Margo is dead, but it wasn't me who killed her," Brett stated.

"I will explain everything later. When a man gets hurt in the field, there are many germs. Carl fixed me up as best he could, but it needed to be cleaned again, wrapped with gauze, and taped. I feel like a wimp when I ask someone to tend to me. Maria feels like my mother, so naturally, I don't mind asking her, but with someone else, it's embarrassing."

"Brett, please. I could never do enough for you, not after what you have done for me. I'm sorry about Margo. I know she was your wife, and you still had feelings for her. I wish she and you could have had a better understanding. She was beautiful. I'm sure when you married her, she was different." Little Dove Two had tears of sorrow in her eyes.

"Little Dove Two, you have no idea how vile she became before she tried to kill Charlie. One morning, a man who worked with Carl came to me. He asked for the wages he had coming. I asked him why he was leaving. He said I can't be near your wife. I wanted an explanation, but I didn't expect the one he gave me. He said Margo asked him to take her away, saying I was mean to her. He advised her to return to the house before someone saw her. She told him that she wasn't going back. She then asked what it would take for him to kill me. He told her there wasn't enough money in the world to make him take the life of another human being. He pushed her out the door, literally. I paid the man for his work. I didn't blame him for not wanting to stay. I don't want to talk about Margo anymore!" Brett told Little Dove Two.

Little Dove Two would love to put her arms around him for comfort, but she knew this was not the right time.

"Okay, you're finished. That's as good as I can put you back together. You should see the doctor in town to be on the safe side. Oh, Lieutenant Markham saw Maria while she was shopping; he wants to come up here to discuss something with you. He also said he wanted to speak with Margo at the church function. It upset Maria tremendously."

"Well, first of all, Markham won't be coming up here uninvited. I don't like that man, not one iota. He has been obnoxious toward my ranch hands. He locked a few of them up on several occasions for no reason. He accused them of causing a row. That wasn't true; they were having a home-cooked meal at the local restaurant. It wasn't them starting trouble at the barbershop.

Someone traveling through town had stopped in for a trim and disrespected a young lady. The barber heard her say that she would get her pa and that no one would talk to her like that and get away with it. The barber ran to the sheriff. The proprietor told the lieutenant it was my ranch hands. No, he doesn't want to come up here."

Brett turned to Little Dove Two and said. "You have nothing to fear. I will protect you.

I need to talk with my mother tomorrow. I would like her to come here to live out the rest of her days. I could make it much easier for her. She has never agreed to live here since my father died, but there is always hope."

Grinning, he changed the subject. "The decorations look very nice. I bet you and Maria worked on them all day."

"When you feel better, I would like to have a ladder so we can finish. I want to put a star on the top. Would you mind if we decorate the big fir in the yard?" Little Dove Two asked.

"Of course, Brett smiled at the idea. I hired two ladies to help with the work that needs to be done. I don't want you or Maria climbing any ladder. I need them here to help Maria when the undertaker arrives with Margo's remains. I'm exhausted and will retire for the rest of the day." Brett stated.

Brett looked pale; Little Dove Two had never seen him so tired.

Little Dove Two went to the sun porch. It was an excellent place to think. The clouds had diminished into a clear sky. The scenery was spectacular, with snow piled high on the mountaintop. Green fir trees shimmered with icy droplets. The snow on the pathway had begun to melt, although more was expected the next day. She thought *I wish it would stop; I'm tired of staying inside.*

She wanted to go out, but someone might see her and ask questions. Brett said not to worry, so Little Dove Two took him at his word. She would not worry … not today … she would do that tomorrow. *I hope Lattermar has good news,* she thought.

I will ask him a few questions when he gets here. Yes, that's what I'm going to do. It's time I started to learn things for myself!

The following day, Brett prepared to leave for the village.

"Brett, would it be okay if I come along? I need some fresh air." Maria asked.

Thankful she decided to join him, he answered. "Sure, Maria. It would be better than talking to myself."

Brett told Maria that he would be ready to leave in a few moments.

He called Lattermar. "Hey, there 'old man. Will you be busy tomorrow?" Brett asked.

"I had planned on visiting you today, Brett, but if you have other plans, I can wait," Latte said, disappointed.

"We're having a funeral tomorrow. Margo died yesterday. Today, I must go to the village and retrieve Little Dove. She would want to be here for the funeral. I will meet you here, say at ten o'clock tomorrow morning? I want you here for the burial. Maria will need your support, too." Brett said.

Latte had a bit of news to tell Brett, but it could wait. "I'll be there at ten sharp. After the funeral, we must talk about the Lovers' Lane murders."

"Tell Little Dove hello for me. I would love to see her again." Latte wondered if she knew anything about Little Dove Two.

I wonder what Brett will think when I tell him I found this briefcase that the detective missed on Lovers' Lane. It was lying in a crevice under a brush pile, just waiting to be discovered. It's good that I went up there before it snowed, or I might not have seen it.

Markham would never have told me about it or the content; I won't tell him either.

He thought about what he needed. Inside is a photograph of a woman who looks a lot like Little Dove Two, except the facial features are somewhat off. I need a strand of her hair to compare to those stuck in the briefcase handle. There was some hair in one grave site near where the other women were buried that didn't belong to the victim. I need to be sure. Nothing adds up. There was another woman there at the gravesite that day, and I'm confident that one wasn't dead.

While at Brett's, I will help myself to Little Dove Two's hair brush, and __Walla __I will get her DNA with no one the wiser.

I don't want to see Brett get involved with another she-cat. Lattermar thought. Tomorrow, yes, I'll wait. Hopefully, I'm wrong, but I wouldn't count on it.

Brett and Maria entered the Indian camp. One of the young braves asked that they follow him to the home of Little Dove.

Brett explained to Little Dove what happened to Margo and that it was an accident she was killed. "Mother, the funeral will be at the ranch tomorrow at noon."

Little Dove held out her arms to her son. He hugged his mother as their tears mingled. Maria watched silently.

Little Dove held her arms out to Maria and said. "You were her mother by birth, and I, her mother of my native village. We tried so hard to keep up with her. I loved her as a daughter, but I couldn't control her.

The braves tried to watch her, to keep her safe, but she always gave them the slip. I wish I could have protected her from herself, but that wasn't possible. I am so sorry, Maria."

Little Dove dried her tears and asked if they had eaten. There was coffee and some good hoecakes by the fire. They sat cross-legged around the fire in prayer and remembrance. Maria was amazed at the delicious food.

"Mother, I want to ask you something. I want you to reconsider returning to my home. I have plenty of room and would love to have my mother and mother-in-law live with me.

I think you both would benefit from it. Both of you are such good people. I love you, my mother, and I want you near me for the rest of our lives. I will make you as comfortable as possible. I hired two ladies from Spur Lacy. They will do the cooking, mending, and other odd jobs; you can do whatever you want. Will you come home with me, mother?" Brett pleaded.

"Son, I know you love me, but this is my home. I love it here. I have lived here with my Indian family most of my life. I will return to your home for Margo's funeral and take extended visits with you, but I want to live out the rest of my days here. I am sorry, my son. I will accompany you, but you must bring me back tomorrow afternoon. I have to prepare clothes for the masquerade party. I will come next week and go with you to the celebration at St Joseph's. Do you think it would be okay if I dress as an Indian? I made a very nice dress?" Little Dove grinned.

"Only my mother would say something like that. The Indian dress will be perfect, Mother, but do remember to dress for a Christmas setting." Brett laughed.

"I will do that, Son. I'm not feeble in the mind yet. During that time, I will spend a few weeks with you," she said.

He looked into the sad eyes of the small woman, and his heart felt broken to see just how frail she had become in the last few years. He wished she would let me take care of her from now on.

The next day, the body of Margo Canterfield was returned to the ranch for burial. Maria stood over the casket to say goodbye to her daughter. She let her tears flow. Saying goodbye was the hardest thing she had ever done.

It was more challenging than when Margo's father died. That one was a blessing in disguise. She then stepped back, giving Little Dove access to the casket of her chosen daughter.

Little Dove walked up to the casket, looking down at the daughter she had tried so hard to protect. Her tears fell freely. She would miss her but knew she was finally at peace. She would now be in heaven where there would be no more pain. The Heavenly Father would wipe away all her tears.

Brett looked at the face of the woman he had loved since they were children. He loved her so much. Even when she had tormented him so badly, tears filled his eyes with memories, but also a feeling of peace. He knew there would always be a place in his heart for her.

"Let me know when you're coming so I can meet you at the top of the mountain. Lately, Charlie the Grizz growls at me; he cannot be trusted. I think it's because he's old and cantankerous," Brett said as he hugged his mother tightly.

"Brett, you have always been the perfect son. I knew you would grow up to be a kind and generous man. You look more like your father than me, and you are like him, with a heart of gold. Please don't ever change. I must ask, who is the young lady staying at your house? Is she one of Maria's family?"

"Mother, that is some story. I found her in the woods about a half-hour walk from the ranch.

She was almost Charlie's lunch. He was coming up the hill almost to the top when I saw her standing beside a tree with her eyes shut. When I grabbed her mouth to keep her screams retained, she thought I was the bear, and she fainted.

When she came back to consciousness, she didn't remember her name or where she came from. I'm working on that now.

All she could remember was that someone had tried to bury her alive, but my P.I. friend, Lattermar, was working to find out. He can acquire the unknown, from who she is to where she came from. We don't want the authorities to know where she is just yet because someone out there is trying to kill her."

His mother's only answer was, "Oh my!"

"I will leave you now with the promise that you will be on my mountain next week, okay?" Brett put on his best grin when he said goodbye. He hated to leave his mother, but this was her wish, and he would honor it.

"I will be there, my son, as I promised. I will let you know the day before, or at least give you time to get me from this side," Little Dove stated.

He hugged his mother as he left her at the village. She waved goodbye to him until he was out of sight.

Brett and Maria rode back home in near silence. Both were exhausted. The roads had opened up as much as one could expect.

Brett thought it would be no problem getting to St. Joseph Church next week if the weather stayed this nice. The clouds that threatened more snow had vanished, and he hoped people could travel that day without getting stuck in snowdrifts.

When they reached the ranch house, Little Dove Two was waiting with dinner slowly simmering on the stove. "What is that wonderful aroma," Brett declared. "It smells superb! Let me guess, it's sweet potato pie."

Little Dove Two laughed. "Yes, sir, I made it today for you and Maria, and there's a pot roast in the kettle."

Maria said. "Umm, Little Dove Two, this is very good. It's the best I've had in a long time that I didn't cook. Your pot roast is even better than mine; everything is excellent."

Brett said. "Well, I cannot say the meal was better than Maria's, but it was delicious. If I said it was better, Maria might not fix me a good meal anymore," He laughed.

"Brett, we both know she can outcook me when it comes to pot roast." Maria laughed.

"After tomorrow, neither one of you will have to cook. That will give you time to do whatever you wish; the two ladies will be here. All of us can go for long walks or horseback riding. Maybe take the buggy to see beautiful sites, and when it's warmer, have picnic lunches under the big trees near the lake," Brett said.

"That sounds marvelous, Brett, but Charlie might be waiting for us out there." Maria shivered just thinking about that bear!

"Well, that sounds okay with me. I need the sun; my tan is fading." He grinned, showing straight white teeth.

The ladies knew that wasn't true; his tan was there to stay. After all, he was half-Indian. The women laughed and nodded with a quirky grin.

"Well, I'm going to retire. I'll see you two tomorrow. Lattermar will be here around ten in the morning. Maria, do you have any cookies made?" Brett asked.

"Yes, I have cookies for tomorrow; I don't want to spoil him." She laughed.

Brett thought. Now, I can get a good night's sleep and not worry about Margo coming to terrorize everyone.

"Good morning, sleepy head!" Maria called to Brett. "It looks like it's going to be a nice sunny day. I feel better today than I have in ages. I slept so hard last night that Saint Peter could have called me, and I would have missed him." She laughed.

Maria's in a happy mood, Brett thought. What's got into that old lady? That was the first time she laughed in a very long time. Oh yes, Lattermar is coming today. She would be a perfect mate for Latte.

What am I thinking? No, I can't lose Maria. She is an essential person in my life.

If he were to mistreat her, I would have to kill him. He has already dropped a hint about asking for her hand in matrimony. I must speak to him about this.

I must find out his intentions before he goes too far. Maria on the beach in Jamaica. The very idea!

"Breakfast is the best time of the day; don't you think so, Little Dove Two?" Brett asked as he sat beside her at the table.

"I always enjoy my breakfast with coffee and a rose," she grinned. "When Maria brought the meals to my room, there was always a rose. She told me you raised roses and vegetables in the basement. Hopefully, you will show me your garden. I have always loved roses. Now, where did I get that? I believe I always loved roses," she laughed.

"Hopefully, we can find out who you are; then maybe you can remember all your past. That will be good." Then he whispered in her ear. "For me, that is."

Little Dove Two blushed. *He makes me feel so giddy when he gets that close.* "Mind if I walk out with you while you have your smoke? There's something I want to tell you." Little Dove Two said with a solemn expression.

"By all means, my lady, join me."

"Brett, I don't know how to say this, so here goes; last night, I heard a blood-curdling howl. It sounded like an animal in distress. Did you hear anything? It was right after we retired for the night.

Brett knew she was still afraid. "Now, if you please, I will show you my garden in the basement." They walked to the basement garden, where the pretty roses bloomed all year long, and his vegetables produced their yield.

"What the heck? Look at this mess! I guess the door was left open, and animals came inside. Looks like Mr. Raccoon made himself at home again.

Maria, please come down here. I think we've had a varmint in the basement again."

"Oh, Brett! Not again. The clay containers are mostly broken. The roses have been turned upside down, and many vegetables are ruined. It just can't be!"

"Easy Maria. It looks like Mr. Raccoon and other animals ran down the rows and knocked over anything in their path. We must catch the varmint. We need to secure the area and clean up. Lattermar will arrive soon, and I need to speak with him."

An hour later, they had put everything back in order. The roses that weren't broken were re-potted.

The vegetables without broken stems were replanted, re-staked, and tied; they saved about half the crop.

Melrose, a young man from the village, met Brett at the basement door and relayed a message. "Your mother wants you to know that she will arrive this morning. She also wanted to know about the Grizz. She is terrified of him."

"We believe he is staying in the caves, but keep a watch out for him anyway. I want you to bring my mother over the mountain; I think it's safe. Don't let anything happen to her. You're not afraid of Mister Grizzley, are you?" Brett laughed.

"I understand. Little Dove is a special person. All the village people love her, and she is one of our elders." Young Melrose nodded. "But yes, I am afraid of that mighty Grizzley!"

Lattermar Arrives

Brett recognized the familiar sound of the carriage and immediately welcomed his guest. "Good morning, Latte. Come in and sit a spell. Hey Carl, have someone unhitch Latte's team. How about lunch? You haven't eaten yet, have you?"

Seeing the look on Lattermar's face, he asked. "What's up? You look like you got caught with your hand in the cookie jar." Brett laughed.

"This may be serious, Brett. We need to discuss Little Dove Two. She is still here, isn't she? I'm not sure what is in this briefcase. You and I need to go through it first, okay?"

Maria came out to meet Lattermar, which brightened his day. "Good morning, Maria. I want to visit with you, but I have business with Brett first. Would you please excuse us? It shouldn't take long." Latte frowned. "It better not take all day; I cannot wait to sink my teeth in one of those cookies."

Maria's face lit up like a red tomato. "That's fine, Latte. I will make some fresh coffee. It should be finished by the time you two are through gossiping." his voice made her heart skip. Was she fond of Lattermar, or was she in love with him? She wasn't quite sure.

"Brett, I came here before I talked to Lieutenant Markham. I returned to Lover's Lane after the detective and police finished their investigation. I found a briefcase with papers inside and a photograph of a woman. Here, take a look at this picture." Brett looked at the picture and was startled by the face.

"My God, Latte, this could easily be Little Dove Two," Brett exclaimed. "Yes, the features are the same, but look closely. There is a difference, too, don't you agree? Little Dove has no scar, and the hairline looks different. There is also a scar on her chin, and she doesn't have one there either."

Brett was very concerned at what he saw.

"I've looked at her closely; there are too many discrepancies for it to be the same without? Plastic surgery, maybe? We need to look at her a little closer. That's not all either; I found a phone number, too. I've tried to call it, but it belongs to an executive at Gloretia Industries in Houston, Texas. They wanted me to state my business, but I hung up. Until I find out more, I don't need to let anyone know anything. You think there might be a connection?" Latte finished.

Brett whistled softly. "The best thing to do is get Little Dove Two and compare the photo with her. Maybe even let her see the photo and get her reaction to the picture. I don't think she is hiding anything from us, but we must find some answers soon. What do you think, Latte?".

"Yes, I think that would be an excellent idea. For Little Dove Two's sake, I hope we can connect the dots before Markham finds her. He keeps questioning me, but I know how he works. Arrest first, then question later. I don't believe Little Dove Two knows anything about what happened on Lovers' Lane, but we must start somewhere." Latte stated.

Brett said. "Wait, Latte, don't upset her too much. Next week is the masquerade party, and she is looking forward to it. She has been through a lot, and I want her to enjoy all she can until we find the truth."

"That's understandable, Brett. Yet, we must confront her with what little we have to go on." Lattermar stated with concern.

"I would like you to hold off until after Christmas. We can pursue this after the masquerade party." Brett said flatly.

"Okay, I will do whatever you ask, Brett; you are my employer. I can get into trouble for withholding evidence." Lattermar stated.

"Let's go see if the coffee is finished. I would almost bet Maria has another batch of cookies waiting for you, Latte," Brett slapped Latte on the back as they entered the kitchen.

"That woman makes my heart flutter whenever she walks in the room, Brett. I can hardly think straight when she's around. I think maybe the love bug has struck again. I'm serious, and this is no joke. I may ask her to marry me when the weather breaks, and we have the time to find out if we want to be together for the rest of our lives." Lattermar chuckled.

Brett gave Lattermar a stern look and said, "Latte, you're a fine man, but I will have to be upfront with you, like before you ask for her hand. I'm about the closest relative she has. I am concerned about your intentions and how you decided to live with her. Beware, my friend. She is like my second mother." Brett's face told Lattermar he wasn't joking.

The two women waited for the men to enter the kitchen. There were plenty of cookies, coffee, much-welcomed talk, and laughter. It filled the house with an aroma of love. They talked about the masquerade party with music, food, and much worship.

Lattermar walked behind Little Dove Two to get another cup of coffee. He placed her hair over her ear and asked, "How will you wear your hair that night, my dear? Will you work golden strands of beads into those beautiful locks or wear them down? You have such beautiful hair. One thing is for sure: it will be beautiful however you fix it." Latte then sat beside Maria, patted her hand, and said. "You, my lovely, how are you wearing yours?"

He just had to know, and there was only one way to be sure. He just did it, and sure enough, there were scars. Sometime, somewhere, Little Dove Two had a facelift! Now, one hair would be sufficient. He looked down, and there on his arm was a hair, exactly what he needed!

He excused himself for a bathroom visit and retrieved the plastic container from his pocket. He took the hair strand and placed it inside. It would be analyzed when he returned to his office. Then he would know whether Little Dove Two had been in the car or near the two bodies.

Brett wasn't pleased with Lattimore when he saw what he did. He thought about asking him to leave, but Maria was enjoying their conversation and visit so much that he couldn't bring himself to end her night of pleasure. She had seen very few of those for such a long time. Tonight, she glowed and expressed contentment. It was all because of Latte!

Mistletoe hung just above the doorway. Little Dove Two had placed it there, especially for Maria and Latte. Maria stepped between the doorjambs as Little Dove Two nudged Lattermar's arm. She pointed to the top of the door and whispered, "You can take it from here."

Latte spun Maria around and planted an unexpected kiss on her lips. Maria's eyes flew wide open, and she blushed the deepest red ever. "Merry Christmas, Maria," Lattermar said with a thoughtful second kiss.

Lattermar was ready to leave but openly said to Maria. "Lady, you are the most beautiful woman I know. May I call on you after Christmas? I don't mean for cookies or coffee either." Latte asked cautiously.

Maria couldn't help but think that her face could have started a fire. She gracefully bowed to Latte and said, "Yes, you may, kind sir. I'll count on it."

Brett and Little Dove Two noticed the glow on Maria's face long after he left. She was even humming a tune.

Brett followed Lattermar outside, then turned to his friend and said, "Well, you looked. What do you think? Has she had a face-lift or plastic surgery?"

"I'm not sure, Brett. There are scars around both ears, but that could be from many things. I have a hair to analyze tomorrow, but that's as far as it goes until after Christmas." Latte said.

The truth can wait long after Christmas, Brett thought.

"Let me know when I can continue. I know Markham; he will be all over me after the twenty-seventh. Maybe I can find out more before he gets back in the office," Latte laughed. "What he doesn't know won't kill him, right?"

"I will talk to you later, my friend," Brett stated.

With that, Lattermar popped the reins for the horses to start back.

Twigs snapped close by, and the horses whinnied. Latte decided he really didn't want to know what was in the bushes. His heart pounded. He was glad when he saw the city streets!

… I made it … "Whew. I know that was Charlie, the Grizzly bear!" Latte uttered.

Little Dove arrived to go to the church with her son, Maria, and Little Dove Two. *I can't imagine why Brett named that girl after me. I'll ask sometime when we are alone.* She thought.

"Hello, Mother," Brett called when he saw her carriage come to a halt. "Melrose, won't you come in and stay a while?" he asked.

"Not this time. I must get back to the village. One of the elders might need me to retrieve something from town. I try to be available as much as I can. When I become an elder, I hope someone is appointed to be my nursemaid. Now, not that I mind being a nursemaid, mind you. I would do anything for one of the elders." He laughed heartily, as he cracked the whip for the animals to pick up their feet and move along. Never did he touch the horses with a strike. Patience was his virtue with people and animals.

"Hi, my beautiful Mother, I love your dress." She wore beads and buckskins and was lovely to look at. Brett always thought his mother was the prettiest lady, so dainty, yet so strong when the time arose.

"Thank you, Brett. I made the dress with one of the hides from this ranch. I bleached it white. The beads, I made myself. It gives me much honor to wear a garment made from the cattle raised by you, my son." Little Dove stood so proud.

Brett provides the village people with meat every year and in between times should they run low on food. They cleaned the hides for clothing. The clothes were much warmer than store-bought clothing. I hope they don't forget the old ways. The young must be taught the olden ways if someday they need to depend on the things they grow. Little Dove thought proudly of her son.

Little Dove walked in the front door just in time to see Little Dove Two ascending the stairs. *She is quite beautiful,* she thought. *She has the look of Indian descent.*

"Mother, I will show you to your room, or if you need to rest a while, it would be fine." Brett offered.

"I will retire now. We will have plenty of time to talk tomorrow. I must hear about the masquerade party again." Little Dove grinned as her son helped her up the stairs.

At the door, Little Dove said, "This isn't the room I usually use, is it Brett? I don't remember this colored curtain."

"No, Mother, but it faces the Mountain and valley. I put Little Dove Two in that room to watch her better. I can exchange the rooms if you would like." Brett answered.

"Oh, no, this is fine, it just seemed different, that's all." Little Dove thought this room was much prettier than the other one, even though there was no way one room could be more beautiful than the other, not in this house. My husband bought the finest of the fine of everything.

Now, his son is his mini-me, and he must have the best of anything that money can buy. Her heart soared with pride.

Little Dove hugged Brett and lightly kissed his cheek. "I will speak with you tomorrow, son. Right now, I need to rest."

"Goodnight, Mother," Brett said as he left the room.

Little Dove Two Was Excited

"**M**aria, it's the twenty-second. Maybe I should try on my costume again to be sure it fits well. It is gorgeous. The silk velvet feels so soft against my skin, and the deep blue color is how I feel inside. Maybe next year, I can laugh at these eerie feelings. It's supposed to be the most joyful time of the year. It took a while for me to get into the Christmas spirit, but now I'm so excited!" She exclaimed.

"Little Dove Two, no one at the church will look as pretty as you. You're beautiful." Maria answered as she pulled the zipper closed. We must put it away before Brett sees you. He might not want you to take it off," she laughed.

"Little Dove, what do you think of this beautiful lady?" Maria called as she watched Little Dove Two turn and spin around the room. The dress hung an inch above the floor, with a full skirt.

Tears stung Little Dove's eyes when she entered the room. *That is the type of dress that Margo wore,* she thought! *I must get a hold of my emotions quickly.* "That dress is most lovely. The color is right for you, too. You are a beautiful lady," Little Dove stated.

As night was closing quickly, Little Dove Two became more excited. "It must be the longest day of the year! I can hardly wait for tomorrow, Maria." She said with a grin.

Maria grinned, but Little Dove's thoughts were of Margo. I wonder if Maria loved her daughter as much as she seemed to love this girl. What am I thinking? Of course, she did. Little Dove then said. "You will be the most dashing lady there. You're quite breathtaking, my dear."

"You don't look like the little wimp that Brett dragged home; you have blossomed into a beautiful flower. Soon, you can model that dress." Maria became attached to the small, exotic young woman.

The coach was outfitted and decorated with tassels, red and gold bells, and red poinsettias. Beautiful, just right for Christmas. It satisfied Brett's taste. Everything was perfect.

Maria wore a red and white taffeta dress with a matching purse and shoes. She was stunningly gorgeous in a white fleece coat trimmed with red.

Little Dove sported a long white dress of dyed hides and an exotic turquoise necklace. Her creation was exquisitely magnificent.

Then came Little Dove Two. Her dress was the deepest shade of blue silk velvet with a high lacy neck, trimmed with sequels. Her shoes and purse matched with shining sequels. Her coat had sparkles and an overlay of lace. Brett felt he would stop breathing by her beauty.

"You women are awesome. I am privileged and humbled to be your escort today, ladies." Brett bowed lowly to the ladies. He felt ecstatic.

Carl and some of the ranch workers were also going to the church. A few leaned on the side of the buckboard, preparing to get seated; one of the men gave a low whistle.

Brett cleared his throat and raised an eyebrow. "It's time to start down."

The men grinned as Brett drove away. "Some men have all the luck, but he has three beauties to escort. That's against nature," one drover said out of earshot. They all had a good laugh. Brett was an excellent boss, and they loved him like a brother.

One coach could maneuver the incline easily, but it was a disaster to meet one! Everyone was comfortable and cozy, with comforters tightly wrapped around their legs. Suddenly, the horse jerked, reared, and bolted. Brett tried desperately to control them.

"Hold on. It's going to get bumpy," Brett yelled. The horses raced to escape whatever was in the bush, but a buckboard appeared right before them! The coach rammed the rear end, sending their occupants flying.

The coach reeled sideways and came to rest against the wall of snow-covered dirt.

"Is everyone okay?" Brett yelled. "I can't see either one of you. The coach between us."

Maria answered. "Little Dove, are you okay? Little Dove Two, you were in the middle. Did we squash you?"

"I'm pinned." Little Dove Two replied in a quivering voice. "I cannot move my arm!"

"Do you think something is broken?" Brett asked Little Dove Two.

"Is everyone okay?" Carl called out as he arrived. "Brett, what do you need? Can we move the coach without harming someone?"

"How about the men? Is anyone hurt or needing medical attention? I know you all took a tough fall, tossed in the air like balloons," Brett snickered.

"The men are okay, someone answered. We've had harder tosses breaking a bronco." They laughed.

"You men get a firm hold on the front. Carl and I will push while the men in front guide the coach. Okay, push!" Brett yelled.

"Stop! Little Dove Two screamed. You're taking off my arm! Eeiow." She was certain the arm was broken, and she had a sick stomach. "Of all the luck, I sure didn't need this to happen."

Why did I hang my arm hanging out anyway? I always do something dumb! She thought.

Brett studied the situation. Fear crept up his back. He knew what must be done.

"Carl, get me a hammer, some rope, and a pry bar from the tack room. We have to tear the coach apart to free her arm. Try to hurry, okay?"

Brett knew Little Dove Two needed medical treatment. *What can I tell the Doctor about her? Since it's an accident, it has to be reported to the authorities; Lieutenant Markham will be breathing down my throat*, he thought.

"Brett," Little Dove Two called to him. "What are we going to do? Can one of the medicine men fix up my arm?" She asked, feeling fear of the unknown. "If I see a doctor, we would be late getting to the church, don't you think?"

"It doesn't matter. The church can wait. We'll take first things first and then worry about whatever else later, okay? We won't miss all of the festivities. It goes on from tonight through Christmas day." Brett was more concerned about her injury than the party.

"There is a good medical doctor in Spur Lacy. He needs to check you out. The medicine man only doctors the Indians. He doesn't use his witchcraft on white people." Brett laughed but was panicked to the max.

The medicine man, or Didanawisgi, had doctored him many times, but he wasn't about to take a chance with Little Dove Two. He didn't know who she was and didn't want anyone coming down on the village people about anything. She must stay away from the village. He didn't want her near the young braves either. Not that he was jealous, but she was defenseless.

Carl and the two men brought another buggy with them.

"Brett, take Little Dove Two to the doctor in the buggy we brought back from the ranch. If you want us to, the rest of us will stay and clean up this mess." Carl asked.

They pried and pulled on the coach, releasing the women. Maria had a knot on her face right under the eye. Little Dove was shaken up but didn't even have a scratch.

Little Dove Two, well, she had a swollen eye and a cut on her left arm. Her right arm had begun to swell. It looked broken. Her once beautiful dress was in shambles. The sleeve on the right arm was torn off.

"My new dress is ruined. It's torn from the bodice down. Brett, I must return to the ranch and change into another dress."

"First, the doctor will check you over, then we'll worry about what you should wear," Brett stated.

"Okay, but I don't want to miss any more than necessary. My arm is okay. I don't want to bother the doctor on such short notice. He will close early today so he can be at the church," Little Dove Two said.

"I feel lucky to have a mask to wear. I couldn't go with swollen eyes; I can tell it's beginning to blacken already." Little Dove Two whimpered.

"Dr. Blackman is going to check your arm first. If he is already at the church, he wouldn't mind going to his office, especially if they are as pretty as you, my dear." Brett replied.

Little Dove Two blushed a deep red.

The drovers took the buckboard back to the ranch. They knew it would be late when they reached town, but they all agreed being late wasn't so bad since no one had gotten killed.

That was the real miracle of this day! God moves in mystical ways.

The drovers entered the church, knelt on the kneelers, and thanked God for His blessings.

Brett, Little Dove Two, and Maria went on to Spur Lacy. The doctor's office was closed, so they went to his home.

The doctor's wife answered Brett's knock on the door. When she saw Little Dove Two, she called to her husband in an urgent voice. "Doctor, come quick, you have an emergency!"

Doctor Blackman was putting his cuff links. He stopped before he got it pushed through the eyelet and handed it to his wife. "Put these up, dear. I may be tied up for a while. Go ahead to the church. I will join you there. Brett, meet me at my office so I can check that little lady's arm."

Dr. Blackman, born Cherokee and from the village, said, "It's good to see you again, Little Dove. How are you?"

Little Dove nodded; "I'm good, Dr. Thank you for asking."

When the Doctor cut away the sleeve of Little Dove Two's gown, she began to cry. It was the first pretty dress she had gotten in a long time.

"What is your name, young lady?" the doctor asked while he worked on her. "I have to put this down in my records. I have to report all accidents to the state department. I know you are of Indian descent, but I must know which tribe so it can be recorded."

Little Dove Two said. "I am Little Dove Two. I came from the village over the mountain. Little Dove and I were visiting Mr. Brett and Maria. We were on our way to the church when the accident occurred. That's all there is to it. It was just an accident. I'd rather you treat me since I am here. It doesn't have to be sent to my family."

Dr. Blackman studied the lady. Never had he seen a Cherokee with a facial structure like hers, but then, maybe one of her parents wasn't the native Indian of that village.

"Yes, ma'am, but I have to report it. It's the law. I do everything legally. You understand, don't you?" he was concerned why she didn't want it reported.

"I understand you must do your job, but it's Christmas, and I just didn't want my family to know I was in an accident, that's all, and I'm not hurt badly." She sounded so truthful.

Little Dove stood up and said. "Doctor, I am an elder from the village. I will see that it is reported as soon as we get back home." She overheard the conversation between the doctor and Little Dove Two.

The Doctor thought. A report has to be filed and turned over to the state department. He would do that right after Christmas, but for tonight, there was no need to call anyone out. Besides, everyone would be busy at the church. There was much to celebrate. Everyone wanted to praise God and give thanks to the baby Jesus.

He grinned at Little Dove. He knew they wanted to hurry, just like him.

Dr. Blackman looked at Little Dove and Little Dove Two and then said. "For tonight, we will not mention this incident to the sheriff or anyone else, but I must complete a report on Monday morning. I can't and won't do anything illegal, and I don't think you would want me to either," he grinned.

"Thank you, Doctor. Monday will be fine; I didn't want something this minor to take us away from the church festivals. We have been planning to attend the festival for quite some time." Little Dove Two said in sincerity.

Brett heard what they told the doctor, and he was glad she thought of it, but he didn't like her telling a fib. It sounded like the truth, and she wasn't hurt badly, and his mother, of all people, had agreed!

My mother must have taken to Little Dove Two, he thought. That's a good thing.

Brett asked Maria. "How do you feel? Do you still want to go to the Church or rather go home?"

"I am okay, Brett. If everyone else is all right, this old woman won't be the cause of missing the celebration," Maria grinned.

She thought about Latte being there, which gave her a warm feeling. *No, I wouldn't miss it for the world.*

"How about you, mother? You took an awful tumble. Are you sure you're not hurt somewhere?" Brett was concerned for the older women; he remembered they developed brittle bones. But she seemed okay, at least for now.

"I am fine, son. I could never be better. I think my son may be in love again. I hope I am right. You need to get on with your life." Little Dove grinned, showing her pride.

"Mother," Brett whispered, grinning from ear to ear with a reddened face. He reached over and planted a small kiss on Little Dove's cheek. "I can't get anything past you, can I?"

Little Dove Two came from the exam room and looked at Brett. "I only had a sprung elbow, so I am fine!" She exclaimed. "I have to get a sling fitted to help hold up my arm. I should be out in about twenty minutes. Can we return to the ranch so I can change into another dress?" She asked Brett.

Brett shook his head, saying it would be okay at Little Dove Two, but he had another idea.

After Little Dove Two had departed the exam room, he turned to Maria and said. "I saw the dress shop was still open as we went to the doctor's house. Would you do me a favor? See if you can find the same dress that Little Dove Two has on. That would really surprise her; she'd still have the gown with no one the wiser. If you can't find it, get her the prettiest long dress they have. What do you think?" Brett anxiously asked.

"I think that's a marvelous idea. Little Dove Two can change here in the Doctor's office before we leave." Maria grinned.

Maria hurried to the ladies' apparel shop. She found the same blue silk velvet gown with the sequel high neck collar and the correct size. The sales lady looked at her strangely for a minute and then exclaimed, "Aren't you the lady that bought that same dress the other day?" With an astonished look on her face.

"That was me; the other one was destroyed in an accident. The little lady liked it so well that we replaced it with the new one." Maria answered.

"It is a gorgeous dress. I don't have many calls for this material. Silk velvet is hard to come by. It's so rare." The sales lady commented.

"Yes, I suppose you're right."

Maria rushed out with her parcel in tow. She had to hurry. *Little Dove Two will be out soon, if not already.* Maria thought.

Brett held the door for Maria. He peeked inside the box before she had time to set it down. "I got it, Brett. It's the same one. She will be the prettiest lady at the party."

"Maria, maybe the Doc should look at that eye. It's getting blue, and it's swollen." Brett stated.

"I am okay, Brett. Quit your worrying. Grown women know when to see a doctor." Maria said.

Little Dove Two walked from the exam room and into the waiting area. "Well, I'm ready to go home. I can't possibly go looking like this." Little Dove Two dropped her head. "I'm sorry, I will make everyone late for church." She couldn't help but feel tears stinging her eyes. She had looked forward to this for about a month, but now, everything was ruined.

"Not so," Brett said with a grin. He handed her the package. This bag is for you.

Little Dove Two opened the bag with the plain paper. Her eyes got big, and she cried. "Wow! Brett, you shouldn't have!"

Before she realized what she was doing, Little Dove Two grabbed Brett, hugged him, and planted a big kiss on his lips.

Little Dove looked at the couple and grinned. She thought, *My son and this beautiful lady.* Seeing a glowing look on Brett's face made her feel happy again.

"It was the least I could do. My team almost killed you, causing you to rip your dress to a shamble. Scared you half to death, and--He whispered in her ear—and you lied to the doctor."

She whispered back. "It was the least I could do. I didn't want any questions asked. The doctor thoroughly examined me, and I haven't had any children. That is a blessing."

"Now, while I settle the doctor's bill, you get dressed so we can get to the church. I want to get settled in before it is too late." He always hated to be the last man there.

The church was too large for Little Dove Two, just too many people. She decided how she would answer if anyone asked questions. *I will say: It's a masquerade party, and no one is supposed to know who is behind the mask,* she thought.

It was stuffy inside, but Little Dove Two would stay inside because she knew safety was in numbers.

This party was one she had ever attended. There were study tables with people reading from the bible and the meanings of the verses. There was a confession booth with the light on and children playing everywhere. Some of the older children were gathered around talking. One room was set up with bingo tables, and the game was ready to begin. In adjoining rooms, many people were on the kneelers, praying. *There were many different things to do,* she thought.

Brett was near when Lieutenant Markham spoke to Little Dove Two. "Hello, you sure look beautiful, my dear. Now, let me guess who is under that mask. As he reached for her mask, Brett was there in a flash."

"Lieutenant Markham, how are you? Maria told me you wanted to visit after Christmas. It's not advisable to come upon the mountain. You know there's a grizzly somewhere that's as despicable as they come."

Then, easing the lieutenant away from Little Dove Two, he asked. "How could you possibly want to come upon my mountain anyway after the way you treated my ranch hands? They were in town just to get haircuts and relax?"

By then, Little Dove Two had moved away from the area where they were talking. She felt sweat forming on her brow, and it wasn't from the heat.

"Brett, how are you man?" Lattermar asked, Interrupting.

The lieutenant frowned at Latte.

He was annoyed at Brett for butting in when he was just about to ask that pretty little lady who she was. But he didn't suppose it mattered. Probably some kid here with her family. But that dress. Wasn't that the one Maria was buying the other day with Brett's money? But who is that? I will find out before I leave here.

Over-ridding Lattermar, the lieutenant continued his conversation.

"Brett, there's been things happened here in Spur Lacy that I think might concern your mountain. I must come up there to speak with you. It is of utmost importance. Robbie told me about his visit with you on your mountain." Markham snickered. "I don't intend to climb a tree; I couldn't if I wanted to. My wife feeds me too well." He shook his bulging belly.

"Well, okay, if you must. Right now, it's Christmas time. Let's have a little fun and enjoy the party," Brett grimaced.

Little Dove Two had moved away from Markham's ogling eyes.

"You must excuse me now, Lieutenant. I hope you understand." Brett nodded and started to turn away.

"Yes, I do, Brett. Who is the lady wearing the beautiful Dark blue velvet dress? I've never seen a more beautiful gown. I bet that was quite expensive." Lieutenant Markham said, right to the point.

"I say, old chap, yes. It is a very nice gown, and it cost me plenty. Who is under the mask? It is a masquerade party, right? That lady is with my mother, Maria, and me. She is Little Dove Two, one of the village people." Brett answered not too nicely.

"Excuse me, I want to speak to a friend I haven't seen for a while. Goodnight, Lieutenant." Brett said flatly, hoping he caught his drift. Next time, it could be different when the ranch hands are relaxed in town. He would gladly pay the fine just to see Markham smacked around a few times. Yes, he would indeed!

Lieutenant Markham knew he'd been rough on Brett Centerfield's ranch hands. It looked like Brett's Indian side might be oozing out. He could get nasty if he wanted, but Markham knew Brett wasn't anyone the law wanted to push. He knew the governor personally, and he wasn't too sure he didn't also know the president; *yes, I better back off,* the lieutenant thought, at least tonight.

Benson Carver entered the church acting as if he was a member. He had on the make-up he had bought earlier. His attire was a perfect disguise. A long robe, a large sash around his waist, sandals, and a sheik's headdress. Now, he looked like one of the wise men.

With a fake beard and heavy eyebrows, the costume was very imaginable. He could have been a wise man in the flesh, except as dashing as he looked, he was also as dangerous as a stirred-up rattlesnake.

He strolled up to the priest and said. "My dear man. I have come from afar to worship the king." With that said, he bowed from his waist and then went to the kneelers to pray. As he knelt on the kneelers, he searched for his prey.

Then, he arose and walked to the front of the church. He grinned and shook hands with everyone. There she was! As big as life. She wasn't dead after all! That's why he hadn't heard about her on the radio. He wondered if she would recognize him.

He strolled up to her and bowed. She stared at him, but there was no apparent recognition. *He wondered if she would recognize him without the facial hair and robe or if she heard his voice again.* He chuckled to himself.

He had knocked her out cold. That was a shame. I could have had all her daddy's money and that BMW. I would have been miles away from here if I had gotten that ride. Benny thought to himself.

I have plenty of pictures and tapes her daddy could hear. I just got too careless. I have to get her back. He thought.

That old geezer at the hotel saw her with me and thought she was my wife. He must be as dense as the rest of these backwoods mannequins. I wonder if he saw her again if he would recognize her. Maybe not with the dress she was wearing tonight! He wanted to whistle under his breath, but someone might hear it accidentally. She is gorgeous! He thought.

She raised the mask just a second to scratch her nose. "That's her! I better be sure before I make another mistake and nab the wrong woman. Suppose I could get close enough to see the scars on her neck. That dim-witted dress has her too covered up; the top of her neckline is covered. I wonder where she's been? If I can't nab her here, I will follow and see who she's with and where she's staying," Benny snickered.

"Until then, I will find the banker's daughter. It would be great if I had them both; then I'd have more money in my pocket, and their daddies wouldn't mind paying for their sweet little daughters. I will have to shoot more videos to make their fathers cringe." He grumbled. "I will abolish both women simultaneously when I'm finished.

Little Dove Two enjoyed the atmosphere of St. Joseph's church. The night was getting colder as everyone huddled around the storyteller. Someone set the thermostat at 68 degrees. The elder ones were sitting close to stay warm. They told about baby Jesus being born in the stable, Christ teaching at twelve, and how Judas sold Jesus for thirty bits of silver. Everyone was interested in the stories as they continued well into the night. When one person was through telling a story, someone else would tell another. All were about the bible, the life and resurrection of Jesus Christ, our Lord.

The night was quiet, and then came a clatter and a big ho, ho, ho! The room was filled with the spirit of Christmas! Everything was amazing. The story-telling and Santa had just arrived, bringing the children toys and candy.

The people of Spur Lacy were exalted as they experienced a wonderful Christmas time together, and Little Dove Two enjoyed it immensely.

The church was packed. There was enough food, at least until the 26th. What a time to remember! They sang songs made from scriptures in the book of Psalms, from the bible.

The children played games and sat on Santa's knee, telling him what they wanted. With a jelly-bouncing belly, he laughed and said, "Ho, ho, ho. I brought you a few gifts this year. I hope you like what I got. I didn't have time to return to the North Pole for more toys this year. There was too much ice for the reindeer to fly Ho, ho, ho.

Little Dove Two was next in line for the restroom; she wanted to freshen up before the nighttime snack. Unaware, a man was just a few feet away, leaning against the wall for a brace. She raised her mask and rubbed her eye. Little Dove Two showed her face to the worst evil imaginable, Benson Carver!

Bennie grinned and said, "How lovely you are, my dear?" Then he turned away before she could answer.

That voice! I'm sure I've heard it before, but where? Little Dove Two thought. That voice scares me. I must find Brett when I'm finished in the restroom.

Little Dove Two turned to leave and ran smack into a young lady as she hurried into the washroom. "Sorry, I didn't mean to bump you," she apologized.

The young lady giggled. "Oh, that's perfectly all right. I should have watched where I was walking," she said smilingly. "I'm Natasia Mason. My father is the banker here. Isn't this the best Christmas party?"

Natasia Is Kidnapped

As Natasia left the restroom, an arm went around her waist. A cloth quickly covered her nose and mouth. She fell unconscious immediately. Bennie lifted the girl's nearly-nothing weight with ease out the side door and into the street.

Bennie laughed. "Well, little princess, the hotel will be fine for you to stay until I return with Miss Goodie's Two Shoes."

Natasia awoke with a headache and quickly realized she was tied to a bedpost. She thought, Where am I, and who grabbed me? Oh my God. I've been kidnapped! I will be still until I find out who I am dealing with. Then they'll understand I'm a handful. She grimaced.

Charles Mason was about to fill his plate with the delightful food. Fiddlers, baked potato, hush puppies, and a salad when he realized Natasia wasn't there. *Now, where did that young lady get off to? She has so many friends; I never know where she is. I want her to eat something.*

"Well, hello, Charles," Mrs. Markham said while dishing up green peas. "I haven't seen you lately. How is that daughter of yours? It seems like yesterday that Bonnie and I had brunch together. I miss her. She was my best friend. I guess Natasia is what? Seventeen now? She has always been so beautiful."

"Yes, she will be Seventeen on the thirtieth." Mr. Mason replied.

"The church is large but not big enough to lose her." Mrs. Markham grinned as she walked away.

"Mr. Mason, you have a phone call in the office. They said it's urgent." The lady from the rectory said.

Charles grinned. "Okay, I'll be right there. Hello, this is Charles Mason."

"Just listen and keep your mouth shut. I have Natasia, and you best do as you're told. Do I make myself clear? I will call you in a few days and tell you my intentions. If you so much as sneeze at the law, she will disappear, and no one will ever know where she went. I'm watching you as we speak, so you best act normal. Go on about your eating and festivities."

"Who is this?" Charles Mason screamed into a dead phone. Mr. Mason was afraid someone might ask questions about the call he received, so he rushed to the washroom quickly without being seen. He had to get his emotions under control. The surprise phone call had stunned him tremendously.

Charles began looking for Natasia, hoping it was a prank. He went to the kneelers and began to pray and to clear his head enough to think. *Should I tell Markham about this ridiculous call or keep quiet? Please, God, take care of my daughter. Keep her safe, please, Dear God,* he thought.

The Panic Button

Little Dove Two was scared. The man leaning against the wall had disappeared into the crowd; she couldn't understand why his voice frightened her so badly. *I best stay with other women, return to the cafeteria, and find Brett. My imagination is running wild!* She thought.

Little Dove Two was sweating as she entered the kitchen, and it wasn't from the heat. She finds Brett talking with some old acquaintances; she slips her arm through his.

When Brett felt her body tremble, he said. "Excuse me, gentlemen, I must speak with the lady."

Brett led Little Dove Two into the corridor so they could be alone. "What is wrong, Little Dove Two? You look as if you saw a ghost."

"I heard a voice that I remember, which scared me silly. I can't remember where I heard it," Little Dove Two answered.

"Was it a man or a woman?" Brett asked.

"A man, but he's disappeared. He's dressed like a wise man. He has a beard, heavy eyebrows, and sandals." She mumbled.

They searched the area but didn't see the man in a Wise Man costume. Then they walked toward the back door; Bennie was coming back inside. Brett sent Little Dove Two into the washroom with a nudge. Brett walked up to the man. With a nod, he asked. "Nice church; I came here when I was a kid. I know almost everyone who lives a hundred miles away. I don't know you; what is your name?" Brett grinned.

"Oh, I suppose not. We are traveling through this beautiful country. My wife and I had just got in our car and started driving. We were headed to Kansas when the snowstorm hit. We decided it would be best to stop, and then we decided to stay a while until the weather lets up." He answered.

"That still doesn't put a name to you, does it?" Brett asked with enthusiasm. "What is your name?"

"Well, this being a masquerade party for the next few days, I plan not to reveal my name. Why are you asking me all these questions? After all, this is a religious gathering." Bennie turned away and started to enter the dining area.

Brett grabbed him by the arm, revealing a De-man tattoo on his right hand. He shoved him against the wall. "Hey friend, I am a Mountain Man and will ask your name again. Then you might not like what happens. Either you will be sent to the local police station and questioned, or I might decide to take you outside and ask you not so nicely."

Bennie didn't want to raise too much fuss, or this man would blow his scheme right out the window and get him locked up to boot.

"Sorry, man, I didn't realize you were that upset. What is all the fuss about anyway? My name is Jeremy Rochester; I'm from Okeechobee, Florida. I only came here to worship, but if that bothers you, I will leave." Bennie laughed.

"That's more like it. I'm sorry if I sounded rude; this town hasn't taken good to strangers lately. Everyone knows everyone else, even the dog's name." Brett said forcefully.

Little Dove Two came from the ladies' room. She was still shaky. "Brett. I don't know where I know that voice from, but I have heard it somewhere before. Did you get his name?" she asked.

"I did. Don't worry; I will be near you at all times." Brett looked deep into Little Dove Two's eyes. He tilted her chin and kissed her full on the lips. The passion between them could have stopped time.

"Brett, this could be a wonderful beginning, but we must wait. I need to wait," she said. Even if push came to shove, she wouldn't have the willpower to refuse him. She was in love with him.

Blankets and cots were set up in different areas for the ones who wanted to rest or nap until daylight,

The rooms were divided into different sleeping areas—some for gentlemen and others for the ladies.

Little Dove Two told Brett she was tired and would rest on a bench; before long, she was sound asleep.

Brett felt Little Dove Two was safe and laid down for a well-deserved rest.

At three o'clock, Bennie made his move. He laid a soft chloroformed rag near Katie's nose and waited. She quickly became unconscious. Picking her up, he swiftly carried her to the door, raced to the motel, and placed her beside Natasia on the bed. He handcuffed and bound their feet and hands and then hurried back to the church before someone missed him.

When he returned to the church, he entered the sleeping group of the men. Bennie thought they would believe he had slept there all night. I will be far away when they miss the women.

The next morning, Brett stretched and headed for the washroom; he noticed Jeremy Rochester (Bennie) was still sleeping. To be polite, he nodded to Lieutenant Markham as he passed by. He could hardly look at him without becoming a wee bit hostile.

After freshening up, Brett went to the kitchen for a cup of java, black as Mother Earth, just how he liked it. While sipping his coffee, he decided to find Little Dove Two.

Little Dove Two was supposed to be asleep on a bench in the center of the room, but she wasn't there. Brett wasn't concerned to the point of alerting Markham. He searched the kitchen, where several people were busily preparing food, but Little Dove Two wasn't there. Now, he was more than a little worried.

He asked the ladies if they had seen her, but no one had. One single lady was fascinated by Brett, said. "My, my, it's good I'm in church. He sure looks fine. Now that's one handsome man. Umm, umm."

Brett left in search of Little Dove Two. He looked in every room. She seemed to have vanished. He went to Fr. Ryan and both nuns, asking if they had seen her. They all said the same thing, not since last night while she slept on the bench.

I cannot report her missing. I don't even know her name, Brett thought, and then he searched for Maria and Little Dove.

"Maria, I think something has happened to Little Dove Two. I'm worried she may be in danger. Last night she heard the voice of a man who scared her badly.

"I wouldn't get too upset; she will probably come in at any moment. I'll check the ladies' room. She may be doing her makeup," Maria responded with frustration written all over her face. "I'll be right back. How about fixing me a cup of that witch's brew while I'm gone? I sure could use some."

Brett grinned. "Witches brew? Nada. Fine coffee."

"What do you think I should do, Maria," Brett asked when Little Dove Two didn't return with her. How can I relate this to the lieutenant? I'll give her another half hour and then go to Markham."

"Brett, Little Dove Two wouldn't have left here without telling someone. You need to talk to Markham right now! Don't wait another minute." Maria said.

Maria had become close to the lady, captivated by her charm and ravishing beauty. Yes, she loved Little Dove Two. Her tears flowed, and she couldn't control them.

Little Dove also became aware that Little Dove Two was missing. "I haven't seen her either, Brett; I will walk around, checking each room as I go."

"Thank you, Mother. If you find her, let me know at once, okay?"

"Absolutely." Little Dove said, with fear written all over her face.

Mr. Mason was walking the floors. Should I take a chance and tell Markham about Natasia? Would that put my daughter in more danger than she's already in, or would it help return her unharmed? That man who called meant business; he will call again to inform me what I must do. If I lose my daughter, my life is over. She's all I live for. No, I won't take that chance. He thought.

Brett found Lattermar in the dining area. "Latte, I need to speak with you. It's urgent." He stressed.

"What's wrong, Brett? I know you didn't just interrupt my coffee and doughnuts. Don't tell me; it's about Little Dove Two again. I swear, Brett. She's going to be the death of you, and if not you, then me." Latte joked.

"Lattermar, this is serious. She's missing. A man spoke to her, and she was almost positive she knew the voice, but she couldn't remember where it came from. I confronted the man. He told me that he was from Okeechobee, Florida. The man is still here. He slept with our group last night." Brett stated with much concern.

Lattermar gave Brett a knowing look.

"Brett, remember the car we found by the lake? It came from Okeechobee, Florida. It was actually located on your property! Markham wanted to visit you after the holidays to see if something odd was happening up there. I discouraged him until I could get a hair sample from Little Dove Two. Brett, she had been in that car, and there was another person's D.N.A., possibly another female. I've checked, but I haven't been able to identify her either." Latte told Brett.

"Lieutenant Markham informed me that the fingerprints we lifted off the car got us nowhere. There were two sets of prints; ballistics revealed they were both female. They checked the prints in all the states, and nothing came up. I want to question that man from Florida." Latte stated.

"Remember the briefcase that I found? It had photographs and phone numbers. There was D.N.A. on the handle. It belonged to Little Dove Two. The entire D.N.A. found was hers. I wish I could have spoken to that man from Texas. Now, about Little Dove Two disappearing. Well, I hope I'm wrong, but bear with me. I'm thinking that maybe Little Dove Two is tied up with those murders on Lovers' Lane. I didn't want to bring that up, but it's time to reflect on that possibility. I like her. Her personality is just awesome. I need you to think back. Do you remember anything she may have said, no matter how small, which might reflect on the murders, any names or places? You need to start thinking of her as another person, not someone you care about." Lattermar stated, looking Brett in the eye.

"Look here, Latte. I have been around that woman for quite some time, and I have never seen anything relatively close to her being capable of murder. She is frightened. I'm positive someone has hurt her in the worst way. She is a victim of circumstance. I know she was nearly buried alive. So stop your rumors before they start, okay? I'm sure she isn't guilty of a crime, but if she were accused of being involved in murder, then I would get her the best lawyer that money could buy." Brett said sternly.

"Don't get so upset, Brett. I only thought that we needed to face the possibility. I don't know how we can find her without involving Markham. If she isn't in the church, then where do we start? Let's go talk to that man that scared her, okay? Then take it from there." Lattermar was concerned, too.

"Let me say this, Lattermar before you start talking out of school. Don't forget who pays your wages, and quite well, I might add." Brett had to corral his emotions.

Brett located Mr. Rochester. "I need to speak with you; you must come with me now," Brett stated in no specific terms.

Ramond Lattermar paced the floor with anxiety, waiting for Brett to produce Mr. Rochester.

Lattermar thought I needed answers fast from this stranger! I'm sure Brett is involved with that little lady, maybe even in love with her. She doesn't realize how lucky she is to have him in her ballfield.

"Well, I see no reason to go with you anywhere. I can see you aren't a policeman or even a sergeant. You're nobody when it comes to law." Bennie snickered.

Brett had the man by the scruff of the neck. "Listen, you! I may not be part of the force, but I could have you jailed before you could spit. Now, you come peaceful, or I will knock you into next week and drag you, understand? That is if I don't break your neck."

The man nearly fell down the steps as Brett pushed him forward.

"Okay, okay. I have no idea what you could want with me. I haven't done or said anything to anyone." Bennie denied.

The two men walked into a small room that the priest had lent them for a time.

Lattermar nodded and said, "I am Romond Lattermar, private investigator. Please be seated."

"Whoa! Wait a minute. What is this all about? I have nothing to tell you. It's time I return upstairs with the others. You don't have the right or authority to hold me here." Bennie shuffled his feet and flung his arms wildly.

Lattermar stood. "As you wish. Mr. Canterfield, would you please send in the lieutenant? I'll ask that he incarcerate and identify this man until I finish my questions."

Bennie's lips formed a tight line. Lattermar was to the point, and Bennie realized he better listen; he definitely didn't want the police involved.

Mr. Mason saw Brett and his private investigator enter the vestibule downstairs. He knew Lattermar was Brett Canterfield's right-hand man. *I wonder if someone else is missing. I will ask him when they come out.*

"What is your name, and what brings you to our neck of the woods?" Lattermar questioned.

Bennie snarled, "I am Jeremy Rochester from Okeechobee, Florida. My wife and I are on vacation. We were on our way to Kansas and saw the ad about the festival. We were looking at deer by the lake, and the car wouldn't start. I must wait until the weather breaks before I can get it repaired."

Lattermar said, "You are lying, and I don't believe that's your right name either. That car at the lake was stolen. Now, let's start over again, shall we?"

Bennie began to squirm. "I need to use the facilities. When I'm finished, I'll return and tell you whatever you want, Okay? But right now, I can hardly wait. You will be here in this room when I return? And the car is mine. It was stolen but had been located and returned to me. I just haven't had time to have the report retracted yet."

"We will be right here," Lattermar said. "Don't take all day either."

"All right, I'll be back shortly, but I'm going to the cafeteria and grab me a doughnut if that's okay." Bennie grinned.

"Make it snappy if you don't want Lieutenant Markham asking you questions," Latte stated.

"Now, if you will excuse me." Bennie sniffed.

Bennie took leave for the men's room.

Lattermar said, "Listen, Brett, Lieutenant Markham needs to be involved with this man. He's lying through his teeth. The car he refers to is stolen, and I would bet it isn't his. I just have this feeling."

"Latte, that's just arthritis." Brett laughed teasingly. Then he said, "I don't want Markham's input. If it comes to that, we will include Robbie Rommeria. He's smarter than Markham ever thought about being. I hate to say it, but I'd rather work with Robbie than that intolerable man."

"Okay, but we can't let this get out of hand. You can't go rough-housing that crazy lunatic." Latte knew Brett could get down and dirty with the best of them. He was well-trained in the Special Forces. He gets mad quickly, and his anger is almost impossible to control when it comes to someone he loves.

Back To Room Fifteen

I wonder what they will think when they realize I'm not there anymore. Bennie laughed as he parked his car at the motel.

The deputy overseeing this place must have gone to breakfast. I should have enough time to get the woman out before he returns. I'll take my chances anyway.

I will visit that old coot in the office; he will gladly do what I tell him when I'm through with him. Then I will leave, and no one will be the wiser. Bennie snickered.

Bennie rang the bell for the clerk at the front desk. The clerk turned pale. "Listen, you old buzzard, and you best listen well. See this picture?" Bennie held a picture of the clerk's two daughters showering in their bathroom.

Bennie had bugged their home one night. They were in the buff with only towels on their heads and laughing at some silly joke.

"See how easily I can get to your girls? Remember, I can enter your home any time, please. When the cops start asking questions, here is all you know. You don't know what time I left. You didn't see if I had anyone with me. You got that old-man? Remember, I can get to any or all of your family whenever I choose, and there's nothing you can do about it. Now, to keep them safe, keep your trap shut."

Suddenly, the man's youngest daughter came in. "Well now, ain't that little girl cute as a button. I bet she's yours," Bennie gave him a wink and then a snarl as he left. The old-man was flabbergasted and terrified.

Nothing in this world could make me tell anyone about that wicked man. He meant every word he said. I will do anything to protect my family. The clerk thought. Anything!

Everything being coshers with the clerk, Bennie loads one woman at a time into the car trunk and speeds away.

He headed toward Arkansas. They wouldn't think about me changing directions. In the next town, I would find a park where the women can use the facilities. That is, if they behaved themselves. Bennie thought.

About thirty minutes later, Bennie stopped at a service station and asked the cashier to use his cell phone.

"Sister Mary, would you please ask Brett Canterfield to come to the phone?" Bennie said in a cunning voice.

"Well, sure, sir. Whom shall I say is calling?" she responded.

"Oh, sorry, sister. Tell him it's Jeremy, and I must speak with him. I'm sure he will want to answer my call." Bennie replied.

"Brett here."

"Listen, you dumb country hick. I have the woman you are looking for. The best thing you can do is wait until I call you again. What is your home number? I will contact you in a few days. I won't harm her without you contact the authorities. Should you notify the police, then rest assured she will be dead. I don't intend to get caught, and you're not smart enough to catch me. You understand me, my friend? That number, now!"

Brett gave the number, and Bennie hung up.

That dumb jerk has no idea where even to start looking. Bennie said aloud. I will probably get more money from Brett Canterfield than little goodie-two-shoes daddy. They both are loaded and want her safe. They both will pay! He continued to laugh.

Lattermar accompanied Brett to the sanctuary to answer the phone. Brett said. "He has her. Now, what am I to do? If I go to the authorities, he will kill her. He is one sick cookie."

"No, he's not sick, he's just mean. That's what the courts always want the public to think. That people are sick because they do some hideous crime. I don't buy it. These kinds of people don't have morals. They could care less what happens to another human. That's what happens most of the time when God leaves their home. Once in a while, someone loses their mind, but he's not one of them. He's greedy and money-hungry. He's nothing but a lowlife." Latte replied.

Brett was very irritated and trying to stay calm under the circumstances.

"Brett, he might be the one who tried to bury Little Dove Two in that grave. I don't know what happened, but I bet he is up to his neck with some ugly scheme when the truth is told. We must be cautious about how we handle this from here on, or he might kill her." Lattermar advised.

Bennie had them right where he wanted them.

I won't hesitate to kill them should I feel threatened. I must stop at that rest area there up ahead. Maybe if I park around back, I can get them in one at a time without much trouble. The medicine I give will make them so sick. They will do as I say. Bennie thought and then chuckled.

He opened the trunk and took the gag off Natasia. He unbound her and then poured some medicine down her throat, making her violently ill.

"Listen, you little squirt, I am going with you to the restroom. I am your daddy, understand?" He gave her hair a tremendous yank.

"You mess up, and I will knock you out. I can do it without anyone being the wiser," Bennie snarled.

Little Dove Two heard what he said. She wanted to tell the girl to do as she was told. He wasn't fooling; he did it to her.

Katie Remembered

Oh, Brett, please help me! I remember everything! Little Dove Two cried silently.

My friends nicknamed me Katie, but my father called me Catherine.

When it's my turn for the ladies' room, I will look for a landmark.

Bennie made me pass out, and I awakened in the trunk of a car. He is one malicious character and does not pity anyone. I made a noise in the trunk while stopping at a Tallahassee parking lot. A boy walking by asked him if a dog was in the trunk. He gave him a shot of something, which took his life. He did this to prove to me that he could do anything he wanted and get away with it.

Benson Carver is from Houston, Texas. He worked for my father as a field representative and sometimes as a bodyguard.

My father always hired a bodyguard when I was away until I returned.

I went to visit my mother's relatives in Okeechobee, Florida. Benson Carve had a business trip in the keys, so my father hired him as my bodyguard until I reached the city, but he kidnapped me instead. My father had trusted him, ha, what a laugh. If my mother were living, she would have had a fit. She was of the Seminole tribe. My father is Dominguez Renold Talley, a big oil man from Texas and a top executive for Gloretia Industries. He also has a transport business at the Houston port.

Well, I better stop thinking; they're back!

Bennie threw Natasia back in the trunk and bound her tightly.

"You know the rules, Katie. It's your turn to use the facilities." He hissed.

"I know the ropes, alright. I know to start crying with my stomach hurting, d-a-d-d-y. Oh my God, that sounds horrible for me to call you daddy, you stinking rat. You ungrateful pig!" She quirked.

Bennie chuckled. "Enough of that, I don't have all day. That spoiled brat Natasia took too much time. I thought she would never stop up-choking. Let's go. Now!"

Katie scrambled from the car. Bennie held her arm, squeezing it tightly.

"You'll ride up front with me when you return, just like before, but you will wear the shocker," Bennie grumbled.

People don't ask questions when a lady rides beside a man.

Bennie used a dog shocker around Katie's waist to control her. He tested it on her at times just for kicks. When she screamed in pain, he would roar in laughter and hit the button again.

Fr. Ryan Called For Silence

Fr. Ryan spoke into the microphone. "Time for the drawing! Everyone, move closely up front. I want everyone to hear the numbers when they're called out. Good luck to everyone."

"I need a little one to come up and pick out a winning ticket. Patty, I see your hand there. Put your little hand through the hole in the barrel and pull me out a winner." Fr. Ryan spoke softly.

"The winner is Sadie Rommeria." Fr. Ryan called out. "Come on up here and receive your prize. There are two tickets to the Vatican City and two thousand dollars to spend on your trip."

Solemnly, Sadie surprised everyone in the room. "Father Ryan, I would like to return the tickets to the church for next year's drawing."

"The two thousand dollars I will keep, Father," Sadie said. "We filled out adoption papers for Creitta and Matthew Drake. I want this money to be their Christmas money and let them know we are waiting for the judge to sign the papers. They will live permanently with us until they are grown." Sadie grinned.

"The monies they inherited will be put into a college fund, and any leftover will be theirs after age twenty-five. I planned to announce the adoption at church Sunday after the papers were signed, but I couldn't wait.

"I asked the children if they would like to live with us before we filed adoption papers, and they said they appreciated that we wanted them to be part of our family. That's all I have to say." Sadie blinked back tears.

The people were shocked but delighted for the children. There were clapping hands, nods, and grins of agreement. Many folks smiled through tears. Sadie and Robbie would be the best parents the children could ever wish for. They were kind, loving, and religious. The type of people those children needed. Then, Robbie and Sadie would have the three children they always wanted to complete their family.

Brett worked his way through the crowd. He needed his mother. When located, he hugged her closely and didn't speak, but she saw tears swelling in those familiar green eyes; she knew something was terribly wrong and not to question.

"Mother, I must go home. I realize it's not Christmas Day, but something has come up. Please forgive me." Brett said, choking back tears.

"It's fine, Brett. I'm getting tired anyway. I haven't seen Little Dove Two much since we've been here. I will try to round her up." Little Dove replied.

"No questions, please, but Little Dove Two won't be going home with us tonight. I will have the buggy ready soon. You're not afraid, are you? I know we wrecked coming down the mountain. Maybe we will have better luck going home. I'll find Maria and tell her we are leaving so she can say goodbye to Lattermar." Brett said.

"Son, I'm never afraid when you are beside me. I trust you with my life," Little Dove said.

"Carl, I want to get my mother and Maria home as quickly as possible," Brett stated urgently.

The foreman knew something wasn't right. He didn't mention Little Dove Two. Maybe she found her people here, and it had upset Brett. He never questioned his boss. Had it been something Brett wanted to correlate with him, he would have said. Brett was a good boss but had a nasty temper. The men were enjoying themselves to the max. The most fun they'd had this year.

Brett climbed into the driver's seat. The crack of the whip sent the horses into a canter. There was something he wanted to do, and it wasn't slow down.

When he reached home, he called the new hands to the stable. "I need these horses rubbed down. Did Carl teach you all how to tend the stock?" Brett asked.

"Yes, sir. Carl was specific about the animal's care. We fed and bedded them for the night." The eldest of the hands answered.

"Good, now I have orders that don't pertain to ranching. I want three men to stay with the stock. The rest of you keep a close eye on the house. If strangers come here, ask them to leave. If they don't, then shoot them with rock-salt. I will be gone awhile. Especially care for my mother and Maria. Do you men understand?" Brett asked.

"Yes, sir. We will care for everything." The man studied Brett's face. "Is there anything else we should know about?"

Brett stood, frozen to the spot. His father's words, which he had spoken many times and lived by, came to him. "Now let me tell you all, and I will say this only once. I never want any of you to question me at any time. I know you are all new to this ranch and don't know my moods or how I think, but if you want to stay employed here, you will learn quickly.

Maria had seen Brett mad before, but never to this degree. He went to the gun cabinet and chose his weapon. Then went into the secret room, hidden from the naked eye, placing enough weapons in a bag to arm a small army. After checking ammunition and filling a canteen, he was out the door and gone.

Brett stopped and stepped back inside. "Mother, you and Maria keep the doors locked at all times. Don't let a stranger inside these walls. If someone knocks on the door that you don't recognize, ask them to leave. If they don't abandon the premises, then pull this lever." He pointed to a small hidden lever. "Pull it down. That will send out a loud ringing to alert the men in the bunkhouse. They know what to do. Stay away from the windows. I love you both. I will return soon." He placed a kiss on their brow.

Brett went to the garage and took out his car. He hoped it wouldn't hang up in the mud before he got to the highway or slide off the road and over one of the cliffs.

It wasn't far into town. The first place Brett stopped was the hotel. He rang the bell for the clerk. When the man came to the front desk, he was stunned at Brett's camouflage clothing, armed with a rifle and a belt of shells slung over his shoulder. "What can I do for you, Sir?" The man asked, not getting too close to the window.

Brett said roughly, "I'm here to ask one question. Don't you lie to me, or I will return and do some real damage. Mister, I am not a man you want to play games with. "Have anyone checked in or out in the last two hours?"

"No, a stranger hasn't been here for several months. No one has checked out either." The clerk answered.

Brett nodded and was out the door. The next closest one was the City Motel. He had never had any reason to deal with motels or hotels, but all the clerks knew him. He had the reputation that people love to gossip about. He had a short fuse when he thought someone was lying or trying to trick him. He had on occasions been known to horsewhip a man or knuckle it out bare fists. He was honest and expected everyone else to be the same.

Slapping the ringer hard several times, the clerk answered and asked. "You need a room?"

The clerk had the frightened look of someone wanting to crawl into a hole and hide from the world.

"I'm going to ask you some questions, and you better not lie to me, or I will come back, and you don't want to know what I'm capable of. "Is there a stranger staying here?" The clerk began to stutter. "Ah, well, I, ah, I'm not sure. Could you describe them?"

Brett slammed the gun on the counter with a thud. "Mister, I won't ask you, but one more time. You either cough up a name, or you won't see daylight for a very long time! Now talk!" Brett yelled.

Tears began running down the clerk's cheek. "He will kill my family if I talk. He is one wicked dude. I'm sorry, I can't tell you anything."

"Listen up, creep. Think about this: which one would you rather face, that maniac or me? What do you think he could do? If he thinks he's about to get caught? Oh, he would be back all right. The authorities will catch him when they are sure who he is. That's a fact. Now talk to me. I plan on nabbing him before he gets away." Brett was about to lose self-control. With patients wearing thin, he was about to become very dangerous and unpredictable.

"Well, this man came in one night and rented a room. I told him the elk hunters had about taken all my rooms and that I only had one left: Room fifteen. I explained it wasn't in good condition. He said he didn't care; he needed one now. When I asked for identification, he went berserk, handed me some large bills, and said, this is enough for the room. Then, raising a gun to my head, he said, and this will buy my silence. He was correct. That man took pictures of my children while they were showering without our knowledge and then showed them to me. The man said; see how easy it would be to harm your family? Yes, I'm afraid. He might kill my family. I have a complete description of him in my lockbox, just in case I disappear; my lawyer is instructed to mail the letter to the police department. That man will stop at nothing. He slapped the girl with him, and she hit the pavement hard just because she wanted to eat at the restaurant!"

"What did he look like? Describe him to me?" Brett said quietly.

"No! Now please leave. I won't tell you anymore. He said he would know if I told because he'd be watching. No, I can't say anything else." The clerk, shakily, backed away from the counter.

"Well, let's see if this changes your mind. A man kidnapped a lady last night, and now he's gone. I bet it's the same man. On his right hand is written _De-man_. If there's one thing I know, he is bad to the bone."

Brett grabbed the clerk by his breast shirt, lifted him off the floor, and then leased him. "Don't make me angry with you, or you will regret you ever laid eyes on me, you got it? I'm chasing that man, and he is getting farther away. He has threatened to kill the woman if his demands aren't met. Let me show you her picture." Brett showed him a picture of Little Dove Two,

He studied it for a while, then seeing the fury in Brett's eyes, he said, "That's the woman that was with him to start with. That's the one he said was his wife. I remember her; yes, that's the one he slapped to the pavement."

Brett could take no more! He grasped the clerk's breast-shirt again and yelled, "Talk! He will kill her if I can't catch him first!"

"He left in a black Chevy sedan. It might be a rental. That's all I know, except I'm almost certain he had two women with him this time. He returned to the room twice and put something big in the trunk. I watched him leave from my window. He couldn't see me, but I could see through the little lace holes in the curtain. I never knew his name. He just laughed when I asked. He had a real smart-alecky attitude. He reminded me of a policeman. His walk or something." The clerk stated.

"Two women! Where did he get two women? He stayed at the church all night. I wondered how he got away so fast; now I know. Did you see which way he went? That would help tremendously. I will chase him to the ends of the earth. I will never give up." Brett was yelling at the clerk now! "Come on, man, talk to me. I need details."

"He turned left from the parking lot, but I don't know which way he turned onto the interstate," he stuttered.

"Do you remember anyone else seeing him leave?" Brett asked anxiously.

"No, most everyone was at the church. I have mostly locals now that the hunting season is about to close." The clerk said.

Brett went door to door, asking if anyone saw anything, but no one had. I will follow my gut feeling, Brett thought. Jeremy Rochester said he was going to Kansas, but I'm betting he went south or southwest. This route is the one I will follow first.

Rochester could be in Canada before I know where he's headed. I will call home every two hours until Maria hears from him, she will give him my cell number. That man is about to get caught real soon.

The Church Masquerade Party ended. The men returned chairs and tables to their original places; the ladies cleaned the kitchen until it shined. And the floors were mopped. It seemed that everyone had a marvelous time.

Mr. Mason walked up to Lattermar and asked. "Has Brett Canterfield left? I needed to speak with him."

Lattermar thought he was just being friendly, so he told him, "Brett went home earlier. The women were tired. I think maybe he enjoyed all the excitement his heart could take. He's getting old." Latte laughed.

The banker hung his head.

Latte, a private investigator, and his friend read the worried look on Mr. Mason's face. "Charles, we have been acquaintances for a long time. What is troubling you? If you tell me, hopefully, I can help you."

"I don't know where to turn. I must be careful; no one else needs to know what has happened. Could we go to your office?"

Mason's facial expression, trembling hands, and tears in his eyes drew Latte's attention.

Lattermar was tired, but he would wait to go home. There wasn't anyone there to miss him anyway. Losing sleep could put a little more money in his pocket. Mr. Mason isn't poor, he reckoned.

"Charles, I need to drop by my house. How about you coming by tomorrow around ten in the morning? Or is it something that can't wait?" Latte said, yawning.

"No, that will be too late. I need advice now! It's urgent! I will pay whatever the price for your service. I don't know where to turn, Latte." tears fell upon Charles Mason's shirt.

"Oh, Charles, I didn't realize it was that urgent. I'll meet you at my office; let me get out of these clothes first," Lattermar said.

Charles Mason was shaking like a leaf when Lattermar met him at the office.

"Latte, my daughter has been kidnapped. A man called and told me he held Natasia and that I would get a call soon. He said he would kill her if I went to the police. I believe him."

What the heck is going on? Lattermar though. First Little Dove Two, and now Natasia.

"Has he demanded money? Or, said what his demands are?" Latte asked with caution.

"No, he said he would call later with instructions. Do you think he will kill Natasia?" Mason sobbed

"First of all, we don't want to think negative. Your daughter isn't the only one who's been kidnapped. The little lady who came to the party with Maria and Brett is missing too. I believe the same man has both."

"Latte, my daughter has taken karate training for most of her life. She can handle herself, and If she gets the chance, she will probably turn him inside out." Mason said with pride. "But she isn't trained to handle someone with a gun.

"I hope she doesn't try anything like that with this guy. As far as him being mean, that's an understatement. We're almost sure he kidnapped Little Dove Two once before. I won't go into details, but I won't mention to anyone that Little Dove Two has been kidnapped. A lot is riding on this." Latte stated.

"Okay, I won't say anything, but what should I do?" Mason asked more anxiously.

"Do what you think is best, but Brett is after that man as we speak. Whatever this jerk demands, go along with him, okay? As long as he doesn't know we've talked about the abduction, he will keep the girls safe. He wants money. I don't think he will harm them." Lattermar said.

"I'm glad I caught you before you left the church. At least now, I have a little light on the situation. I won't go to Markham either. With Brett's training, he can do more than the authorities. He has the guts to hunt the man down and kill him if necessary. Markham would just put out an APB on him and the car and probably get both girls killed. When you hear from Brett, be sure to give me a call. I will let you know if I get a call from the kidnapper." Mason said.

"Good idea, Charles. I will see you later. Now, I have a friend I would like to call. Please excuse me." Latte said.

Charles Mason walked to the door, then turned and said. "Thank you, Lattermar. I needed that talk. I wish the other girl well, too." He grinned and closed the door softly as he heard Latte begin to speak to a lady friend.

Back At Bretts' Home

At nine-thirty, on December twenty-fifth, the telephone rang. "Hello Maria, has anyone called for me?" Brett asked.

"Not yet. All is quiet here. The only one called was Lattermar. He wants you to call him when you get home. He said it's imperative. There will be a hog killing over at the Thompsons next Wednesday, and he wants me to attend with him to get some fresh meat. It sounds good, but I wanted to check with you first." Maria said cheerfully.

"I will call Lattermar, but you and my mother stay at the ranch. The ranch hands will protect you with their lives. That keeps my mind at ease. I have this gut feeling that something bad will happen while I'm away." Brett sounded uneasy.

The telephone rang in Lattermar's office. He hurried to answer, thinking it would be Maria. He could hardly think of anything else lately. The thought of her was on his mind as he answered the phone. "Lattermar's private investigative services, may I assist you?"

"Maria relayed a message that you needed to speak with me. What's up Latte?" Brett asked.

"Brett, you aren't going to believe this. Mason's daughter, Natasia, has been kidnapped too. What do you make of this?" Latte said.

"Well, I know he has two women. The clerk told me at the motel. That's where this creep has been staying. I tried to follow him, but I haven't had any luck. I don't know which way he's headed, but I'm headed toward Arkansas."

"That Jerremy guy called Mr. Mason once. He said there would be another call with details. He's afraid that the maniac might get kill crazy, not care about the money, and then end the girl's life. How far are you from home?"

"I will cross the state line in about an hour, Latte. I'll contact you later. You have my cell number, right?"

"I have your number; you be careful. This guy acts a little too crazy for me. He's brilliant. That man has had skilled training from somewhere. Bye." Latte hung up.

He drove a long way and watched the girls. It was hard to hold his eyelids open.

"Well, Katie, I think we will stop for the night. That trailer park would be a good place to hold up. No one will bother us, and I can get a little shuteye." Bennie said. He got out, pulling Katie with him. "You open the trunk and unbind her legs. If she yells, I will finish you both off. You hear me, Natasia? You best heed what I say. I'm tired and in a no-nonsense mood."

Natasia was bound and crying. Katie whispered to her. "Don't let him see you cry. He will be meaner to us." After she pulled the tape off her legs and mouth, Natasia said. "I have to go to the bathroom."

Little Dove Two (Katie) whispered. "Be very quiet, Natasia, or he will beat you within an inch of your life. He really will kill us if we refuse to cooperate with him. He is in one of his nasty moods." Natasia nodded.

Katie walked beside Natasia to the restroom, and Bennie trailed right behind them. He wasn't laughing anymore. He looked more scary than usual. There wasn't anyone in the toilet, so Bennie stood in the doorway.

There was a look of recognition in Natasia's eyes. Katie watched Natasia nod toward her side. There, Katie saw the end of a screwdriver. With lip movement, she silently told Natasia, "No, don't." She had tried almost the same thing with bad results. He beat her nearly to death.

As the girls left the rest room, Bennie walked close by them. Natasia dropped to her knees as though she had sprung her ankle. Bennie was right there.

"Pick her up. If she tries to stick me with that screwdriver, I will knock her out. I'm not in the mood for her foolish games tonight." Bennie hissed.

Katie looked at Natasia. "He will kill you. Throw that away."

I can't believe he saw the handle; I was so careful. While he sleeps tonight, I will kill that man, Natasia thought.

Both girls were bound so Bennie could sleep. Suddenly, he jerked Katie by her hair and whispered. "Lay down in the seat. Natasia, you lay down in the back seat. There's no need to put you in the trunk, as dark as it is. There aren't any cars on the road right now. We're getting back on the highway."

When he pulled back onto the highway, Katie noticed he was going the opposite way from the way they came. She said nothing but wondered why he changed directions.

As they entered a small town, Bennie had to fill the gas tank. He stopped a mile or so away and slammed Natasia back in the trunk, gagged her, and said, "You best be quiet, or I will have to kill the attendant, and I don't mind that at all."

They entered the service station and were about to pull up to the gas pumps when Bennie suddenly sped away. Little Dove Two looked out her window. Was that Brett? Oh my God! Bennie spotted him, too. The car rose to one hundred miles per hour. Soon, there was nothing to see except darkness.

Bennie stopped several miles down the road at another station and filled the car with gas. The girls were scared and now only allowed to relieve themselves on the side of the road.

They were headed back toward their original destination. Indeed, Bennie wouldn't go back to Spur Lacy, but that would be suicide. There will be a town sign soon. *I know these streets; they're the back streets of Spur Lacy! Now I know he's a nut case.* Katie thought.

Bennie had scouted this area before and stayed in this line-shack while searching for Katie after she disappeared from Lovers' Lane.

Before taking the girls to the cabin, Bennie checked to ensure it was still empty; it looked like it had been vacant since he left.

He hid the car in the underbrush and went to the cabin, dragging the girls by their hair up the cold, snowy pathway.

The girls were told to find wood for the stove. When they hesitated, he yelled. "Get out there and get the firewood. Don't be lazy, or you will freeze to death."

He held a big flashlight, watching while they worked.

"Let me be clear. I stocked enough food to last the entire winter. There isn't a house around for miles and

miles, and grizzlies roam freely. Don't try to get away from me; you may be frozen or eaten by a Grizzly. You're not wearing enough clothing to last twenty minutes in this cold. I have to make a phone call. Stay inside while I'm gone."

Katie explored the room. Four beds, with lumpy mattresses. A table with six chairs. An icebox. A wood stove. Windows with bolted shutters. Wood floors. Rafters for the ceiling. There is no escape. Natasia looked at Katie and said, "What does he want from us?"

"Nothing, he wants your father's money. He kidnapped me, and my father has paid for over a year just to keep him from killing me. When Bennie returns, he will have a stupid camera to take pictures of us nearly nude and send them to our fathers. He says he will send our father a little finger if they don't pay.

After that, our faces will be disfigured, and then we will be sent home in a wooden box cut up into little pieces. I have reason to believe that Bennie would do precisely what he threatens. Listen to this: I was taken to a plastic surgeon and had a facelift. The Doctor changed my face; Bennie called my father and told him he wouldn't recognize me the next time. He is one mean kook. Had I not let the surgeon operate, he would have killed my father. I didn't know it, but that was his original plan."

"He needs to be in prison!" Natasia cried.

Don't cross him, Natasia, and do not speak any of your family names. He will use it against your father if he can gather information.

The door opened, and there it was: all his camera equipment. Bennie set it up and got ready for the shoot.

"You ain't much to look at." Bennie threw Natasia on the bed and ripped her dress. "Now sling your hair back and smile."

"I won't do it," Natasia screamed. The deranged man looked at her as if she had lost her mind. Then he roared with laughter.

"Oh, but you will, my sweet," Bennie said, grabbing for the girl. Natasia was too quick for him. Her foot found its target under his chin, and the other foot slapped his head half around. He hit the floor. When he got up, she punched him, which would have made a boxer proud! With the breath knocked out, Bennie staggered and fell right onto the pistol!

He grabbed the firearm and aimed it at her midsection. "Well, well, and I thought you were a pipsqueak." Bennie hit her with his fist so hard that Katie thought he broke her neck. As she began to get up from the floor, he pulled off his belt and began striking her creamy white skin until she was black and blue and produced a black eye.

"Bennie, that's enough! You're going to kill her, and then you won't get any money. Bennie! Bennie! Control yourself," Katie screamed.

"Now, my lady, you will lay on your side with your hair flipped back and do it now!" He snarled.

"Okay, Katie. I'm finished with the pictures. Now, you best be quiet and leave me alone, or you will be next.

"**B**rett Canterfield residence, Maria speaking." She was expecting Lattermar to be on the other end. There was lots of static on the other end, but no voice.

Finally, after some time, a man whispered, "Let me speak to Brett Canterfield."

No caller ID came up; Maria asked, "I'm sorry, he's out at the moment. May I take your number and have him return your call?"

"No, what is his cell number? He is expecting a call from me." The rude voice yelled.

"Don't get ugly with me, young man, or I will hang up on you," Maria snapped.

"Look here, whoever you are. Brett knew I would call. I must speak to him. Now, his number or Katie is dead!" the voice yelled angrily.

"I don't know any Katie. When Mr. Canterfield returns, I will tell him about this call." Maria hung up with a slam.

Bennie was fit to be tied. He jerked the tape from Katie's mouth. "That old woman said she didn't know any Katie! Didn't you tell her your name?" Bennie yelled.

"If I spoke with her, she would recognize my voice," Katie said.

"That might work. Okay, come on, you can try that, Bennie agreed."

"Hello, this is the Brett Canterfield residence, Maria speaking."

"Maria, this is Katie Talley. I need Brett's cell number. I must speak to him immediately. He gave it to me once, but I must have lost it."

"I don't know any Katie Talley. I think you must have the wrong number. Brett has never mentioned your name before." Maria was hurrying to turn the recorder on. That is Little Dove Two on the other end; she was sure of it!

"I lived there with you and Brett for some time. I was nearly eaten by a grizzly bear on the Mountain. That's where I am. I mean, that's where Brett found me. Do you remember? I'm Little Dove Two."

"Little Dove Two! Where are you? We have been so worried." Maria exclaimed.

"I can't tell you, I don't know. The same man that kidnapped me before has me again! I need Brett's cell number, please!"

"Okay, hold on, I wrote it down. Aw, here it is. Are you coming home soon?" Bennie slammed the phone back in its cradle.

"What was the meaning of that? That's where I am? Do you know where you are? Have you been in these woods before?" Bennie asked.

"No, I haven't been in these woods before. It was a slip of the tongue. Maria is daffy as they come. She can't remember to get in out of the rain." Katie lied.

"This is so you will remember not to do something like that again." Bennie slapped Katie's face hard. "Don't ever let that happen again! If it does, you will pay dearly, and you know what that means, or maybe I'll make that old woman pay." Bennie laughed.

The lieutenant had known Robbie Rommeria for many years.

And yet, he would have never guessed what he and Sadie had planned.

"Robbie, that was one of the nicest things ever. Your wife is such a thoughtful woman. Why didn't you tell us that you and Sadie would adopt the Drake children? Sadie should have kept the vacation package for her honeymoon. I bet she never had one."

"Well, Lieutenant, it has been hectic here at the station. I haven't had much time to think about anything else. Internal affairs have been down my back about the murders. I can't function as I normally do." Robbie answered.

"By the way, have you planned to visit Bretts Mountain yet? I remember you wanted to go up there after the Christmas celebration at church, or did you talk to Brett at the church instead?"

"Well, I started to say something to him, but he's still miffed over his men at the barber shop that day." Markham snickered. "So I believed it best if I waited a while before I started questioning him. He can get angry real fast over his men."

"Yeah, well, I tell you what. You best watch for that Grizz when you go up there; he's one bad boy. Brett might just turn his back," Robbie chuckled. "Can't say as I'd blame him."

Markham grinned. Robbie was just trying to scare me. He would change his tune if I sent him, but then I wouldn't get to rub Brett Canterfield raw either, and I love doing that. I will make a note to give him a call tomorrow morning. I think of Brett Canterfield as being a self-righteous baboon.

Brett should have taken the job here when the chief offered it, but he didn't need the money, and upholding the law was only when he felt like it. I don't care if he is a close friend of the senator. He's nothing to me but a problem. We had a few scrapes when we were children. Everything always had to be exactly right. There could never be anything a little out of place. Oh well, I guess by gone's should be by gone's, but it's hard to retract bad memories.

He was always the one who got the girl. Look at whom he married, Margo. She was my lady, but he didn't know it. I was dating her, too, when she would come up on Brett's Mountain to get away from her father. Her old man always hit her, but her old man feared Benjamin Canterfield, Brett's father. When Brett's old man spoke, everybody listened. Margo would meet me when Brett went to tend the ranch, and actually, she was in love with me, but Brett had the money and power. She was beautiful and spunky. I was so in love with her that it made me crazy sometimes. I have to stop thinking!

Bennie chuckled. It's time to scare old daddy Mason, to keep him on his toes. I love to see distress from a worried man. After all, it was the police force that made me highly callous. He should be at dinner right about now.

"Hello, Charles, this is what I want. You will transfer twenty million dollars to my banking account in the Cayman Islands. When I get the money, Natasia will be freed. Her welfare is up to you." Bennie snickered.

"Wait! Don't hang up. Is my daughter okay?" A frantic Charles yelled into a dead phone. His tears flowed as he screamed. "What kind of ostentatious character am I dealing with? I best call Lattermar."

Lattermar was ready to phone Maria when the phone rang, "Lattermar private investigators," he answered.

"Latte, I just got a call from the kidnapper. He demanded twenty million dollars. I didn't get to say a word. He just told me his demand and hung up. What do I do now?"

"Charles, get the money together. Please, don't give it to him until he produces proof of Natasia's well-being. We will try to get a trace on the call. When is he supposed to call back?"

"He didn't say when he would call back. Latte, I am scared for Natasia." He answered.

"I understand, but don't let that jerk know it, or he will bleed you dry. I will be there by eight in the morning. I think it's safe to say the kidnapper won't get too pushy until maybe Thursday. I will contact Brett and let him know what's going on. See you tomorrow, Charles."

Lattermar dialed Brett's cell. "Brett, Did you know Maria received a call from Little Dove Two?"

"What! No, I had no idea she talked to Maria!" Brett had mixed emotions. He was angry at Maria for not calling to notify him that Little Dove Two had called and was angry because he hadn't located the sedan. *I best get myself under control before I make that call.*

"Brett, that's not all. Charles has gotten a ransom demand, too. He is supposed to get a call telling him where to send twenty million dollars, but I can take care of that. Where are you?"

"I'll be back in Oklahoma sometime tomorrow. I haven't seen hide or hair of them. I'm hoping Maria can give me something to work with. Staying out here is a waste of time. It's like looking for a needle in a haystack."

"Little Dove, I need some advice. I realize Brett said we were not to leave the premises, but we are running out of supplies. Brett has been gone four days, and the cupboard is getting bare. Do you think I should call him? I don't want to anger him."

"Maria, we should stay in the house and space our food. There's plenty in the basement. We can do without meat or have the ranch hands butcher a calf. Brett was very explicit when he gave the orders."

Little Dove knew her son. He was just like his father. When he gave orders, he expected them to be carried out to the max. No exceptions.

Maria heard the phone ring. "Hello Brett, good to hear from you. I was just about to lie down for a spell. It seems I am so tired lately."

Brett grits his teeth, but he could never yell at Maria. She was too kind to him.

"All those festivals you attended," he laughed, "that and all the flirting you've been getting lately from a certain fellow I know."

"Maria, Latte told me you spoke to Little Dove Two. Tell me. Start from the beginning, and don't miss one word, okay?"

"Brett, I turned on the recorder! I will play it for you. Listen to this." Maria said, proud that she had done something that would maybe help.

Brett was amazed at the information Little Dove Two had given. She even knew her name! That is excellent news. "Play that again, Maria, so that I can catch every word. Oh my God, she is on the mountain. 'Where you found me.' Yes, this was very helpful. In the woods!" *Okay, old man Carver, now you will see what I'm made of. It may take me some time, but your history. I will find you and get the girls back.* Brett thought.

"Thanks, Maria. That was great. The recorder was a great idea. I'm glad you thought to turn it on; maybe I can find them now.

Would you call Carl? Ask him to go to the Indian village for me. I need Two Toes and about thirty men on horseback. I want every acre searched, from the lake to the Kansas line. They are to look for a man and two women but do it secretly. Do not try to apprehend the women. Let me know when they find them.

"Is Latte there with you?" Brett snickered.

"No, he isn't, but I wish he were. You always keep us in the dark about everything." She fussed.

"That's because I love you. I don't want you to worry about anything." Brett answered with a grin.

Bennie decided to get the ball rolling.

He hadn't contacted Katie's old man in several weeks and felt it was time for Dominguez Talley to wire more money to his bank account. *I'll send another picture with her hair pulled around her neck, so he won't be able to tell if it's his Catherine.* He laughed.

Talley believed Bennie was out in the ocean somewhere on one of his drilling rigs, making him all kinds of money; He never even gave one thought it could be his bodyguard holding his daughter captive.

The two women looked at Bennie like he lost his mind. Natasia looked at Katie in wonderment. Katie just shrugged her shoulders and gave the jester he was nuts.

The girls were tied to chairs; it scared them, and they nearly flipped over as Bennie jumped to his feet,

"I won't be gone long," he said and hurried out the door.

The room was beginning to cool off, and the coals were turning to embers.

Katie was the oldest and felt responsible for Natasia. *I must get loose and get her to safety,* she thought.

The girl's arms had rope burns. They looked at one another; although afraid to escape, they twisted and turned their arms, trying to loosen the ropes. Katie knew they could not survive in the wilderness without shelter. They must stay here until found.

Bennie made his phone call.

"Gloretia Industries, how may I direct your call," the receptionist asked.

"I need to speak with Dominguez Renold Talley. Bennie said, and don't tell me he's not in. He never leaves his office except to go to the bank."

Bennie was ready to make his demands when Mr. Talley answered the phone.

"Hello Talley. Your sweet little daughter needs a few more things, and my money is running low. I can't buy anything else without more money, so do what you usually do: send twenty thousand dollars to the same account in the Cayman Islands bank. I'll know when it gets there. Catherine is fine. I will bring her the next time I call so she can speak with you. Goodbye, Dominguez.".

Bennie laughed and hung up the phone. "I'm sure good old Dad will come through. He hasn't failed me yet."

Dominguez would be irate when he discovered who was blackmailing him, which pleased Benny to the core.

"Brett Canterfield is next! Hello Brett, I have Little Dove Two. If you want to see her alive again, you will do exactly as I say. Deposit twenty thousand dollars into my account at a Cayman Islands bank. Here's the routing and account number; write it down. If you don't deposit it, I will send Little Dove Two to you in a box. She's such a nuisance that I'm ready to dispose of her!" Bennie laughed and hung up.

I don't know if I want to dispose of these two women or have them live on an uninhabited island for the rest of their miserable lives as my slaves. They would eventually become accustomed to me and might serve me well, which sounds good. He laughed hysterically. I never thought about this before; it might be fun. I need a little humor in my life. I've had to work for everything I got until I dreamed up this scheme. It's sure paid me well.

Things didn't look the same as Bennie started back up the mountain. Horses had traveled the path in front of him. I wonder if someone went to the line shack? I let the fire burn nearly out before I left, and the gag was tightly bound around her mouth. Those girls couldn't make enough noise for anyone to hear, but I better not take a chance. I'll creep up slowly and check it out. I don't want to compromise my position. There's too much money at stake to make a ridiculous mistake.

As he rounded the corner, he saw smoke rising from the chimney, but no one was near the cabin.

The horses he followed had turned into the woods ahead of him.

The girls were still bound, but Katie had fallen over trying to escape.

Before Bennie sat Katie upright, he kicked her and asked her not so kindly. "What do you think you're doing? You cannot escape from me. Is that clear? Katie, you, of all people, should know not to try. I would hunt you down again. Do I have to punish you? The belt again, or this time maybe something more drastic. Is that what you want? I can't believe you're dim-witted enough to try running away! The next time you're punished, I will see how well you can withstand cigar burns." He sneered.

Bennie untied Katie. "You go fix dinner. I want fried pork chops and mashed potatoes. It better not take too long either; I'm hungry," he shoved Katie toward the stove.

Carver was a frantic man when it came to getting his way. Katie knew not to defy him because he enjoyed being malicious at any fastidious moment. The monster you only hear about in books. He never laid a hand on her sexually, but she knew he would kill her if she didn't follow his instructions.

He loves her daddy's money, so that keeps her alive.

The Braves Searched

Grey Wolf and his three young braves combed the woods north of Bretts's home. They found fresh tracks between the waterfall and fir trees near the north pasture. They followed close until they saw a campfire.

As not to be noticed, they stayed among the trees. They wanted to keep their presents unknown until they could see what the men in the camp were doing.

Carl had told him not to be seen, but this looked more like hunters, not a man, and two women.

Grey Wolf motioned for the eldest brave to follow him to where the men were camped. They sat around the campfire, sipping from a bottle and eating. Grey Wolf needed to see what they were eating; they had brought jerky. He was grateful because he didn't want to deal with rustlers. He had other things to worry about, like finding the girls.

As the Indians dismounted, two men from the camp pointed and yelled, "Halt, stay where you are, who are you?"

"I am Grey Wolf from the village over the Mountain. What are you men doing here?"

"Well, Indian, it's none of your business." He snickered, now pointing his rifle at Grey Wolf's midsection.

"I'm sorry, but it is my business. There are signs all over stating, 'no hunting,' there are grizzlies here, and they are extremely dangerous." He said firmly.

"I suppose now, you're going to tell me you own all this land, and we must leave because you say, am I right?" he sneered.

"I do not own this Mountain range or any of this land. I am just warning you of the bear and drawing your attention to the fact you are on private property." Grey Wolf stated.

"Well, now you have warned us that we are not welcome. Now, what makes you think I won't kill you and your friend there and bury you both right here on this spot? Come to think of it, maybe I will do just that." The man laughed while taking a long swig from the whiskey bottle.

"I cannot stop you from shooting me, but look into the trees on the hill before you do. Several guns are pointed at you, Mister; you are close to being shot. I was hoping you would lay down your guns slowly. My men might get the wrong idea if you keep holding me at gunpoint." Grey Wolf spoke calmly.

The men laid their guns on the ground as Grey Wolf suggested. There were at least two Indians there, but where there were a few Indians, there were usually more than a dozen, or so they had heard. It's best not to take chances when you know you're in the wrong. That's an excellent way to get shot.

"Now, since that is settled," Grey Wolf said with his arms folded across his big Indian chest. "I want to know what you men are doing here?"

"Well, we were hunting elk, but when we didn't get one, we decided to stay a little longer and do a little fly fishing. We didn't see the sign' that you speak of." The man said, squirming on his seat next to the fire. "Can you tell me who owns this beautiful lake? We need to speak with him." He said.

"I will tell you this: he doesn't like anyone drinking alcohol on his property, and he has a grizzly bear running loose here in these woods. He would be furious if he knew you guys were out here."

The man said with a hateful attitude. "Well,? What is his name? We will ask for ourselves. That is if you don't have an objection to that!"

"This, and all you can see, for ten thousand acres belong to Brett Canterfield. You can locate him south of here, about four miles. You can't miss it. Watch for the huge log home high on a hill, but I imagine you will run into his ranch hands long before you reach his home." Grey Wolf stated.

Grey Wolf demanded. "I need to see who else is in the tent. I'm looking for someone, and we won't leave until we're sure who is in there; you all come out now."

The tent flap raised, and another man emerged. "I don't have a gun. I'm the cook. I don't hunt. I only fish when I get the chance." He answered, shaking in fear. He was terrified of the Indians.

"I take it forgranted; you men will stop at Bretts before you do more fishing or hunting? I will be watching you." Grey Wolf said, mounting his steed.

When the braves returned to the village, they located Two Toes and reported their findings. They thought Brett would want to know about the men hunting and fishing. "When you see Brett, tell him about the hunters. Most of them were intoxicated." Grey Wolf reported.

Brett contacted Two Toes at the village. "Have you seen or heard anything yet?" he asked.

"We rode North, South, East, and West. Not a hide nor hair of them. We checked the caves and the high country. The only place left to search is the valley. Grey Wolf and his men found men hunting and camping by the falls. He advised them to contact you or leave."

"Okay," Brett said. "I will check them out. Right now, though, I have something more important that I must attend to. I thank you and the Braves for helping me search for the women. I will see that all of you are handsomely rewarded."

"We are pleased to help you. You have done so much for us, Mr. Brett; this is the least we could do. Have you heard anything from the kidnapper yet?" the Indian asked with concern.

"I got a ransom demand. I will do what the kidnappers say. Whatever it takes to keep her safe. I will check with you and your men tomorrow. Should anyone see or hear something that's out of the ordinary in the fields, let me know at once. I am exhausted, and I need to rest now."

Back In Spur Lacy

Lattermar found out the blood type was rare, mainly of European descent. *Brett said he would be home this afternoon. It's about three thirty now, so he's probably somewhere on the mountain. I will go by his house and say a big hello to Maria before I see him. I haven't seen her since he's been gone. Maybe she will have some cookies made. They are the best,* he thought.

Lattermar decided to call Maria.

"Maria, are you going to be home this afternoon?" Lattermar asked.

"Hi Latte. Yes, I will be home. It's good to hear from you. Brett should be home anytime now. I'm sure he will want to speak with you.

"Maria, I'll be coming up on the Mountain soon; maybe Brett will be home when I arrive. You haven't seen Charlie lately, have you? I don't want to walk upon that Grizz. He can be one cranky critter, he doesn't seem to like anyone, and he's not trustworthy. I think he had rather eat a person than be their friend." Lattermar chuckled.

"You're probably right; he's not much of a friend. He keeps some people who are not wanted away from up here, like Lieutenant Markham. That cop gets under Brett's skin. I wish he would tell him off. They didn't get along when they were younger, so there's no way they could get along now; anyway, I'll see you when you get here. You won't be long?"

"I can hardly wait to smell that sweet aroma in your kitchen. The house always smells so good." He grinned. He could picture Maria in the kitchen wearing that cute little apron, flittering around, trying to hurry with the table setting.

Lattermar arrived on Bretts Mountain thirty minutes before Brett.

"Welcome home, Brett," Maria called when she saw him walking up the path from the garage. She hoped he brought home good news.

"Hello Maria, it's good to be home.

"I've been contacted with a ransom demand. The man said I must send twenty thousand dollars to a Cayman Island bank within Twenty-four hours to keep Little Dove Two safe, but I haven't seen Little Dove Two to know if she's still alive. He's a sleazeball. What do you think?"

"I don't know Brett, but Lattermar is here in the parlor; he would know more about that than me. He has some news to tell you, too."

"Okay, Maria, I'm going to get a bath and rest a few minutes before I speak with him. Then we can all sit down, have some cookies, and talk."

"When you're finished upstairs, we will most likely be in the kitchen." Maria grinned, still remembering what Lattermar had said about her sweet-smelling kitchen.

Just as Brett was climbing the stairs, the telephone rang, and Maria answered, "Brett Canterfield's residence, Maria speaking."

"Maria, this is Lieutenant Markham. Is Brett home? I need to speak with him, please?"

"Yes, he is, but he is in the shower. Could you leave a message? I will have him return your call when he is available."

"That is fine, except I must speak to Brent tonight or visit him at home, which would be best if possible. I know he's busy, and I am the last man he would want to speak to, but this is extremely important."

Maria didn't want to anger Lieutenant Markham. He could be one of her worst nightmares, so she decided to be civil and set a time for him to visit, including Lattermar. "Lieutenant, how about six o'clock tonight? Would that be too soon? If that isn't, we can set another time." She said.

She felt it would be best for Brett if Lattermar were here also. Maybe he could defuse some of the tension between the two men.

"Tonight will be just fine. I have some things I need to go over with Brett about those murders on Lovers' Lane. I know he would want to be included with this information."

"Yes, I'm sure he would. Brett is interested in that case. It is terrible for something like that to happen in our small community. Do you have any leads yet? Oh, I'm sorry for asking. You cannot tell me anything. We will be watching for you. The bears are probably in hibernation, but to be safe, we will watch out for you to get here. I'll let Brett know you're coming."

"Thank you, Maria, and since I'm coming upon the mountain, is there anything from town you would like me to bring? It would be no bother since I will be up that way. The roads are still nasty but travelable. I thought it might save you a trip to town."

"No, that's quite all right, Lieutenant. I plan on shopping in town this weekend anyway. I can pick up what I need then, which will get me out of the house for a while. I need to get a little sun and some fresh air, but I thank you very much anyway." Maria answered very pleasantly.

"Brett, I know you just got out of the shower, but I need to tell you, the lieutenant will be here at six o'clock. He has things to tell you about the murders on Lovers' Lane, and since Lattermar is already here, maybe the three of you can figure out what happened together; three minds are better than one."

"When Markham comes up the Mountain, he better watch closely; the Grizz might not be in hibernation now that the weather has warmed up a bit. He will be out roaming before long, looking for berries, and he likes the grass underneath the snow. That silly bear still eats bark from the tree." Maria grinned. "As I gathered eggs this morning, I saw bear signs in the yard. It looked like he or another bear had presumably stripped the bark from the tree beside the gate last night. That tells me he may already be out of hibernation. It could easily have been Charlie.

I wonder if he is still as pretty as he was when he was younger. He was quite a beautiful animal. Although, I am still terribly afraid of him." Maria shivered as she remembered how the Grizzley hurt her, and he almost succeeded in killing Brett that day, but he's a magnificent animal.

"Really? I best meet Markham before he reaches the Hillcrest. It wouldn't do for him to meet Charlie. That hateful old bear simply won't tolerate strangers coming up the mountain. He might decide the lieutenant is his meal." Brett said, grinning at Maria.

Brett thought Markham would never want to come on his mountain again should he meet Charlie. I am pretty cautious about that old cantankerous bear tonight.

"The evening meal is prepared. I'll set a place for Lattermar; I don't think he gets a home-cooked meal very often. He would enjoy eating with us tonight." Maria grinned, waiting for Brett to answer and hoping he would say yes.

"Of course, that's fine Maria, there's no telling what Latte has to tell us. It may take us quite a while to solve his problem." Brett answered, looking through the mail.

"Maria, I need to ask you something before Latte arrives. Did you know he plans on asking for your hand in marriage? He will ask me before long for my approval, and I need to talk with you before I answer. I know he fascinates you, but do you love him? Would you want to spend the rest of your life with him? It would be best to do some soul-searching before answering any question of that nature because that is forever. I won't ask for your answer now, but we must talk. I will not permit anyone to harm you in any way. You are my second mom, and I love you." Brett spoke in a worried voice. "Lattermar has been my friend for many years, but Maria, you are my priority."

Maria knew Latte was interested in her but had never spoken about marriage with sincerity. It confused her when Brett thought someone needed his approval for her to marry. If she were his child, that would be understandable.

"Brett, I don't know what to say. I know he's interested in me but has never said anything about marriage. I don't know my answer, but you will be the first I tell. Do you think he would make a good husband? What if he wanted me to leave Brett Mountain? I have lived here for ten years; I'm not sure I could. This house feels more like home than any place I ever lived. Let's not speak anymore of this tonight," Maria answered.

I'm going to avoid Lattermar. I don't think tonight is the night I want to get engaged. Maria thought, heading for the kitchen.

Back At The Cabin

Katie knew she was taking too much time with the potatoes.

"Let the kid come and help me over here. I need her to peel the potatoes while I make the pork chop batter, or better yet, you help me. It's taking too long to do it by myself." Katie called out to be Bennie.

"Don't be stupid. I'm not going to cook. That's a woman's job. My job is to keep you two safe and get money off your good old daddy's. I'll send the kid over there, but you better not try anything. I'll be watching every move you make. The very idea of me cooking that'll be the day!" Bennie snarled.

Katie nodded toward the window; the hinges on the shutter were broken loose, but it could be a chance for their escape.

Natasia looked at Katie, rolled her eyes, and shook her head no. She was afraid to move. She still carried a black eye and could barely see. She didn't believe her body could withstand another beating like the one he gave her a few days earlier.

But that day, he held a gun on her, and she could do nothing to defend herself. Maybe, just maybe, Katie's right. "Katie, do you know how to get out of here?" Natasia whispered.

"What's that?" Bennie yelled from across the room. He was seated beside the fireplace, warming his feet from the trek down the Mountain. His hearing was extremely keen, but he couldn't decipher what they were saying.

"Natasia just said her side hurts," Katie answered. *My word, he has good hearing. I hope he didn't understand. Bennie seems to be more irritated now than the first time he kidnapped me. When he goes to sleep, I'm going to try to escape. I don't know if I can take Natasia with me, but I will try. Should Bennie get more angry, he will kill both of us. I hope to find my way to Bretts' home or the highway. Both places are a long way from here, but I must save us from this brutal man,* Katie thought.

Katie gestured at the window, and in the dust, she wrote. We try tonight. Then, she quickly erased it.

"What you two doing? Trying to plan a getaway? I may have to tie you both real tight tonight. Katie, you know better. Natasia, you're learning, don't make me prove my point."

After eating, Bennie returned to his chair by the fireplace. Since they were in just one room, he could watch them from any place he sat, and after all, they had no place to go. He snickered.

I could rip them apart easily or shoot them, which would probably be the best and the quickest. But then someone might hear the gunshot. Hmm, I didn't think of that before. I better not use the gun. If I have to, I can cut them into small pieces. Bennie thought *they would look like the man in the BMW.* Satisfied with his idea, sleep overcame him.

Bennie decided not to tie them up. He wanted them to get a night of sleep without being bound. Unknown to the girls, Bennie planned to move them. He knew they couldn't go anywhere.

Katie waited until Bennie was snoring and then crept to the window. She pushed against the seal to see if it would release, and sure enough, it did! She knew they could get out but figured they better wait until Bennie returned to town. Then, they would make their move. Katie knew if they got caught, he would kill them. He was at the limit of his sanity.

The Lieutenant Visits

When the clock struck six, both men prepared to meet Markham at the hillcrest before he became scared to death. He was petrified of Charlie.

When they reached the top of the crest, they could see Markham's carriage. Lattermar snickered and said to Brett, "It would be so funny to growl like a grizzly and scare him. If he considered it was Charlie, he would whip the horses terribly, trying to get off this Mountain and probably wreck."

Brett grinned, remembering how bad he used to be to Markham. They could never get along when they were younger, but to scare him would really be funny. He would have loved to see Markham's face, should he think it the Grizz.

"Maybe joke around another time," Brett stated.

There always seemed to be something that Markham had against him, but he could never figure it out. It didn't matter now that they were older.

"Hello Brett, Lattermar, good to see you. I had my eyes peeled for the Grizz. That old bear can make the hair rise on my head. I've seen a lot of big bears, but that one is the biggest yet!"

"Maria saw signs in the yard today. It may have been another bear, but I doubt it. He comes to the house when he comes out of hibernation for me to feed him, but Charlie's getting way too aggressive. Let's hope he's not hungry, but if he is, maybe he doesn't like Lieutenants," Brett laughed.

"Now, don't go scaring me. I wanted Robbie to come here, but he wouldn't even listen. He said he was never climbing another tree."

"Can you keep him away should he appear to us aggressively, Brett?" The Lieutenant asked.

"Well, I'm not really sure, Lieutenant. I don't know if my dart gun would stop a twelve-hundred-pound bear. I know one day I will have to put Charlie down; he is almost unmanageable now. I don't feed him like I did. I just put food out quite far from the house." Brett answered.

When they reached the house, the moonlight was shining brightly. All three men were aware that they might not be alone.

There he was, bright as day, Charlie! All the men froze. They remained still, hoping he would leave. He was a beautiful creature, but make no mistake, he was very dangerous. If he became frustrated or angry, he would definitely attack.

Brett knew this, but the other two men took it for granted that Brett could handle the situation. Brett wasn't so sure.

The horses in the corral stomped and whinnied. They didn't like the bear either.

Charlie turned towards the men, opened his mouth, and roared his dislike of the situation.

Brett knew this big Grizzly would tear apart anyone he met tonight. He also knew he had gotten so big the dart gun was useless against him.

The front door opened, and there stood Maria. She threw Charlie a handful of cornbread, which she knew never to feed a bear at your home, but Maria knew Charlie would attack. She had to take desperate measures.

Tears began to roll down Brett's face. After all these years he had fed and cared for Charlie, now was the time he must put him down. He would kill a human if he got the chance.

Brett had no rifle, and Maria could not bring him a gun. He had no idea what to do.

Maria closed the door and returned with Bretts 30.06. Tears rolled down her cheeks as she pulled the trigger, knowing quite well this would be a fatal blow. "I'm sorry, old pal, but this time I have to shoot to kill," Maria said. The bear lunged at the woman but fell to his death two feet from where she stood.

With tears in his eyes, Brett bent down and caressed Charlie's fur. "I must contact the Indian village and let them know that the

Grizz is deceased. I know they will want his hide and all the meat. I don't want to see any food wasted from any animal. The meat will still be good come morning."

"Everyone, come on in and make yourselves at home," Brett said quietly.

"Brett, maybe you can lend us one of your bedrooms tonight. I believe Markham and I would like to stay over. It's late, and Charlie isn't the only Grizz on the mountain. On the other hand, make that two bedrooms. I don't want to sleep in the same bedroom with Markham. He probably snores." Latte laughed.

Maria set another place for Markham, even though he told her he had already eaten. She insisted he at least eat a piece of pecan pie the cooks had baked that day.

When they had finished their dinner, they went into the parlor to sip their coffee, and naturally, the conversation went from how good the pie was to, 'I wonder how long it will be before we find the girls.'

They began catching up on things that mattered around Spur Lacy. Soon, Maria and Little Dove retired for the night.

The next day, the sun shone brightly by mid-morning, promising a beautiful day on that glorious mountain. The ranch hands began to stir, doing their daily chores.

Brett called out to Carl. "Hey, Carl, send someone to the village and let them know that we killed Charlie last evening. I need one of the young men to pick up the meat and hide. The meat is still good, but the carcass needs to be taken care of today."

Maria decided she would be the cook today. The new cooks protested it, but Maria knew how to handle the newly hired help. She didn't know what she would do. People on the ranch need bacon with eggs and biscuits, gravy, and some good old coffee to start their day with good vibes. Brett planned for the two women from Spur Lacy to do all the cooking and cleaning, which had been her job.

He says he wants me to have leisure time, which would be good, but just to a point. I know for sure that I would really get bored, Maria thought.

"Breakfast is served in the dining room. I'm sorry about your bear, Brett, but I didn't know what else to do. I hope it doesn't ruin your day." Maria said.

"My, my, what have we here? It was the best-looking breakfast I have seen in a long time, and the cook, too. You would make somebody a real fine wife." Lattermar exclaimed.

He wished they were alone to tell her how much he cared. But that would be another time because there were too many problems to solve today.

Maria blushed and turned to her stove so no one could see her face. She really liked Lattermar but just needed to get breakfast over right now.

"Thank you, Latte, for the comment, but it's just a country breakfast we serve daily."

Little Dove looked at Maria and grinned. She read her like a book. She was definitely in love with Lattermar; it showed in her face. Maria returned Little Dove's grin.

After breakfast, the men retired to the parlor. Maria brought in the coffee urn. She knew it would be a long day for all the men, and it gave her more time to be close to Lattermar; she grinned as she sat the urn on the sideboard.

It was time to get serious about things that had recently occurred.

Brett began the conversation. "Markham, I know you came here with something you wanted to discuss with me. I know it concerns the murders, which could be quite interesting. Let the cards fall where they may. We should begin with what we know and how we could possibly help one another. That is, if Markham doesn't become an ostentatious obnoxious cuss. You would walk ten miles to get the better of me, Markham, but I always welcome my guests, no matter who they are." Brett and Latte laughed under their breaths.

Markham started. "What do you guys think happened? Brett, have you had any odd things happening here on the ranch lately?"

Brett snapped. "What kind of odd things are you talking about, Markham? Some things have happened, like Margo dying. She lost her mind, you know, and didn't know her name. She would come in at night while we slept, walk the halls, destroy my garden in the basement, leave the doors open, and then scream like a panther. I don't think she knew us at all. My mother, Little Dove, did her best to care for her by taking her to the village for protection. The Braves watched over her, but at night, she returned home with a crossbow under her arm. I believe she would have shot anyone that came in contact with her. What is that look, Markham? Is there something specific you would like to know?"

"Well, I saw a third woman with you to the party. I didn't see her today. Whom might she be?" Markham asked.

"Lieutenant, no more secrets. We need to work together. I found the lady you saw with us in the woods. Her clothes were tattered, and she didn't know who she was or where she came from. She kept thinking she would be arrested but didn't know what for; we decided to find out everything about the lady before you put her in jail on some trumped-up charge. We learned her name after the same man who had kidnapped her did it a second time. He now holds her again for ransom. We are trying our best to keep her from being killed." Brett said.

"Brett, you could be in trouble if you knew that girl was at the murder scene on Lovers' Lane?"

"Listen to me, Lieutenant, we are here in my living room. You cannot prove anything I say, and furthermore, I didn't know she was at the murder scene. I heard that later." Brett was trying to be civil.

"Right now, that's the least of my worries. We must work together and find the man holding her against her will. He is very evil and doesn't seem to care if he hurts or kills another human being, and he takes pleasure in inflicting pain. This man is the type of man we're dealing with." Brett explained.

Markham asked. "What do you think we should do? If this man is violent, like you say, then why are we not to believe this dangerous freak would kill her, even if he gets the ransom? I think he will kill the girl anyway, no matter what. What is your opinion on this Lattermar? Do you think it's wise to pay his ransom?"

Lattermar whistled. "I don't know, I've been thinking about that, but I know if we don't pay, he will kill them for sure, and are we to believe that he wouldn't kill them if we do pay the ransom? Well, that's something else; I don't know what to think. I don't know who we're dealing with. I need to speak with this man before we pay any ransom. I think he might be a link to both kidnappings."

"What do you mean both kidnappings? Does he have more than one girl? Come on, spill it; who else does he have? How long has he had someone else? Look, let's work together on this. We agreed to put the cards on the table and see what we have." Markham stated, beginning to get angry.

"That was just a slip of the tongue; I don't know whether he has anyone else," Lattermar answered, looking at Brett with a question in his eyes; should we tell him?

The look on Brett's face said no, so Lattermar didn't say anything else to Markham.

"Okay, here's what we got: a BMW with the dead man in it. Two women were slaughtered beside two gravesites that were being dug, and a girl was already half buried in a grave and would have been dead in another half an hour. We found DNA in a car down by your lake, Brett, that doesn't match any of the victims. We found blond hair and a rare blood type. Now, if we could match that blood type with someone and the hair, we might be able to get somewhere with this investigation." Markham stated.

Maria walked by the door; she didn't mean to eavesdrop, but when they said AB-negative, a light bulb came on in her head. She knew there weren't many people with that blood type around here. The only one she knew of was Margo.

Maria froze in her steps.

"I'm sorry; I didn't mean to be listening to your conversation, but I did overhear and feel that I should say something. Margo's blood type was AB-negative. Her hair was blonde. I don't know if this will help you or not."

Markham looked at Maria as though she had been slapped him. "Maria, you have no idea how much that helps. The only bad thing is that Margo has been buried. Her body would have to be exhumed to identify her DNA. I would hate to have that done."

Lattermar cut in. "Let's wait until we get the girl back. She may be the key to the murders. I'm not saying she did the murders. I'm saying she was there, so she might know what happened."

"That sounds reasonable. Now, let's concentrate on where the man could be hiding. Does anyone have an idea? We haven't heard not one-single-thing at the station." Markham looked at Brett as if he held something back.

"Lieutenant, I had the braves looking over ten thousand acres of range. They looked everywhere they could think of on horseback but found nothing." Brett answered sadly.

"Lieutenant, I got a hair sample from Little Dove Two. I had it analyzed, and it did not match any of the other women's DNA. I don't know who was around the other stuff, but it wasn't her. I found a briefcase after your men finished with their investigation. It had a name and photographs of a woman that resembled Little Dove Two. She has had plastic surgery. The facial figure is different, but she is of Indian descent. Her father's name is Dominguez Renold Talley. I tried to contact him, but I haven't been successful. His daughter's name is Catherine Margaret Talley. That is our Little Dove Two. Tomorrow morning, I will try contacting him again. I thought maybe Mr. Tally would speak to me quicker than he would the police, which is the reason you weren't told. Your people scare the daylights out of a normal person. That's why you can never get the information you want when you ask questions." Lattermar told the Lieutenant, unapologetic.

The Lieutenant snapped. "You're overstepping yourself, Lattermar. We have to ask people questions with an ongoing investigation. You withheld evidence, and you, of all people, knew better. You should have turned in anything you found out there. It was still an ongoing investigation, but since you didn't, and no one else knows about this, we should continue our conversation after you speak to this man named Talley. Maybe you will find something useful in this case. God knows we need help from somewhere."

"By the way, Lattermar. Did you learn anything about who could have been connected to the man in the BMW from his workplace? I'm still having trouble with who kidnapped Max Robertos. Why would anyone take a BMW out to Lovers' Lane to kill a man?" The Lieutenant was puzzled.

"The wife said it was probably one of his girlfriends. I checked with the women he may have been involved with, but no one has jumped out at me. The ones we have talked to all have reliable alibis." Lattermar replied.

Brett slapped the table. "So, the only thing we know for sure is that we have a dead man, two dead women, and a missing girl from a half-filled grave."

Lattermar scratched his head. "I'm not exactly sure what, but we are missing a link here. Lieutenant, when you return to the station, would you check on convicts and police officers? Look for a man with a tattoo on his right hand that reads _De-man._ This tattoo is odd, but it's written on Jeremy Rochester's right hand. It reminds me of a gang symbol. He gave Brett his name at the Church."

"That's a place to start. I will check with records while Brett contacts Talley. Lattermar, see what you can dig up on Max Robertos's wife. Hopefully, we can connect some of the dots. These horrific crimes must be stopped. We can get together again tomorrow night and compare notes. Is this agreeable with everyone?" the Lieutenant asked.

The other men nodded with consent.

"I need to tell Robbie something more than shooting the grizzly, even though he would like that. He will enjoy it even better that Maria killed him. Robbie likes her. Think of something, people. He knows I came here to find out if odd things were happening on Brett Mountain. I can't go back empty-handed, but I definitely can't tell him what we have talked about either." Markham commented.

"Tell him I didn't know anything. Robbie remembers me well enough that what I say is what I mean. If I remember correctly, Robbie won't mention it again because he says you're a slave driver; you never let him have time off to rest." Brett laughed.

"Is that what that little pipsqueak says? I don't know what to think about the hired help these days." Markham laughed.

"Then I'll see you both back here tomorrow afternoon. We will see where it goes from here. Hopefully, it's enough to put some light on the case." Brett said. "The road should be open tomorrow; you can drive your automobiles here. Yesterday, I got through with my all-terrain vehicle, which wasn't too bad. It may be slick in places, so use care."

They shook hands, went to the door, and left.

As they waited for Carl to hitch the team, Brett caught something from the corner of his eye. It was like a flash, but he was almost sure he saw someone on the other side of the tack room.

He didn't mention it to the other men. I will check it out later once they have gone, he thought.

As Brett strolled toward the building, he called to Maria. "I'll be back in a while. I need to take care of something at the tack room." He was almost sure he saw a little girl there.

With the men out of sight, Brett investigated his sighting. As he rounded the back of the building, there she was!

"Mr. Brett, I found this little wolf cub about a week ago. Mama won't let me keep her. She said there would be too many pups later on. What can I do with it now? The pup is so smart that I can hide a piece of my clothing in the snow, and she finds it real fast! I already love her. She plays, romps, and chases rabbits." The little girl said through tears. "Her mother died in a trap, and her siblings died from the cold or starvation. She was in bad shape when I found her. I fed and nurtured her. She looks real good now, doesn't she?"

Brett said quietly. "She does, indeed. She is still too young to fend for herself. I will take her under my wing. You did a swell job. You are very kind not to let an animal suffer. I will take her off your hands if you promise to come daily to care for her. Is that a deal?"

Her little eyes lit up, "Oh, Mr. Brett, you are the best! I promise to be here every day to help you tend to her. Thank you, and my momma will be glad too."

"You are very welcome. I found a bear cub like that once. He was a big, handsome fellow. Like you, I had a soft spot in my heart for an abandoned small fry. I kept him for many years." Brett said.

"What happened to him? Did he run away?" she asked, her eyes big with curiosity.

Brett explained softly. "No, he became vicious as an older bear. He would hurt people. I had to destroy him."

"But you kept him so long. I don't know how you could destroy an animal after you get so attached. I bet that hurt your heart, huh? I could never do that." Her eyes were big, and her face told it all! "Never in this world could I do something like that!"

"Listen to me, little one. I am a man who loves all animal and human life, but there is a great difference between humans and animals. We love our pets, but some animals cannot be tamed. Charlie was one of those. He was born to live free and lead the life of a wild animal. We are human. When an animal harms a human, they have to be destroyed. That is something that can not be allowed. We are dominant over all animals. We must protect them, but human life comes first. Do you understand?" Brett explained in detail to the little Indian girl.

"I understand, sir, but it would be hard to kill the animal you love, right?" her face was sad to think she might have to destroy the wolf pup when it grew older.

"I will be back tomorrow. I have to let Mama know where I will be. It's a long way over the Mountain, but I will try to be here before noon." She said.

"Wait a minute. There's something I might let you have for a price. Hey Carl," Brett called. "Bring out the black mare; we may have a buyer for her."

The little girls' eyes lit up with astonishment and wonderment. "I can't pay for a horse." She said. "I have no money."

"Now, who said anything about money? I said we might have a buyer. Do you know the meaning of the word, trade?" Slowly, the little girl nodded. She wasn't real sure what Mr. Brett meant.

Brett grinned and spoke softly. "Well, we are going to trade. I will give you the mare since you promised to come every day to take care of the wolf pup, and while you are here, you must feed your mare. Is this fair?"

The little girl clapped her hands and squealed with delight.

"Oh yes, Mr. Brett. Wait until Mama hears, she won't believe it!" she was so excited that she grabbed Brett and hugged him tight. "I love you, and I will never forget what you have done for me!" She cried.

"What's the mare's name?" she asked..

"Well, you can name her if you like. She has the look of a molly. That's what we call her, but we don't call her by name often, so it would be okay for you to change the name. What would you like to call her?" Brett asked as he knelt beside the tiny, small fry.

"I will call her blue blaze. I bet she can run like the wind. That is if you're sure you don't care that I rename her," she said, looking down at her toes and swaying side to side.

Brett laughed. *What a cutie,* he thought. *She is just perfect—smart little one, and pretty too. I can hardly wait to meet her parents. I know they are so proud.*

Realizing she didn't know how to ride, she held the reins. "This is embarrassing, Mr. Brett. I can't take the mare. I don't know how to sit a horse," she explained.

Brett laughed. "You know, I thought maybe you didn't know how to ride, so I gave you a mare that won't throw you, and should you fall off, she won't step on you or kick you either. Now, all we have to do is teach you to sit and rein her. That shouldn't be hard to do. I see you like horses, and you will try your best to learn."

Brett looked down at the wee girl. "Carl, please send Yancy out here. He can give you a few pointers about riding. That is, would you like him to? He is very gentle with horses."

Considering she was small, her mother might not appreciate a horse this size. The mare was right at ten hands high. Molly, now Blue Blaze, was too tall for the child to saddle.

"How old are you?" Brett asked.

"I'm almost eight." She stated proudly and then stretched, trying to look another two inches taller.

"Will someone saddle and bridle her for you?" Brett asked.

"Oh, yes, I won't have a problem with that. Someone is always around helping out at my house," she grinned.

Brett hadn't had communication with a child in a long time. "I tell you what, I haven't ridden for a few days and need to see Two Toes, so I'll ride home with you to the village. I need to speak with your father about the horse and you coming over the mountain daily. Will that be okay with you?" he asked the child.

"Yes, that would be fine, but I have no father; you can speak to my mother, though," she grinned. "When do you want to leave?"

"Well, as soon as Yancy gives you a really quick lesson, I don't want you to fall off before we get to the village." Brett laughed as he looked at the child.

I lost my little girl when she was about this age. I wonder what she would have looked like today had she lived. I wonder if she would be as polite as this wee one. Brett thought.

Once again, Brett felt the pain from his daughter's death. He missed her so much and still had nightmares about his children's fall.

"Carl, please let Maria know I went to the village. I won't be very long, okay?" Brett called out as Yancy came from the tack room to teach the lass a quick lesson.

As Yancy taught the child how to sit on a horse, the wolf cub brought a scarf to Brett. It belonged to the girl.

"What have we here?" Brett asked as he took the scarf from the pup's mouth. He looked up at the girl sitting straight in the saddle. She did say the wolf pup could find anything she hid. Well, well. She may have something here. Maybe it will be a tracking wolf. Hmm, very intelligent.

Yancy called from the corral. "She will be a pro before long, Mr. Brett. Hold your legs tight to her sides, lass, so you can feel her movement as you ride. Does the saddle feel like it fits you? Or do I need to take up the stirrups some more?"

"It feels fine, but I know nothing about a saddle." She answered.

"Brett, you can ride anytime with the wee one to the village; she will be fine. Keep her behind you until you get off the narrow ledge. I don't see a problem, but Blaze doesn't need to get spooked. The lass already knows how to restrain her. She is a swift learner. Do you need me to ride with you this time?" Yancy offered.

Brett called to Yancy as he and the child started towards the mountain. "No, I will be fine. I need someone to feed the wolf pup and put her in the barn where I kept Charlie when he was small. Be sure she has enough water, food, and bedding. The nights are still brutal."

The Line Shack

I must go to the next town, Bennie thought. *I must check my money in the Cayman Islands bank to ensure the good old daddies padded my account.*

I need some supplies, and it's been twenty-four hours. I'm betting good old daddy won't like bruises I'll put on her body or pictures of her all beaten up if he doesn't comply with my demands.

If I get the money, there's a non-inhibited island where I could take the girls and let them live their miserable lives; that's a consideration to study.

"I will be away for a while. I'm going to gag and tie both of you to your chairs so you can't make any noise. The door will be bolted from the outside, so should anyone come here, they'll think it's vacant." He snickered.

He put on his coat and closed and locked the door.

Something new was in the making. The girls looked at each other wide-eyed and realized Bennie was crueler than usual.

Katie knew Bennie had something else on his mind, which would be terrible this time. *We need to escape, and as soon as possible!* She thought.

After Bennie left, the girls began kicking and trying to loosen the ropes bound to the straight-backed chairs.

The cold outside is extreme, and they don't have enough warm clothes to keep from freezing to death, but the girls knew they could carry enough blankets to cover up in and dried jerky to eat. They could survive for a time.

I don't know if there's anything we could use as a shelter or how far we are from the caves on the Mesa. We might be in the Valley close to the lake. We must take our chances before Bennie gets back, Katie thought.

Katie tilted her chair sideways; it fell with a crash, breaking the arms off and releasing her. She removed the tape from her mouth. *At last, I'm free,* she thought, *now to get Natasha loose.*

"We must get out of here and fast! He will be in a hurry to get back, especially if he gets the money!

Natasha, are you okay? We better hurry. When he returns, he may kill us both. He's losing his sanity more all the time. He needs to be locked up in the crazy house or put in prison for the rest of his life for the things he's done. Natasia, grab the bread we made and all the blankets you can carry while I see if I can open this window. We had better not be here when he gets back." Katie said.

"Do you think we can get away, and if so, do you think he will find us?" Natasia asked. "I don't want him to find us. He would kill me with that gun before I had a chance to defend myself, but if I could just get a hold of him without that gun, I could take him down. I have trained in martial arts most of my life on survival, but I don't know what kind of survival rate I will have among animals in the wilderness. I am definitely ready to find out!"

Katie grinned. "I think I'd worry more about him than wild animals. They're not as dangerous. Okay, one more push, and this window should fall. There it goes! Let's go, Natasia. Throw the blankets and the food out first, and then I will help you through the window."

"It isn't dark yet, so maybe we will have time to find out where we are or at least get far enough away that he won't be able to find us; the further, the better. I know there are caves in the Mesa, so if we go up the mountain, maybe we can find them. It's worth a try; anything is better than staying here," Katie said. "Are you okay, Natasia?"

Natasha pointed to the underbrush. "Katie, what is that over there? I'm not sure what I saw. It was an animal. Did you see it? I don't think my eyes are playing tricks on me; I am scared to death."

"I have no idea what you saw; maybe it was just the wind blowing the underbrush. I know you are scared, Natasia, and so am I. But the farther we push into the dense woods, the safer we will be. I don't know how good a tracker he is in the forest. Hopefully, not a good one," Katie stated.

"Katie, what happened to you before? I understand that you know this man. What has he done to you?" Natasia asked.

Katie whispered. "I would love to tell you, but we don't have time. It is too quiet right now. We better not talk. I hate to think what evil thing Bennie has in store for us, especially me."

The banker didn't wire his money. Bennie will give him another call, but only one more chance.

Bennie yelled in the phone. "Mason, I told you what would happen if you didn't wire the money like I told you. Do I have to send you some of Natasia's body parts, or are you going to do what I say? The ball is in your court. Either you pay, or she dies! You got that old man?"

"Okay, I will wire it to you, but you better not harm her, or I will send someone to cut your throat. I promise you this. When you get it, you better let her go!" This time, Mr. Mason hung up on Bennie.

Bennie wasn't used to someone hanging up on him. Hang-ups were his lousy doings. He stood there looking at the phone as if it had burned his ear. He slammed it down with a bang.

I will get his daughter, beat her black and blue, and then cut off one of her fingers. I wonder what he will think when he opens the letter with a body piece inside. Bennie thought.

Katie Heard the crunching of snow; She knew he had returned. Katie grabbed Natasia by the arm and held her finger to her lips in a quiet signal. They stood beside some overlapped ponderosa pines that had grown closely together, protecting them from the scanning eyes of Benson Carver.

"Where are you?" Carver called out to the girls. "You can't get away. You will freeze to death out here. I will find you. I know you haven't gotten very far, and you can hear me. I brought some food. Aren't you ladies getting hungry?"

Bennie walked near the girls. *I'm unsure how long they've been out here, but they must be cold.* He thought *if I could get them to move, I could grab or shoot them.*

Bennie turned in the direction of a rustling sound. "I heard you there; come on out. I will start shooting if you don't, and pretty blame soon." He yelled.

Katie held Natasia steadfast. Natasia wanted to run, but she knew that's what he wanted. They watched as Bennie came face to face with a pack of gray wolves. Katie knew it was time to run.

Bennie yelled. "Oh, my God!" as he backed slowly towards the cabin. "I thought it was the girls. Get! Get! Get outta here, you blame wolves."

Katie grabbed Natasia by her hand and ran swiftly. If the wolves weren't too hungry, they wouldn't become supper. When they reached a clearing, Katie knew nothing about wolves, but they grabbed twigs and started a fire, thinking the wolves wouldn't come near. If Charlie the Grizz wasn't hibernating, they might be his supper. They realized there was much danger in the forest.

"Natasia, I don't know much about the woods. Do you want to climb a tree for the night? Or take our chances on the ground with a fire? I have walked in the woods but never camped. I hate to tell you this, but a Grizzly bear is here in these woods and is one ornery cuss. One time, I was almost his lunch." Katie reflected.

"Whatever you think is fine with me," Natasia said. "I only see animals on the road or in the zoo. I don't know anything about wild animals."

Katie asked. "Well, your life is at stake, too. I won't take charge of this situation; it's your choice, so what do you suggest? I brought a hatchet from the cabin. We could climb a tree and cut the branches as we climb. That way, bears can't climb up after us. There are also Cougars out here. I'm not trying to scare you, but you have the right to know."

"Well, I have never climbed a tree, but let's climb a tree," Natasia shivered.

"Katie laughed and said, "I was a tomboy, raised on a large ranch, and trees are my specialty." The girls sat and laughed. It was good to be free; they happily yelled, "Yippee," and danced around holding hands.

"I have never been incarcerated, but being Bennie's captive felt like it. Bennie, that old granddaddy of evil, was going to kill us. I just know he was." Natasia quirked.

"We better move toward the bigger trees. It will be dark soon. If we don't hurry, we won't be able to see how to climb. I hope we find a tree with big branches at the top so we won't fall out while we sleep." Katie giggled.

Natasia frowned. "I never thought about that. Ugh! How will we stay atop a tree without falling out?"

"Use our imagination. It's thrilling if you think about it. We're going to camp in a treetop." Katie laughed.

Katie thought. *I'm so scared I could cry. I don't know how long I can keep being the big sister. If only I knew where we were. Tomorrow, I must decide which way to start walking. Aw, fiddlesticks, I'm lost. I hope we find safety in a tall tree for the night.*

"Natasia, look, there's a tree we can climb. I will push you up to the nearest branch. You were in gymnastics, so you should be able to pull yourself up quickly. On the other hand, I will have a little difficulty. Katie grunted.

Katie pulled herself up, a little at a time. She cut the lower limbs so animals couldn't climb up behind her. I can't imagine waking up looking eyeball to eyeball with a mountain lion or a cougar. I know they could probably climb up here with us if they chose, I just pray they don't. Katie thought it necessary to climb high in the tree.

Katie yawned and said, "Natasia, lock your legs around the branch closest to you. Stay aware, and don't sleep too soundly. I will do the same. Whatever you do, don't fall out of this tree. To break a leg or bone would be devastating. We will be all right come morning. We need to be very careful. It's a long fall."

Natasia was sore from the beating Bennie gave her. She hid the pain as best she could, but now her side was really throbbing, and there were splinters in her hands. As she sat there in the dark, she thought about how easily this man put his hands on her person and how quickly she became livid.

She fumed. "Katie, if we get the chance, I want to beat that Bennie to a pulp. I will show him just what I am made of."

Katie steamed. "Natasia, if we get out of this alive, that will be enough for me. Benson Carver was once a policeman from Texas, but I don't know how smart he is at tracking. That's where my father met and hired him. Since he knew the system, my father figured he could help his company. Good old Dad didn't realize what he hired."

A red streak crossed the horizon as Katie opened her eyes.

She sat very still and listened. Nothing was moving - wait - too silent - Natasia was still asleep. A coyote yelped in the distance. What is that rustling in the underbrush right underneath us? Katie wondered.

It can't be! She thought. *Bennie is standing about ten yards from the tree where we took refuge. He is looking at the ground, studying our footsteps!*

Katie nudged Natasia. When she opened her eyes, Katie nodded towards Bennie. Slowly, they pulled their legs up so he couldn't see them.

Bennie was outraged; he snarled like an animal as he moseyed toward the ridge. He found tracks, and then they just disappeared. *Smart little winches,* he thought. *They covered their tracks as they walked. They couldn't have got very far in the dark.*

Silently, the girls dropped to the ground and hurriedly backtracked the way Bennie had come. Then they went into the brush toward the mountain. Katie knew the caves were up there, but not precisely the location. The caves would be a shelter for them if she could remember what she had overheard when Carl spoke to Brett about them.

Horse hoofs! Someone is coming down the narrow ledge. I know better than to yell. Bennie wouldn't hesitate to kill them, too.

Katie grabbed Natasia's arm, signaling her to squat and be silent. The horse walked near the women and on up the trail. Although they didn't want to be seen, the girls followed closely. Bennie would have been right on their heels if the rider had pronounced their presence.

Wood smoke filled the air from nearby. Katie considered having the warmth from that fire so much that she had tears in her eyes. She knew they were close to someone's dwelling but didn't know if they should let their presents be known. They waited to recognize their location.

Katie squeezed Natasia's hand. "This is the reservation! We will be safe. Little Dove and her family live here. Let's ask for help."

It was still early, and very few were awake. Katie could hear someone moving around inside one of the houses. She knocked on the door softly. A man peered at her like an enemy through the glass storm door. "What you want," he quaintly asked. "Too early for visitors."

"I need to see Little Dove. Is she back from Mr. Canterfield's? I don't know which house she lives in." Katie grinned.

He stared at Katie like she was from outer space. "You, her friend? What's your name?" he bluntly stated.

"Yes, she is my friend. My name is Katie. Mr. Brett Canterfield calls me Little Dove Two. I was named after her. She is his mother.

"What are you doing here in the village? Does she know you are here? Come sit by the fire while I brew some coffee." He said with a changed attitude. Katie said the right thing when she mentioned Little Dove and Brett Canterfield.

Katie began telling Adahy, an Indian, about some things that had happened. The quiet morning was shattered when someone knocked at the door. Bennie had followed them. There he was, as big as life!

Adahy stared at the man grimly as he stepped aside for Bennie to enter.

"Well, well," Bennie said. "Looks like you found my wife and daughter. That's a good thing. I'm tired of looking for them. They got lost in the woods last night, and I have been so worried. I will take them and go now. I'm sorry they bothered you at such an early hour. I must get the wifie to a doctor. She is not well, afflicted, you know. She tells some mighty tall stories. The doctor says she lost her mentality." Bennie said sorryfully.

Adahy stood along the wall. His hand was on the pistol in his waistband. He said. "Hold on, hoss. We need to talk before you go taking the ladies away. If what you say is true, then I will send for the shaman to have a look-see. I don't know you. What is your name?"

Bennie sneered. "Now see here, Indian. I might not look like much, but I love my little wifie and my daughter. I'm leaving now with them. Am I making myself clear? It's awful early in the day to die."

"I can't permit that, mister. I must insist they remain here." Adahy seethed.

Bennie grabbed Natasia by the hair and held her like a human shield before him. "Well, whatever you think, Mister Indian." He pointed the pistol near Natasia's temple. "I could care less if they live or die. They're nothing to me, and I don't mind telling you; I could kill you easily enough, too. Now lay the gun on the table, or all of you will surely die. I have nothing to lose. It's all in your hands. Whatever happens here will be your fault." Bennie stated with malice.

Katie looked Adahy in his eyes. "It's okay, we will go with him. He will kill you and never blink an eye. I thank you for your kindness, but we must go now. I don't want anyone else killed." She walked over to Bennie and gritted her teeth. "Let's go. He hasn't done anything to you. Leave him alone."

Bennie sneered at Adahy. "See what I mean? She's loco. Turn around. I don't want you to see which way we go."

Adahy did as he was told and turned his back to Bennie. Whap, the pistol hit its mark. Adahy was on the floor. Bennie tied him up and taped his mouth with duct tape. He carried it with him to bind the girl's mouths. "I am just too awesome for my own good." He snickered.

Bennie shoved the girls out the door.

"Listen, you two idiots. You do as you're told, or you are going to be guilty of someone's death. I have had it with both of you. We are going back to the cabin now. I have to find another place to stay. We must move probably to Chicago. Illinois. I already had trouble in the state of Missouri. I wanted to stay close to the Oklahoma line, but no, you two won't behave. I have tickets for passage toward the Bahamas, but I'm not ready for that move yet."

Bennie taped their mouths so they couldn't ask why there were tickets for the Bahamas, but Katie understood precisely. *He didn't say to the Bahamas! But toward the Bahamas. Where is he planning on taking us?* She thought, *scared stiff with tears burning her eyes.*

Natasia's eyes were wide with freight, too. Neither girl could move their hands. He had bound them so tight the blood was restricted.

He shoved them down the mountain as fast as they could travel. Bennie would jerk them back on their feet by their hair when they fell.

Bennie thought about killing them and being on his way, just get it over with. But the thought of money kept getting in the way. These women are dumb. If they knew what was good for them, they would behave. They're liable to go too far, and I can't control the – I need to kill inclination!

Bennie hurried as the cabin came into view. He wished he had killed that Indian, but he would have had to beat him to death. A gunshot would have awakened everyone in the village.

It had taken a few hours to get back to the line shack. Someone would have found the Indian by now. People would be on their trail real soon.

He threw the blankets into the trunk, leaving no room for the girls. Forget the blankets. *The girls go in the trunk. I can buy more blankets with the money the banker wired to the bank,* he snickered.

Without consideration, Katie and Natasia were shoved in the trunk; he hit their heads hard against the trunk floor. "You both better be quiet. I will stop on the next dirt road and send you to the netherworld if you're not. Is that understood?" Bennie yelled and glared at the girls with squinched eyes.

The girls nodded their heads. They knew to do as they were told, or he wouldn't hesitate. He would carry out his threat. He slammed the trunk lid shut with such force it made the girls' ears vibrate.

They had pushed Bennie to the limit of his stability. He was becoming more radical every day. If someone didn't rescue them soon, Katie knew he would bury them out there somewhere in the wilderness, and they would never be found.

Katie heard a whine as Bennie was getting things from the cabin. She recognized the cry of a wolf pup.

Where did that come from, she thought? *That's someone's pet!*

Brett expected little Adsila to be early, but she was late getting over the mountain.

"Well, good morning, little lady," Brett called to the little girl on the big black mare. "How are you today? You are a bit late, and I bet the pup is hungry. I haven't heard a peep from her all morning. Come on, we will see what she's doing."

She slipped her tiny hand into the big hand of her admirer as she skipped beside him to the barn. When they entered the stall, there was an opening in the back, a slit just large enough for the wolf cub to escape. There was no pup to be found.

Tears filled the child's eyes, "I guess she wanted her freedom too. She is too small to survive on her own, though." She lowered her head so Brett wouldn't see her tears.

Brett grinned with a look of confidence. "Wait a minute, that pup is very smart. She came with you from the village. I'll bet she went back there looking for you. Let's see if we can find her. What do you say?"

Adsila quieted her tears, saying. "Do you think so? When can we go? I shouldn't be so anxious, should I? Momma has told me to be patient and not to get my hair caught in the wringer."

Brett laughed and then grinned at the small fry. "Let's get some breakfast first. Then, get started on the hunt for your pup. You haven't eaten yet, have you?"

Adsila (meaning blossom) grinned and answered. "Not yet. I left too early. Momma didn't have it ready."

Brett said. "Maria will love to have you eat with us. That is if you would like to. I know Little Dove would love to see you, too. She hasn't seen any of the village people for some time."

"Little Dove is here? I know her. She is a nice lady, and I love her very much. She lives close to my grandfather." Adsila grinned.

"Okay, it's settled; we are headed for the kitchen." He laughed as the child raced him to the door. Of course, he let her win. "I must say, you are very fast, Adsila. You could outrun Blaze."

Maria watched Brett and the child running across the lawn. She hadn't seen him laugh like that in many years. He seemed happy. Adsila might be the medicine he needed to live again. "Well, it's about time for you to come in and eat. Go wash up while I set another place."

The child bumped into Maria. "Sorry, ma'am. I was racing Mr. Brett; he is fast, but I outran him," she giggled.

About that time, Little Dove came into the kitchen. "Oh my," she exclaimed. "Who do we have here? Well, if it isn't little Adsila. How are you, child, and how is your grandfather, Adahy?" Little Dove asked.

"Oh, he is great. I was supposed to gather eggs for him today. I must do that when I return." Adsila laughed.

"He gets around good for his sixty-eighty years. I am very fascinated by him. He is a wonderful man. I must visit him soon," Little Dove implicated, hoping her son didn't see her face flush. She was very fond of Adahy! Yes, Indeed.

Brett didn't miss the look. *I'm glad she has a male friend to talk to for companionship; he might be the man she needs.* He thought.

After breakfast, Brett and young Adsila went to the tack room to saddle Brett's horse. "Well, young lady, we can go to the village now. I want to see Grey Wolf anyway. There is something I need to ask him. He was out hunting yesterday while I was there. Hopefully, I can catch up to him before he leaves again."

As they approached the village, Brett could hear dogs barking. It was so cold that many of the people wanted to sleep while others were beginning to prepare for their day.

They tied their horses at the hitching post and entered the hardware store. Brett wanted to know the price of grain, but Mr. Ahanu (he laughs) was about to close; he didn't always stay open.

"I knew you would be coming soon, Brett. The food you have stored for the winter must be gone by now. I know you have always checked prices here first, then in Spur Lacy. I always have the lowest prices." Ahanu laughed. "We are very appreciative of the beef you send us during the winter."

"Yes, old friend, this is true, but today I will buy. The store in Spur Lacy can not beat your price. Can you deliver on Saturday? Carl expects me to order the grain today."

"That I can do. Expect it early. I close at noon on Saturdays. Got to have my rest, you know." He laughed.

Brett pointed his finger at the old Indian in acknowledgment and grinned. As he walked out the door, he heard Adsila scream. Ayeeeeee. Brett ran to the child and held her.

"What is wrong, Adsila?" Brett asked. "Where have you been?" The child cried so hard she could only point to the house down the street.

Brett ran to the house she indicated and entered. There, he found an elderly man on the floor. Brett bent down, removed the gag, sat the gentleman in a chair, and untied him. The man glared at Brett for a moment, trying to focus.

Adahy looked at Adsila and said. "Your pup was here last night. I fed and watered her. You spoiled her too much; she slept right next to the fire. The lady that was here wore your scarf because she was so cold. When they left, the pup followed them. I'm sorry, pumpkin, she wouldn't stay."

Brett felt a chill inside. The elderly man was slowly returning from the shocking experience, so using much caution, Brett asked. "Adahy, what woman was here? Can you describe her?"

"I can, and also the other girl, too. That man I will never forget. He was a demon from hell."

Adahy told Brett about the intruders early that morning and about the man who yanked the hair of the girl called Natasia.

"A little after daybreak, I heard this low knock on my door. When I opened it, there stood two girls. They were cold. I brought them in to warm. That's when I gave Katie adsila's scarf. The man came in a few minutes later. I think he had followed them. He held a gun to her head. Then the girl called Katie got between me and that Bennie guy. She protected me with her life. I was scared, but I would have shot him anyway, except he said he would kill the girl. He took them and left," Adahy recollected.

"Do you know how long they have been gone, Adahy?" Brett asked as he paced the floor.

"I do not know. I was unconscious," the Indian answered.

Brett was out the door like a bat. He waved to the child and said, "I will see you tomorrow, Adsila."

Searching intently, Brett went behind the houses, looking for footprints. Suddenly, the wolf pup appeared with Adsila's scarf in his mouth. Brett knelt and looked the pup in his eyes, repeatedly saying over and over. "Go find the girl."

When he sat her on the ground, the pup looked at him and ran into the woods. Brett knew then this was an exceptional wolf-cub.

Brett followed her as close as he could. She was fast, stopping to wait, when she got several feet ahead of him. They traveled several miles around the Mountain, just wide enough for one horse at a time, and down the ledge where most people wouldn't try to walk.

The pup sat down. Brett picked her up, stroked her fur gently, and whispered in her ear, "Go find the girl," he repeated it repeatedly. She began running again.

Brett hoped the pup hadn't forgotten where she found the scarf.

They went deeper and deeper into the valley, with the underbrush getting more dense. Brett was afraid he had made a mistake following the pup.

Then he saw it, the line-shack! So that's where he's been hiding. The tiny cabin sat in a valley surrounded by hills to help keep out the cold.

Brett dismounted. He crept slowly to the top of the hill. A small amount of smoke rose from the chimney. He noticed a window missing in the back but couldn't see if anyone was inside.

He knew if he rushed in, the man would kill the girls. The wolf pup ran ahead as though he could rescue the girls. *Good pup,* Brett thought.

Brett crawled through the underbrush and saw tire tracks. *I'm puzzled; it was a good hideout, so why did Carver leave? Most likely, the man was scared Adahy had told someone what he did to him, and the Braves would find and kill him over what he did to the Elder.*

Right under our noses, and we couldn't find them. Maybe I can see which way the car went. With the pup in tow, he mounted his steed; slowly, he went down the grade toward the highway. Brett wondered how that man

could climb the steep grade without an all-wheel terrain.

Spur Lacy is about twelve miles to my right, but I can't tell which road they took. I'm going into town and looking up good old Lieutenant Markham. Maybe he had luck with the hand tattoo. I can report this incident while I'm there.

The road is pretty slippery, Brett thought.

I don't know if I should ask the lieutenant to put an APB on Jeremy Rochester. If Jerremy thinks he's cornered, desperation will set in, but then again, if the police aren't aware of the situation, he could slip right through the cracks and never be found.

With money being wired to a Cayman Islands bank, there would be no way to trace it back to him, and that man knows we would keep sending money to that bank as long as we thought the girls were still alive.

But again, he might kidnap another girl and dispose of the ones he already has. What a horrible thought!

Mr. Mason and I sent the requested money, but we haven't seen Little Dove Two or Natasia. Twenty million dollars isn't chicken feed. I pray he keeps them alive. Or maybe he plans to kill them when he can't get any more money from us. Whew, I know that answer.

I almost had the girls within my reach. That's enough to make me want to kill that rotten hyena with my bare hands. He's as low-life as they come.

Reaching the sheriff's office, Brett sat on a bench in the outer room and waited for Markham. "Lieutenant Markham, did you find out about someone getting a <u>De-man</u> tattoo? We need some answers soon."

"Brett, come into my office. I indeed found some things. First, the man we are hunting will be difficult to apprehend. He was one of Houston's finest. He was a homicide detective for fifteen years. He knows all the ropes. It makes me wonder how long he has been doing this. His name is Benson Carver. Initially, he is from Houston, Texas. He was accused of taking bribes, but the charge didn't stick. Then Benson was accused of beating a witness to death, another charge that didn't stick. Taking money off drug dealers, no conviction. The list goes on and on.

The tattoo on his hand was meant to let the scumbags know he wasn't to be messed with. That was a recognizable mark among the drug cartel. He's smart as they come.

Slick talker. Dresses in the latest fashion. He acts with perfection in whatever crowd he's in at the time. High-stake kidnapper too, I'll bet." Markham continued.

"Should he take the girls out of the country, they would probably never be heard from again. He is also a make-up artist. He can change his appearance in fifteen moments in a bathroom. Did you get a good look at him at Christmas, Brett?"

"Since you asked me. Well, No. I didn't see the man without make-up. He had on a robe and wore a beard. I know it was a disguise now, but it looked so real.

What are we going to do? We could get the women killed if we push too hard. I think he's crazy." Brett said.

"No, Brett, he's not mad. He's just mean as they come, more like a demons. He can have passports made up in thirty moments. By looking at the documents, neither you, the feds, nor I could tell whether they were falsely acquired. He is the most educated character that you will ever meet."

Brett needed clarity. "Okay, Lieutenant, where do we go from here?"

Markham said. "Whew, we know the color and make of the car, plus the license plate number. The bad thing is that he may change the color or obtain a different vehicle. You never know when you are dealing with an artist who is trained this well.

I think he will try to get to another state. I have set up roadblocks throughout the state, but the police expect him to try getting through the back roads. If he tries to run one, the officers are ordered to shoot to kill. We realize we are risking the girls' lives, but Benson Carver must be stopped.

He can't be allowed to leave the country, which is probably what he intends. If he gets the girls out of the country, we will never get them back."

"Whatever must be done, it needs to be immediate. There is no time to waste. Benson knows I'm not very far behind him." Brett stated. "I was within about an hour of catching him. He was hidden in one of my old line shacks, but I don't know how long he was there. The girls escaped him and went to the village. He caught them and took them back to the cabin. One thing I can't understand is why he came back to the mountain."

"The hardest thing to see is right under your nose. The man knew you would look for him elsewhere, so he circled back. He probably left for a while to throw you off his trail.

He had to look different. I bet he changed his appearance every day. He may be a longhaired hippy by now. Just try to remember the shape of the eyes. That is the only thing that won't change. He may even use a colored contact lens." Markham reflected.

"I'm heading home, Lieutenant. Let me know if you hear anything. I don't know where to start looking from here. Let me know if I can assist you at any time. Keep me updated." Brett said.

The wolf pup yelped constantly but was still where he had tied it. He swooped down to pick it up when he spied an item hanging from a car trunk. He stayed squatted, watching and listening. There was no sound coming from the inside. he noticed no one in the front seat either, so he strolled over to get a better look.

The car was a dark green, nothing like the color Carver had been driving. But it was a sedan, almost the same as described. As he got closer to the car, he said. "Little Dove Two? Are you in there?" There was no answer, but the pup started pulling at the white garment.

Brett didn't want to leave the car unattended to call the lieutenant, so he stayed beside it until a lady came by walking her dog. "Ma'am. I need your help. Would you please go to the police station and ask Lieutenant Markham to come outside? Tell him it's Brett, and it's urgent!" He spoke with insistence.

The lady didn't answer but went to the station and returned with Markham. She didn't come back to the car but informed the lieutenant of Brett by pointing to where he was squatted. The lieutenant rushed to Brett's side with his weapon drawn.

"What do you have there, Brett? I can see a white piece of clothing, but what is it?"

"I'm not sure, but it belongs to Little Dove Two or an Indian girl named Adsila. The pup keeps pulling at it. She tries to get anything Adsila has worn. Little Dove Two had some pieces of her clothing from the village, given to her by Adsila's grandfather." Brett stated.

"Let's see what is in that trunk, shall we?" Markham said as he checked the front for keys or a trunk button. He called for one of the deputies to assist. They had to pry the trunk open manually. There was a piece of a petticoat inside with duct tape and rope.

The girls had been in the trunk right out front of the police department in broad, open daylight! Brett thought *that man must be either stupid or the most daring cuss ever born.*

While they examined the things, they found one thing that stood out on the sleeve of the white petticoat. The words Bahamas and Ill were written in lipstick, a significant clue for Brett and the Lieutenant.

Brett said. "Lieutenant, we need to check all the ships and cruises going toward the islands, but not necessarily for the Bahamas. You are right; he is trying to get out of the country, but where do we start?"

Bennie needed passports, and he knew where to get them done fast.

"Sit still, girl, or I will pop you again!" Bennie yelled at Natasia. "You have to look correct. I can't have you looking like a rag mop. Now be still!"

Katie watched Bennie put make-up on Natasia. It sure made her look different. She looked much older, at least eighteen, with the paint and a wig. It would be hard to recognize the girl when he was finished. He made her pose for a picture; Katie figured it was for a passport. That's why everything must be exactly right.

I hope someone finds my clue. I didn't have time to finish writing; I almost got caught as it was. Bennie is trying to get away! Katie thought.

I believe we're in Chicago. Maybe that's where he plans to catch a ship or boat. Who knows about Bennie? Katie thought.

Bennie barked at Katie. "Are you losing your mind, or did you hear me tell you to get ready?"

Katie hurried with her makeup; Bennie had no patience for being slow. She didn't want the belt again. Her skin felt like needles, and the bruises were still red and blue. He had beaten her and Natasia when they ran away to the village. It was less than expected. At least she could sit. She couldn't sit for a week the last time he beat her. She thought, *I'm usually kind-hearted with a good disposition, but I wish that man were dead. He hurt me so much,* just as the edge of the belt grazed her thigh.

"I said hurry up! I don't have all night. The man will be here in a few minutes, and you better be ready. I don't have to tell either of you what will happen if you don't behave, you got it?"

I must have the passports by the day after tomorrow. That's when we catch the boat." He snickered.

Bennie snarled. "Katie, remember, you are my wife, and Natasia is our daughter. If anything goes wrong, I will kill you both first and then myself."

Katie looked at Natasia. They both knew he meant every word. They must do as he said, or they would become a statistic and be buried in a shallow grave or perhaps at sea. Katie trembled with a bundle of nerves. Bennie had inflected too much pain and agony on her body and soul.

"Stop shaking, Katie! I won't have it. Sit still while I get the lens corrected. I won't tell you again!" Bennie yelled.

Katie decided to try a new tactic. "Bennie," she grinned with the nicest voice she could muster. "I've been thinking, if you would lighten up on us, we would be a lot more cooperative to you. We need a little breathing space now and then. We both understand it's all about money. We want to help you spend it too.

"Well, well, now. I do declare. I think maybe you have finally begun to see my point. I bet you would like to spend some of your daddy's money." He laughed. "There will be plenty for you both, as well. That is when we get to where we're going."

By now, you both know I can keep you forever if I feel like it." This time, he looked at Katie from her head to her feet, making her want to crawl in a hole and up-chuck.

"Bennie, you've had me with you for over a year. I gave you the slip a few times, but that was to see if you would look for me." Katie lied, trying to keep up the charade.

Natasia's mouth fell open; she looked at Katie as if she had a hole in her head. When Katie walked past her, she closed her mouth with her finger and said very sternly, "What's the matter, little girl? Does this surprise you?"

Grinning, Katie said. "I decided that if I can't win, then join them. It's an old saying I heard my entire life. Well, I like the idea." She winked at Natasia while her back was turned to Bennie.

"Now, that's more like it. I can use someone on my side. I still don't trust you, though. I will keep my eyes on you." Bennie commented as he ran his hand across Katie's shoulder.

Katie froze. Her eyes flashed, and she sassed him with her hands on her hips. "Listen, Bennie. I may go along with the money bit, but you keep your grubby fingers off my person." "I said that I was in it for the money. For the rest of your life, you can do it as you want. I will never be your woman. Let's get that straight right now."

Bennie shoved Katie lightly. "That's real cute, Catherine. Do you think I would look for a woman somewhere else? Well, I already do that. I will go along with you for now, but you don't have me convinced. Now, let's get back to the photograph. I have ten minutes, tops!"

I will play along and see what she is trying to do. She thinks I will trust her just like that. Ha. I don't think so, Bennie grinned.

"What?" Katie asked when she saw Bennie grin.

"Oh, nothing. I was just wondering what it would be like if I didn't have to worry about you giving me a hard time." Bennie quirked.

Katie knew she was playing with fire. She tried to get away from him before, to no avail. *When and if he starts trusting me, maybe I can tell someone where we are and protect Natasia simultaneously. This plan isn't much, but it's the best I can develop. He will probably see right through me.*

She tried to look happy, posed well, and sat very still for the picture. That was the hardest thing Katie had ever done. She was desperate and would do almost anything to escape. It would be too late after they sailed into international waters.

Back At The Police Station

Brett calculated. "Lieutenant, let's look at that undergarment again. There was something else on that cloth when we examined it. Something we may have overlooked."

The lieutenant handed the garment to Brett. It was bagged, ready to go to the evidence room. Brett turned the petticoat over and looked closely at the writing. "Lieutenant, that isn't ill, as being sick like we thought. That stands for Illinois! Little Dove Two, or Natasia, was trying to tell us they were headed for Illinois. Make sure the roadblocks are in place, especially towards that state. I feel that I am right about this." Brett demanded.

"Whoa," Brett. "It sounds like you are heading this investigation. We don't need to have a discrepancy about who is in charge. We are no longer kids; let us get that straight right now! It's my investigation and my job, not yours." Markham snapped, apparently angered.

Brett is still trying to be the top dog. Nope, it's not happening. This time, it's in my ball field, he thought.

"Sorry, Thomas. I have just been up too long. I'm going home to rest." He grinned.

"Lieutenant Markham jerked at his Brest coat. Okay, go home. I will keep you informed." He said flatly. *I can't believe he just called me by my given name, and he can be so persistent.*

"Here is my cell number, Thomas. I might be outside and wouldn't want to miss your call." Brett said, holding his head high; he stormed out the door.

Brett thought. *Well, Markham, now that you're out of my hair, I'm headed to Chicago. The port has ships entering and leaving the United States. Bennie will probably use some import/export company to escape. Well, beware, Mr. Carver. I will catch you, and you won't like it. I best call home since I'll be gone for several days.*

"Maria, please ask Carl to pick up my horse and the wolf pup in Spur Lacy. I left them at the general store. Also, I have already bought the grain we need from Ahanu to be delivered before noon on Saturday.

"Sure, Brett. We have a new filly this morning. She and the Mama are doing fine. It looks just like Molly." Maria said proudly. "Molly was so gentle; it's unbelievable that you gave it to Adsila."

Brett had wanted another colt with Mollie's color for a long time.

After speaking with Maria briefly, Brett hailed a cab for the airport.

I haven't been in the windy city for a long time, Brett thought as the airplane touched down. *From what I can see, it has grown much more significant, with many new buildings. Then again, I wasn't paying much attention when I was here the last time. I was on business and had my mind on the price of beef and how much money I would receive should I export the cattle overseas.*

Now, I must find a needle in a haystack!

Brett contacted a man he had met during the cattle deal. When he was in Chicago before, he carried a lot of money with him, so Brett asked the police to assign someone to protect him. This time, his request would be very different.

Pulling his cap down low to help conceal his face, Brett entered the police department. It was near the waterfront. Knowing Benson Carver was a shrew man and had connections in Chicago, Brett thought he should take extra precautions. Walking to the front desk, he noticed a man reading a newspaper, a big giveaway; the man was looking for someone. Brett went down the hall to the men's room and called the front desk.

"I need to speak with Howard Skeits, please," Brett said.

"May I have your name, please? The desk clerk asked very politely but to the point.

"Brett Canterfield, from Oklahoma, please be discreet. I don't need my name advertised. It is very important. Thank you." Brett stated.

"Howard Skeits here, how are you, Brett? I haven't heard from you, as you folks say, in a coon's age. He laughed heartedly.

"Well, I have a request. I need information as quietly as it can be gotten. Can you meet me for coffee somewhere?" Brett asked.

"Well, I can, or you can come into my office," Skeits answered.

"I need professional help. If you could meet me somewhere, I will make it well worth your time. It will be a cash deal. Howard, perhaps you could get someone to cover your position during your absence." Brett grinned.

Skeits laughed. "Oh, that kind of need. Okay, how about I meet you in the café around the corner from the station? Would that be acceptable?

"Yes, that will be fine. I'm in the conference room at the police station. I noticed a man sitting on the bench that I had rather not see me. He's known as Jodie the Snitch." Brett laughed.

Brett slipped out to the street without being seen. He knew the snitch would recognize him and that Jodie knew he carried money on his person. If he had told other people about Bretts' Mountain, that wouldn't have been a good thing to speak about on the streets of Chicago.

"Hello, Brett. It's good to see you. What kind of help are you needing, my friend?" Skeits asked, sliding into the booth.

"Well, it's similar to the last time except much more serious. I need information about a specific thing going down. Is there a ship docked that would transport human cargo to an island somewhere for a price? It will be most likely within the next week to two." Brett pulled the pictures of the two women and a man from his wallet. "This is the cargo I speak of."

"Skeits whistled. "Whoa, this may be harder than you think. Human cargo is so dangerous that we rarely hear anything about it. The ships' captains have such good connections with the export/import company that it is almost impossible to penetrate their system. It can be done, but it would take time, and it doesn't look like that is something you have."

"We've been chasing this man and those two ladies for quite some time. He kidnapped them on Christmas Eve. We almost had him once, but he's an expert at eluding. We haven't been able to put a location on them until now. One of the women left a clue on a petticoat."

Brett stated, pointing to Katie's picture along with Benson Carver. "He is an experienced make-up artist and an ex-homicide detective from Houston, one of the worst to apprehend. Benson has gotten away with so much crime it's unreal. It seems to thrill him to damage other people's lives. He cares about no one's feelings, and he will kill anyone that gets in his way. The police from Spur Lacy are desperate to apprehend him. The lady in the photo is a friend of mine, a very close friend."

"I will get on this immediately, but I need Jodie. I know you don't want him to know you are in town, but he is the best I know of for this type of work. I won't mention your name if that's how you want it. He can get around ship's people much better than I can." Skeits said.

Brett looked Skeits in his eyes. "If Benson Carver knew I was here looking for him, he would dump the women in the lake or city disposal, so please ask Jody to use caution."

"I will be discrete, but it's hard for a Private Detective to get nosy without someone getting wise."

Markham Brews A Scheme

Lieutenant Markham went to Chief of Police Perry Davis. "Chief, we should be doing more in Max Robertos's case. The DNA we found in the BMW doesn't match any we found anywhere else at the scene. I would like to have Margo Canterfield's remains exhumed. Her mother said she had the AB- blood type, which we found in the stolen car at the lake. Brett told us she had lost her mind. Maybe she had something to do with the murders. I think it's worth a shot. This way, we could be certain whether she was there that day." Markham stated anxiously.

Chief Davis yelled at Markham. "Are you out of your mind? You want me to order an exhumation on Brett Canterfield's wife with him out of town? You must be nuts! I would never do such a thing without first informing Brett of such an action."

"He's at the ranch, sir. He's waiting for me to call him if anything turns up with that half-breed Little Dove Two." *Brett should have known I'm not going to do much when it comes to helping him. After all, he stole Margo from me, even if he didn't know it.* Markham snickered.

The chief stood up and shook a pointed finger at Markham. "Lieutenant, there is a short line between getting suspended without pay and keeping your job. Brett Canterfield is one of the most respected people around here. You best do whatever it takes to help him retrieve Little Dove Two. What's wrong with you, Markham? Has your love affair with Margo finally pushed you over the edge? I bet Brett doesn't know about that, does he? No one around here would have told him just how dirty you were, and you best keep it buried with her."

The chief fumed. "Sometimes I wonder about you. You don't have the brains God gave a goose! Furthermore, Brett isn't at the ranch. He's in Chicago. You are excused, you maggot."

Markham jumped from his chair and flounced out the door. He was never so mad. "The chief had no right speaking to me like that.

I have done my best to keep law and order," he said aloud. "Now, I will do things my way."

"Good morning, Lieutenant Markham. How are you? Would you like some coffee and doughnuts? The stove has already been turned off, or I would offer you breakfast." Maria said with a grin.

"Thank you, Maria. This morning, I'm here on business. I was talking with Chief Davis, and he expressed the need to exhume Margo's body to test her DNA, but he didn't know how to approach you with the request. I told him you would understand if I came up here and spoke with you about it. This way, we could end the question of Margo being at the lake. It's preposterous thinking she was there or had anything to do with those murders on Lovers' Lane. Markham said, trying to seem unhappy. I am so sorry," he stated.

Maria's grin faded and was replaced with a look of remorse. "Well, if that's what he thinks, it must be done. Brett isn't here now, but I will speak to him about it when he returns." She said solemnly.

"Well, that's the point. The Chief wants the exhume as soon as possible. I thought you could give the consent since Brett isn't here. The chief could get a court order, but if you say it would be okay, we wouldn't have to bother the judge." Markham suggested.

"Okay then, I suppose it must be done. Now, excuse me, I have my work to do." Maria stood, looking tight-lipped at Lieutenant Markham, as she held open the door for him to leave.

Maria thought *He went too far this time. I have walked around that man for the last time.* "Hello, I need to speak with Chief Davis, please. Yes, I will hold."

"Chief Davis, this is Maria Gonzales speaking. I understand you want to exhume Margo's remains for an autopsy. Well, that would be okay, but you must have a court order signed by a judge before a procedure of this nature can be done. I just spoke with your Lieutenant." Maria said softly.

"Ma'am, I didn't send Markham up there, and he will be reprimanded when he returns. I told him to leave that alone. As the investigation continues, we're not sure what we will need. I do most apologize for his behavior." The chief said. Maria grinned, holding her mouth to keep from laughing.

It's time for him to pay the price of betrayal. He was supposed to be Bretts' best friend, but rumors around Spur Lacy told a different story. Markham was trying to get Margo to marry him instead of Brett. He was dating her until the week of their vows. He is a slime bag, Maria thought.

Maria snickered. *Margo realized Brett would cater to her every need, but Markham, well, everything was just for Markham. He wanted her money, and she had her daddy's millions. I wonder what he will do now: find another rich woman who needs a comforting shoulder? I should keep what I know to myself, and I shall, but I want to see him squirm. He needs to be taught a lesson!*

The desk clerk whistled under her breath when Lieutenant Markham arrived for work the following day. "Hey, Markham. The chief wants you in his office, pronto!" she said quickly.

"Markham, you are on suspension until further notice!" the chief yelled as he entered the room.

The grin on Markham's face faded. He stood there, as still as the statue of Robert E Lee.

He had already formed the words of what he would tell Chief Davis and that the excavation could begin.

"I told you not to mention the exhumation of Margo Canterfield, and what did you do? You went to her mother! That is one of the most ill-informed things you have ever done. You know there has to be a court order for an exhumation of human remains, and we're waiting for the coroner to finish his paperwork. Now turn in your badge and firearm, and get outta here before I really get mad!" the chief fumed, slamming the papers on his desk.

With force, the lieutenant slammed his gun and badge on the desk. His face was red from being humiliated and being put on suspension. I will get even with you, Chief, and Mister Brett Canterfield! he thought as he hustled out the door.

"Robbie, come in here for a minute, please!" the Chief called out. Right now, he was extremely furious with Markham.

"I need someone to fill Lieutenant Markham's position. I don't know if it will be temporary. Who do you think would be most qualified?" Chief Davis asked.

Robbie said. "I don't know right off hand, maybe Henry Paulsen. He is a good man and easy to get along with. I knew Markham went way too far. I should have reported his actions to you before now. I'm sorry, chief."

"It's not your fault, Robbie. I would have had to see the proof of what he was doing. Send Henry into my office. I need to get the paperwork started." The chief said.

Markham thought as he boarded the plane for Chicago. *Brett Canterfield caused me trouble for the last time. I will show him. He won't get the glory this time. No matter how decorated he is, I will solve these murders by myself, even if I have to shoot him in the leg. It's my time to shine!*

Ships Loading On Lake Michigan

The winds on the dock were bone-chilling as Benny waited for his Contact man.

I wish that man would hurry. I am cold and need to get this over with. Aw, finally, there he is. He thought.

Bennie stood as the man approached. "Look here, my friend, I will pay you very well, but I expect the best of everything. Do I make myself clear? Our rooms must have the most exquisite food with extraordinary service. I am wealthy, and my ladies must have anything they desire."

The Sea Captain sneered at Bennie and said. "You're not what I expected. Put the money upfront, and you can have anything you want. I will accommodate you however you wish."

Bennie had a beard, wore a felt hat, and sported a long black coat and leather boots. He looked more Amish than a Texan.

Money was no entity right now. Bennie forked over his ransom money like it was paper. He had plenty in his valise. While he counted out the bills, another man watched.

Jodie counted the bills with field glasses. Nineteen thousand. That's a lot of money being handed to a man on a ship. I often see that man in the office and at the shipyard. Under dealing! Yep, that's it. Now, let's see where the fancy-dressed dude goes.

Jodie followed Bennie to a sleazy apartment near the dock. I wonder what he's up to? I will get as close as I can. Jodie wore his disguise: a scruffy beard and tattered clothes which looked appropriate. He staggered up to the side of the building, a typical alcoholic.

He took the bottle from his breastcoat and started the pretense of being a drunken street bum. That was all he remembered. He awoke in the city hospital with a concussion.

A policeman guarded the door just outside Jodie's room when he awoke from a coma. "Hey, I have to see Howard Skeits he yelled." The guard ran to Jody.

"I see you're awake. That private investigator just stepped out for coffee. I will get him." He stated.

"Wait. What day is this, and what time is it?" he asked.

When the guard gave him the information, Jodie was pleased. He hadn't missed too much. "I believe the private investigator can use my information." Using hand jesters, he waved the guard to hurry and get Skeits as quickly as possible.

The information was ready when Skeits entered the room. Jodie told him what he saw at the port. There was another man with Skeits. Brett Canterfield!

"Hey Howard, This information is for Canterfield, right? I wrote what I saw on a plain sheet of paper, but it's gonna cost you more than the few measly two hundred bucks." He sneered.

Skeits nodded. "Jodie, do you want to stay in the streets and continue doing what you do? Or do you want to spend a few nights in jail? I can have that arranged too, you know. We need that information now. Let's have it."

"Okay, keep your pants up and your dander down," Jodie grinned and told Skeits what he saw between the two men. He didn't have time to get the transporter ship's name because someone cold-cocked him, but he knew he could as soon as he was discharged.

It wasn't long before the nurse discharged Jodie, promising to be more careful and not fall from his top steps anymore.

The Coroners Oficial Report

The coroner read the report. "Chief Davis, the death of Max Robertos was determined that he died from a stab wound made by a sharp instrument, possibly from a cross-bow arrow. It penetrated the heart, causing him to bleed out. The cuts were from a bowie knife, which many people still carried. A cross-bow also killed the women. The wounds were consistent. There was enough AB-blood found to consider that whoever did the murders had a rare blood type. That is the person who killed all three people. Also, there was Blonde hair. The DNA from the hair was AB- so when DNA matches the same blood and hair, you will have your killer."

"Thank you for the report. Now, to put the pieces together. I will need a request signed by the judge to exhume Margo Canterfield's remains. The body will prove, I'm sure, to be the rare blood type. She lost her sanity when her twins fell over the mountain to their deaths. I fully believe she is the one who killed all three people, but we need her DNA to be certain. She was also blonde." The chief said

The coroner replied. "I will send the request to the judge early tomorrow morning. I am so sorry for all the families involved. This murder is the most horrible thing that happened in Spur Lacy over many years."

The Chief said. "Robbie, you and Paulsen go to Brett's home and give notice to Maria and Little Dove. They will see us in the family cemetery, so we need them to know what is happening before we start digging. I hate to disturb the dead, but this is a must. I wish Brett were here to calm the women folk. They loved Margo."

Robbie nodded to the chief; this would be hard for him. He always liked and respected Brett. As a bystander, he had often watched Brett cry with sadness. Brett adored Margo; it broke Brett's heart when his children died. Then, he almost gave up when Margo lost her sanity. He didn't want to go on and might have ended it right then had it not been for Maria, Margo's mother, being the saint she is. Maria held what was left of Brett Canterfield together. She actually nurtured him back to mental health. She insisted he go back to church. That seemed to help turn him around.

"I will go in the morning as soon as I get the exhume papers from the judge," Robbie said.

The next day, Robbie told Paulsen as they started up the mountain. "What a nasty way to start a day, but it's my job. It's a shame because they are such wonderful folks."

"Well, good morning, Robbie," Maria said as she opened the door. "We just had a visit from Markham the day before yesterday. Would you like some coffee or tea? I have both."

"Maybe some other time, Maria. Today isn't a social call; I must serve an official paper giving us the right to exhume the remains of Margo Canterfield. I am so sorry." Robbie stepped back and bowed his head with tears while Maria read the papers. "I dislike this very much, Maria, but it is my job."

"I expected this, but not quite so soon. I wish Brett were here. Could it wait until he returns? I think he would want to be here." Maria asked.

Robbie shook his head. "I am truly sorry, Maria, but the backhoe will be here in an hour or so. I wish I could help, but my hands are tied. This order comes from higher up than me."

Maria nodded. "I understand, Robbie. I would still like you, and I don't know the other fellow there with you to come in and warm up until the tractor appears."

"Thank you, Maria. You are so kind, but we should stay out here."

The men unloaded the excavator at the gravesite. Robbie noted the site to Paulsen.

The coroner concluded. The remains of Margo Canterfield were sent to the lab immediately after being removed. The coroner sent the results to the chief when the tests were finished. Margo has the same DNA and the same hair fossils.

Robbie said. "Chief, since she is the one who killed the man and the two women, I would like to know just what happened out there. Margo didn't go into town and bring Max out to Lovers' Lane. I am certain there is still more to this than we know."

Chief Davis looked at Robbie and said. "Well, when Brett finds the girl Bennie Carver kidnapped, I think we will get our answers. She was there when all this went down. I bet she saw everything that happened. I can hardly wait to hear from him."

The Ships Were Loading

Jodie checked at the ships to see if any had left the harbor while he was away. He nosied around each one to see what they were loading and talked to the crew, taking a break.

The crew thought him just a loud, nosy bum. They laughed and fed him a line of lies. Jodie made most of his money snooping. He had been around the ships and crews for many years.

Jody knew that one of these days, a ship's crewman would take his life. He thoroughly enjoyed what he did for now. He met interesting people along the way, and with his practice and training, he could separate the truth from the lies.

"So, ye gonna set sail fer de ilens tamare? I be a sayn goodbye ta ye den." Jodie said to one of the crew.

Jodie loved to use slang words on the deckhands. They thought he was just an old dude. They even nicknamed him 'the creepy bum.' He wanted to snicker but knew better. It could give his disguise away and blow his cover, which would be disastrous.

The ship's mate let Jodie hang around with him, even following him to the galley. He sat and ate with the crew members; they all enjoyed his company and his jokes, giving Jodie time to investigate some without anyone causing suspicion. All the ships were different but essentially the same.

Jodie went to Skeits with his report that night. "I located the ship hauling passengers. It is called the Admiral and sets sail tomorrow at nine-thirty sharp."

"I haven't had a chance to get aboard the other three yet, but I'm working on it. I asked if they ever let people pay for passage to another port or island. The one crewman said, not this one, but check out the one named Jersey if you want passage. That one will let you board for anywhere."

"The man laughed at me. He told me, 'Fellow, you don't have the price of a biscuit; how do you think you could pay the price of a ticket? That one has a hefty tariff.' He thought I was just a waterfront bum, but that's my cover." Jodie laughed.

Not even Brett knew Jodie was an undercover cop. He had his job down pat and was good at it. "Tell me, Mr. Canterfield, what are you doing here anyway? It can't be because Skeits is your good friend." Jodie laughed a hardy ha, ha.

Brett sat beside Jody and said. "I never suspected that you had been assigned to me as a personal bodyguard when I visited Chicago before. Jodie, you are good. I believe you got careless at the sleazy apartment building the other night just because you were tired."

Jody snickered. "That man should never have been able to sneak up on me. I must be getting old,"

Brett said with a bit of sarcasm. "Well, the cat is out of the bag. I'm here to find a kidnapper. He is a nasty varmint holding two women hostage. He loves to torment people, and revenge is his middle name."

"Describe him to me. I'm out there all the time looking for idiots." Jodie suggested.

"I don't think so. This man is one it would take an expert to conquer. Skeits and I will keep that to ourselves. We don't need a snitch or bum to get involved." Brett laughed. *That's all I need for someone like him to let Bennie know I'm here in Chicago. He looks like he just crawled out of a gutter somewhere. Yuk. He needs to take a bath.*

Jodie threw up his hands and said, "I offered. I know when to bud out. I know when I'm not wanted." He jived, winking at Skeits, as he left the room.

Outside, away from the others, Jodie laughed heartedly. *This case is serious. I had better wait around for Skeits to let me know the reason.*

Brett said goodnight to Howard Skeits and headed for the hotel. Jodie met Skeits in the anti-room. "Listen, Jodie. Don't take any chances with this guy. He is an ex-homicide detective from Houston. He's a real bad dude. He's been arrested for many crimes but never convicted, yet he is as guilty as sin. Have you seen a stranger anywhere doing anything out of the ordinary?" Skeits asked.

"Just what I told you earlier. Do you have a picture of the man Canterfield mentioned? I need to see it. I know what I'm looking for, but not who. Do we need to fill Canterfield in on who I really am? Is there a reason he can't know?" Jodie asked. "Brett doesn't believe I was a real bodyguard assigned to him."

"When we started this type of police work, if you recall, we decided not to let anyone except the chief and the judge know about what we do. Brett doesn't know I'm a homicide detective, either. We are to maintain and keep our identity hidden so we can work undercover when we're needed. I think this is one of those times. Those girls are in real danger. If that man suspects anything, he will kill them and maybe himself. We must be cautious and not reveal ourselves." Skeits said.

"Look at these pictures closely. The two girls probably won't look like this because the man is a make-up artist. We will just have to act on instinct. Watch their walk. They are from the mountains. At least Natasia is. The other one is actually from Texas. Their fathers are wealthy. Maybe even more prosperous than Brett Canterfield."

Jodie took the pictures and looked closely at the eyes, weight, and height. He had a photographic memory. To recognize them would be hard but not impossible.

"Skeits, the man I saw in the limo was about this man's height and weight. He doesn't look like this photo, though." Jodie was fascinated at the resemblance. "The man I saw looked like a plow-boy. This one looks like a preacher. Man, what a difference. If this is the man, he is good with make-up, and I think I'm looking at the same person. I wonder if it was this man that conked me on the head."

"I'll go to that building later tonight and look around. You never know what a fellow might shake out of the woodworks," Jodie grinned.

"Okay, I will see you in the morning. Try to find out what you can with the Jersey ship. We can't let him get away with those women." Skeits stressed.

Markham Caught A Flight

The plane Markham boarded made an emergency landing, so his flight didn't arrive until the wee hours of the morning.

Markham headed to the police station, nearest to the waterfront. "Anybody here?" he yelled while banging on the desk. "I need to speak to someone. It's important."

A sleep-eyed dispatcher came to the front. "Keep your shirt on. I just went for a soda and chips. What's the hurry? It's three o'clock in the morning. What do you need?" He asked.

"My name is Detective Thomas Markham. I need to speak to the detective in charge. I realize it's early, but I have been looking for the police department for quite some time. I am trying to find a man who kidnapped two women." Markham stressed, straightening to his full height of five feet ten inches.

"You come back tomorrow, and I'm sure she will see you. I just asked you to quiet down. At this precinct, the police officers cherish every shut-eye moment they can get. We have a lot of crime around here, and they're on duty most every night." The dispatcher stated.

"Okay, where is the closest hotel? I will get some shut-eye and be back early in the morning. Did I hear you right? Did you say the detective is a female?" Markham snickered.

"I sure did, and a darn good one too." He snapped.

Markham grunted and left for the hotel. *I will deal with the female detective in the morning. A woman detective. Ha! Women!* He thought.

The lieutenant was up early: a man on a mission. As soon as he showered and dressed, he was at the police station. He strolled in as if he were on their payroll.

"I was told to come back this morning. Well, here I am. I want to see the detective right now!" He yelled, obnoxious and demanding. "Where is the detective? Markham yelled again.

The dispatcher jumped with anticipation. She gave Lieutenant Markham a frozen stare. The clerk said. "Mister, sit down and be quiet, or I will have one of the policemen escort you to a cell. Do you understand?"

"You can't talk to me like this. I followed a kidnapper from Oklahoma, and I need assistance from your local law office now! I don't have time to waste." Markham stressed.

"Believe me, I don't care," the dispatcher hissed. "Now sit down!"

Thomas Markham stuffed his hands in his pockets and shuffled his feet across the floor. "Let me know when the detective comes in," *They can't do this to me,* Markham thought as he picked up a newspaper and tried to read today's headlines, but he was so angry he couldn't concentrate on what he read.

That was a very ignorant thing to do. Put me on suspension without pay. I will get even with Chief Perry Davis. I will solve this case and make him look like a fool. Markham thought as he began pacing the floor. He returned to the bench seat and sat down on the newspaper he had been reading.

Jodie checked in at the Police Station on his way to the shipyards. There might be something going on he would want to pursue.

At the Police Station, a stranger was sitting on his newspaper. "Hey, mister, may I please have my newspaper?" Jody asked politely.

Markham looked him up and down. *A town bum,* he thought, *and he wants me to get up, as angry as I am. No way.* "I don't see your name on it, butt out," he snapped. "Don't just stand there; go away somewhere. Flush yourself down the toilet. It might get some of the crud off you."

Jodie stood and glared at him. "Who are you? I don't remember seeing a dragged-out idiot like you around here. Get off my paper. I won't ask you again." He said with a crooked grin.

The dispatcher interrupted. "Hey, Jodie, how's it going?" She knew what was about to happen in under two seconds. "Meet Lieutenant Markham from Oklahoma." She frowned.

"I am trying to be civil here, but you know how moody I am before my coffee and newspaper!" Jodie grimaced through clenched teeth. "Now, get off my paper."

The lieutenant was being obnoxious and sat still, not moving an inch.

Without warning, Jodie grabbed Markham. He gave him a whap, and he hit the floor. Jodie walked over and picked up his paper.

The lieutenant got up, brushed his clothes off, and yelled at the dispatcher. "Are you going to sit there and let him do that to me? He body slammed me!"

"Detective Jodie, would you please escort mister Markham to a cell? The charge is unruly conduct. I will personally sign the arrest warrant." The dispatcher laughed.

"Wait! You can't do that. I'm working on a case. I may be from another state, but a bad person must be apprehended in your city. He kidnapped two women from Oklahoma!" Markham yelled.

"I can't believe you're a detective," Markham said as Jodie escorted him to his home away from home.

"Well, believe it. I am an undercover agent, and all the force knows me." He smirked. "Don't ever cut a man down because of his dress. I could have been Jesus. You wouldn't have known the difference." Jodie said as he pushed the lieutenant into the cell and 'click,' locked the door.

Jodie called Brett. "I wasn't supposed to call about the kidnappings. Skeits will explain why I'm involved with your case later. Right now, guess who I saw this morning? One of Okalahoma's finest. Lieutenant Markham. He disrespected our Detective. I interceded and locked him up for disturbing the peace. Good riddance, too." Jodie laughed. "He's an obnoxious imbecile. What do you suggest I do with him?"

"I don't care for that man very much, Jodie. Keep him incarcerated as long as you can, will you? He is always interfering where he doesn't belong. He isn't at the top of the line if you know what I mean. I will contact the chief back home and see what's happening," Brett commented.

The Dock In Chicago

The morning begins with a beautiful but frigid day. The sky is clear, although the wind off lake Erie confirmed winter still hung around.

Bennie knew he had to return to the waterfront, but he still had some last-minute details he must take care of before they started the long trek to the island.

The magnificent uncharted island lay in the South Pacific.

Bennie was sent there once on a survival expedition while on the force. He remembered the hot sandy beaches, palm trees, and the abundance of fruit. It was like a paradise in the sun. He named the island 'Paradise de Peace.' He believed the women would like this island to live out their lives.

He did not pity little rich girls. *They always got everything they wanted. Just tell Daddy. It never failed, Daddy's little girl. Ugh!*

I will have my peace when I get my mansion built, and my slave girls will help develop it. I will erect it among the coconut trees or the palms. I will have them beckon to my every need, from my house shoes brought to me to fresh squeezed orange juice for breakfast.

Bennie couldn't help but daydream. He could hardly wait! Palm trees, sand, and hula girls.

He had money, so he would have someone pick him up and take him to the mainland for supplies. He would buy enough to last a long time. "I got it all figured out," he laughed loudly.

Bennie didn't know that Lieutenant Markham and Brett Canterfield were in Chicago. He thought he had given them the slip, and they were still running around in circles looking for him in the little heck town.

I have no worries, he thought. He could go down to the ships anytime he wanted and talk to whomever he pleased without worrying about being arrested.

They were some dumb cops. I was right under their noses in Spur Lacy. Several times, I was in the Albert Jones hardware store with Markham standing beside me. That dumb flatfoot looked me in the eyes and said good morning. Bennie roared with laughter.

I wonder what they thought when they found the car at the lake. I bet that blew their little pea brains; they're probably still trying to fingerprint it. They didn't see my prints on it. I dusted it too generously. I would have gotten away if it hadn't been for that blonde hussy catching me with the BMW. She thought it was her car. I still can't believe what I saw her do. That poor dumb stiff didn't know what hit him. If she had known I was there, she would have killed me too. She was fantastic with that crossbow.

Captain Roberts was the Pilot of the ship named Jersey. He looked at Bennie and said, "I don't know if I should trust you or not. Are you mixed up with the law or anything that would cause the authorities to come asking questions?" That man looks too dressy, wanting to go to one of the uncharted islands and asking when the ship would return to the island again.

"No way. My wife, our daughter, and I want to live there, away from the hustle and bustle, but we will need medical supplies, food, and other things we can't produce from the island," Bennie explained.

He made it sound so honest that the ship's captain was convinced that what he had said was true. "Okay, be here at one o'clock sharp tomorrow. This ship waits for no one; even if the passage has been paid, I won't hold the ship up. Not even a minute. Do we understand one another?"

"Yes, yes, we understand each other."

Bennie snickered. *You foolish man, I may decide to stay on the island forever with my newly found family, or I might decide to return alone and bring new ladies to the island for my slave girls and their daddy's money to make my harem bigger. I can't believe I'm so intelligent.*

Jodie knew the man in the sleazy apartment had left. He watched him hurry toward the docks but had no idea where the man was going. Jody wanted to follow him, but the need to investigate the apartment complex came first.

Jody believed that the man who left the apartment was the one Brett was looking for.

He waited ten minutes and then walked silently up to the second floor. He heard no sound, just eerie silence. He knocked on doors as he passed them, stopping just long enough to know there was silence on the other side.

When he came to the last door on that floor, he thought he heard a muffled sound. He shoved the door open, and there they were, 'the women!' he hurried to remove the ropes from them, but as he did, the younger woman gave him a roundhouse kick before he knew what hit him. It put him in a daze from such an unexpected hit to the head.

She yanked her gag off and coughed. "Gag that man, Katie," she yelled. "It's bad enough to be kidnapped by a pro, but I'm not going to be held by any hobo. We have to hurry before Bennie catches us. He won't be gone long. He had to see that man again to finish the cruise details."

Katie grabbed the rope and taped Jodie's mouth before he regained his senses. He couldn't muffle out one word. The women grabbed their blankets and ran.

Katie, being the oldest, felt somewhat responsible for Natasia, even though Natasia had these skills, which she used very successfully. "You put that bum on his butt," Katie laughed hysterically. "We are free one more time. This time, you lead. The last time I got us caught."

"I have no idea which way to run. I know we must get away from here before he catches us again. That varmint won't be gone very long. The ship's captain was supposed to be waiting for him as soon as he arrived. What do you think? Which way should we run?" Natasia had the idea to run away from the sounds of the ship's foghorn, which she thought the crew members had tested every hour since they had been in the apartment.

"I don't have the least idea. I can only think, run! We can figure out what to do after we know we are far away from Bennie. I think he will kill us if he catches us this time. He's so enthused about that blamed island. I don't want to be on an uncharted island with him for the rest of my life! That is the most horrid thought I ever had. I had rather die!" Katie stressed!

Bennie went back to the apartment. Climbing the stairs, he heard a shuffle. He drew his pistol as he opened the door slowly. "Who the hell are you?" He screamed at Jodie.

Seeing the women were gone, he ran outside and looked for them. "That's the stupid bum I knocked out the other night. I thought he understood he wasn't welcome here. Now, where did they go?" he yelled loudly.

"You will pay dearly this time," Katie, do you hear me?" Bennie screamed.

"That was Bennie screaming. Run faster. He will kill us this time, Katie." Natasia said.

The girls ran as fast as they could. Every time they went around a corner, they stopped to check and ensure he wasn't on the street in front of them. They were cold as icicles and knew they must find shelter before dark.

Katie shoved her purse under her arm as they ran from the apartment, giving them some money.

Bennie let Katie see what it felt like to have cash on her person, even though she couldn't spend it at a store. Katie thought he was teasing her, but this money would help them along the way.

"Natasia, we need to call the police and have them pick us up. Let's go to this restaurant and ask to use the phone. What do you think?"

"Good idea, but let's not get cornered in there by Bennie. He wouldn't hesitate to kill the people inside, us included." Natasia said, breathless.

"While you use the phone, I will stay outside the door and watch for Bennie, okay?" Katie said.

"I'll be right back, Katie."

A few moments later, Katie was surprised to hear Natasia call to her.

"Come in here. Katie, I need you!" Natasia excitedly called!

Katie thought she couldn't have already called the police. Maybe she's just scared. "I'm coming, Natasia. What's up?"

"Oh my God! How did you find us?" Katie screamed as she ran into Brett's arms. "How did you know we were here?" her knees buckled as Brett circled her with his strong arms.

Brett stood silent and held Little Dove Two for a spell before answering. Katie was crying tears from fear and joy. He did follow Bennie. Bennie, she thought! "Brett, Bennie will be not far behind us. He will kill anyone that gets in his way. We need to get to the police, and quick!"

Howard Skeits stood up and bowed. "At your service, ma'am," he stated. "We were just going to get a cup of that delicious witch's brew. Care for a cup? Maybe a plate of Bar-B-Q ribs? They have very delicious food here. Good cooks here, too," he grinned at Katie.

"Listen, the man that kidnapped us will be here real soon; he is evil. He has an assault rifle and pistols. They all have silencers. He won't hesitate to kill everyone in here. The two of you couldn't possibly stop him. Katie and Natasia began to cry. They were scared beyond belief.

"How did you girls get away?" Skeits asked. The thought just hit him; someone had helped them escape, and that person would be in danger, too.

"There was this bum that came into the building looking for a place to get warm, I suppose. We thought maybe we were being kidnapped by another man, so Natasia gave him a what-for with a roundhouse kick." Katie grinned at Natasia. "My hero," she said with pride.

"Do you remember where you were kept?" Skeits asked. "Try to remember where it's located. It is very important. That bum is a detective assigned to help find and rescue you two." Skeits turned ashen as he spoke. He knew Jodie was in dire danger.

"Detective Skeits here, dispatch, send all the men you can muster to the riverfront. Send in S.W.A.T. One of ours is in essential danger. Jodie is somewhere in one of the old apartment buildings. A dangerous, belligerent man may have captured him. Stay alert." Skeits demanded.

"Finding anyone in the dark will be hard, but we must try. It's almost dark now, and it's going to get colder. We must find Jody quickly, or he will freeze to death." The detective stated.

"I saw a mural painting on the window in the back, some kind of saint, I think," Katie said. "I hope that helps."

"You bet it does, little lady. That is the old glass factory. Four buildings have murals on the windows. That means he must be in one of those. I have to let the others know so they won't spook the man and cause him to do something stupid. I hope he doesn't shoot Jodie." Skeets said, concerned. "I don't want to lose a good cop. He is one of our best."

"I am so sorry. We didn't know Jody was a policeman. He was dressed like a bum. I would never forgive myself if I am the cause of a policeman getting killed." Natasia wept.

Brett said, trying to calm the women, "I didn't know he was a detective either. I thought he was a bum too," he laughed, "until Lieutenant Markham arrived on the scene, causing us difficulty."

Bennie decided to lay low for the night. He figured the two brats had contacted the authorities by now. How stupid! I should have taken one of them with me. Who was that man, tied up in the room where they had been? I will find out who that guy is and who the heck I'm dealing with. He might not be just a bum. I think it's dangerous to return there, but if I hurry, I don't think the police have had time to get to the apartment yet.

Kicked the door open, Bennie hurried into the room where Jodie was tied. He removed the gag from Jodie's mouth and jerked the tape off. "Who are you?" He yelled at him. "You smell like a cop, am I right? Are you a stinking cop? Yeah, you're a rotten cop. Okay, here's what we're going to do. We are going for a little walk. I am going to the pier, and you will be my escort." Bennie laughed. "What is your name? I don't want to holler, hey you." Bennie said, shaking Jodie for attention.

"Da name is Billy, sir. I'm just a homeless feller. I stay here, on these docks, and pick up what the crew leaves behind whenever dey leave. My hands are cold. Them dar girls are mean. I jest come here ta get warm a spell, and dae grabbed me and tied me up en left. What's a going on here anyways?" *Oh boy,* Jodie thought. *I hope he buys my yarn. I have to convince him, or I'm a goner for sure.*

Bennie sized Jodie up. "I really don't believe what you told me, but come morning, I can find out. Say the crews know you? Well, we will see." Bennie tied Jodie's hands close to his sides in front of him so it would look as if his arm was broken, then dragged him down the stairs and out into the cold night.

They walked toward the piers and found a hobo jungle near the apartment. He knew he would be safe there. He had arrested too many of them before, so he knew how to think like one.

While they were walking toward the hobo camp, Bennie could see the police entering the buildings right behind them. *I just made it,* he thought.

When they got into the hobo camp, one of the homeless ladies recognized Jodie. He was her friend. Jodie shook his head at her. She kept her silence.

As they entered, Bennie told them that the man with him was paralyzed, and he had to keep him tied so his arms wouldn't dangle. They ignored him, except for Jodie's friend; she approached him and said, "You want me to tend to him tonight? I will be real good to him."

Bennie roughly shoved her aside and said harshly. "No, I don't want you to tend him. Now get away from me."

They had coffee brewing there in the camp. The old woman handed Bennie a tin cup, "I know it's surly cold tonight. Here, this cup of coffee might warm your bones a might." She was just being nice. She handed Jodie one, too.

Bennie took the cup. *I hate bums,* he thought, *but I am cold, and this could benefit me with the warmth. At least help keep me awake.* He and Jodie sipped their brew and enjoyed their cup with the help of the homeless lady. Suddenly, there was a thud. Jodie watched as Bennie tumbled over. The old lady quickly untied Jodie.

"You didn't kill him, did you, Erma? I will always be grateful to you, " Jodie said as he bent, kissing Erma's cheek.

"You saved my life. You are my hero, Erma."

"Nay, he ain't dead. But he'll have a mighty headache tomorrow." she giggled.

Jodie bound Benson Carver's hands and feet and, oh yes, gagged him. Jodie asked the men in the camp to keep him until the police arrived.

Jodie called the station with the news that Benson Carver was being detained in the hobo camp, "I would appreciate it when you pick him up; to be sure to thank Erma. She was the greatest. I would never have survived the ordeal had she not given him some of her potion. She's one good friend to the department."

Jodie also informed the chief that if there should be a reward, Erma was to receive it. She had captured him barehanded.

Brett was at the police station when they brought Bennie in. "Well, what do we have here?" He said. "You look like a pile of horse manure." Everyone in the station laughed and agreed.

Markham thought he heard Brett Canterfield. "Brett is that you!" he called from his cell. "I'm in here, man. Please, you got to get me out. They're going to lock Benson Carver in here with me. Brett, I need help!"

Brett grimaced at Little Dove Two. "I hate to, but he's one of our own." Brett shrugged his shoulders and went to the desk. "I know he's an aggravating cuss, but if you let me, I will take him off your hands."

The people there at the station agreed. "Let that idiot go back where he came from and never come to Chicago again!" The detective said.

Skeits and Jodie escorted Brett and Lieutenant Markham to the airport. Benson Carver was handcuffed to Markham. Lieutenant Markham protested against the kind of treatment he was receiving from Brett.

Brett would love to have a few minutes alone with Benson Carver. It was good that Lieutenant Markham kept him cuffed to him. If Brett had got hold of Bennie, he would have beaten him to death.

Just who does he think he is? He's not any lawman, yet he gives orders as if he's entirely in charge. I will get even with him yet! Markham thought.

As they boarded the plane for Spur Lacy, Brett turned to Little Dove Two and whispered, "I can't wait to get home. I am tired of chasing the woman I love all over the United States. Whoa, I haven't asked you yet. Are you married? And if you're not, may I ask for your hand in matrimony?"

"Brett, I'm not married, but I would like to wait a while before I answer that question." She held her breath, hoping he would understand. She had to have some space before she made any decisions. "I will answer you before long; just give me some time, okay?"

The flight was canceled for a day when they got to the Denver layover. It began to snow again, and the runway was icy.

The airlines leased rooms for Brett, the girls, and Lieutenant Markham, who also had to share a room with Benson Carver, although not to his liking.

"You keep him with you, Markham. I might kill him if he's with me." Brett seethed.

"Shut up, Brett, I will get even with you for this," Markham smirked.

"Now, Lieutenant, you know I kept you from staying there in jail. Have a little pity, won't you? Just a little?" Brett laughed heartedly.

Markham threw his empty cup at Brett and then laughed with him.

Katie called her father and told him that it was Bennie who had held her captive but that she was safe now, thanks to Brett Canterfield; then she explained to him a little about what had happened.

Her father said, "Catherine, a one hundred thousand dollar reward was offered for your safe return. I need to know where to send the money and whom to address the check."

"Well, Dad. I want to tell you, never in your wildest dream would you believe who caught Benson Carver. The one that captured him was a little old lady with the audacity of a lion at a hobo camp in Chicago. You can address it to Erma, under the care of Detective Jodie, at the Chicago North Side police department. He will see that she gets it. She is one special lady." Katie grinned.

When the plane landed at the Spur Lacy airport, Chief Perry Davis was there to greet Katie, Natasia, and Lieutenant Markham and take Benson Carver into custody.

"Chief, I must tell you, I don't know what I would have done had it not been for Lieutenant Markham. I want to thank you for sending him. He had a lot to do with finding that varmint, Carver." Brett grinned, looking at Markham as he shook the chief's hand.

Lieutenant Thomas Markham stood in silence, with his mouth gaped and very close to shock, as the words soaked in as to what Brett had just said to the chief. He couldn't believe Brett had just saved his job!

Markham turned to Brett and said, "I didn't do much. It was my job." he grinned and said thank you silently with his lips as he left for the station with Benson Carver in tow.

Then there was Dominguez Talley. "Daddy," Katie screamed as she ran to her father, wrapping her arms around her only parent. Their tears mingled as he held his daughter tightly.

"Catherine Margaret, I could not have lived if that monster had killed you. I want to get my hands on him just one time. I have never been so scared in my whole life. If your mother were still living, she would claw his eyes out. There wouldn't be a jail that could have kept him from her. She would have put up his bail bond money and had him released so that she could slit his throat." Dominguez Talley said while hugging his child.

"Father, there is something I must know. Bennie was my bodyguard when I was young, and I really loved him, just like an uncle. He kidnapped me to hurt you, and he knew the pictures he sent would destroy you because there was nothing you could do about it. Father, what did you do to Benson Carver to cause him to hurt me so badly to get even with you? He also said before he died that he would kill you, me, and then himself. Please tell me!" Katie pled.

Dominguez was tearful as he looked upon the beautiful face of his daughter. "I will tell you someday, but not now. Something horrific happened years ago. When the time is right, I will explain everything to you. Are you telling me he didn't tell you anything?" Dominguez said.

"No, Father, he didn't," Katie replied.

"He likes to hurt the innocent; that's his character. I will tell you about our family and the Carvers one day, but right now, I'm not prepared." Dominguez turned his face away from his daughter so she couldn't see his tears.

Several people from the town were there to meet Brett and the others; they were happy the ordeal was over. Little Adsila was there with her grandfather, Adahy. When Brett got off the plane, she ran to him with her arms opened wide. He scooped the child in his arms and said. "I sure missed you, little one. Do you still have the wolf pup?"

"I sure do, and tomorrow, I will bring him back to the barn." She whispered. Her grandfather winked as he said. "Yes, before her mama paddles her for not leaving it in the woods." The older man grinned.

"Oh, and since we made it through that ordeal, Brett, my name is Catherine Margaret Talley, but please, call me Katie! All my friends do," Katie grinned.

Invitation to the Talley Ranch

Dominguez Talley, Brett, Katie, and Maria congregated at Bretts' home on the Mountain. It had been a long and tiresome trip for all involved.

The sight of Brett's beautiful mountain home was impressive. *This man is wealthy,* Dominguez thought. *I must investigate this man before Catherine gets too involved. He might not be the night in shining armor she thinks he is.*

"Brett, you have a beautiful home. I would love to see your ranch tomorrow if you have time. I'm interested in how you run things here, and you're invited to visit my ranch in Texas. It is quite different than this one," Dominguez said.

"I would like that very much, thank you for the invitation. When things get back to normal, I will take a few weeks off to get my nerves untangled and maybe get in a little fishing. I haven't done that for some time." Brett answered.

Later that evening, Brett asked Katie, "Can you tell me what happened to you on Lovers Lane? Who tried to bury you alive, and how the women were murdered? Do you know how the BMW got involved? I should wait until tomorrow, but I'm so curious; I know it was horrible for you, but everyone will eventually have to know." Brett said solemnly.

Katie nodded. She tried without success to block it all out after her memory returned, but it was constantly on her mind, always vivid. It was most horrifying. If Katie revealed what Margo kept repeating, it would destroy Brett; he would never want a relationship with anyone again. Especially not her if she told. Katie began to shiver.

"It's alright, Katie. Try to get some rest. We will talk tomorrow," Brett said, kissing the top of her head. "Goodnight, little one."

"Now, if I may," Brett grinned. "I will have one of our maids show Mr. Talley to his room. There are plenty of rooms here. His bodyguard will sleep in a different room. This house is very secure.

Everyone, have a pleasant night; that is after we have a midnight snack."

They all headed for the kitchen to nibble on the left-over fried chicken that Maria pulled from the frig. The cooks had even made a mincemeat pie. The pot roast was still warm in the crock-pot, with all the trimmings. "I can't believe there's so much food left after so many people have eaten." Mr. Talley stated.

"We never know who might be hungry and drop by unexpectedly. We always ensure plenty to eat, just in case." Brett answered.

When Katie was finally alone in her big bed, she thought about how being kidnapped could change her life forever. *I will never feel the same, and I will never completely trust another man. Benson Carver fixed that for me,* she thought.

Early On The Mountain

Adsila ran to the tack room, looking for Brett. She brought the wolf Pup as agreed. "He isn't here, little one, but he will be soon. Come down to the bunkhouse. The wranglers would love to meet you. I have bacon and eggs cooked. We can eat while we wait for him. The men have heard a lot about you. You are one special little lady to Brett. Hey guys, listen up. We have a lady present, so beware of your jokes. Adsila is Brett's new friend, so make her welcome," Carl said.

The main house was quiet; the cooks made breakfast while Maria and Little Dove sipped coffee. Katie was also in a silent mood, but a cup of witches' brew was all she needed to start the day. Her eyes were so swollen from crying that night they would hardly open. *I don't ever want to relive that again,* she thought. Tears stung her eyes again for the hundredth time.

Little Dove wrapped her arms around Katie and held her steadfastly. She didn't speak for some time; she just let Katie cry it out. Then she wiped the girl's eyes with her kerchief, looked the lady in the eye, and said. "Listen to me, young woman. You are powerful. You went through an ordeal that most women wouldn't have survived. Women are stronger than they think when put to the test, and this was most challenging, but you are strong. Now dry your eyes and stay focused. Carry on with the things you know you must do."

Katie knew Little Dove was right. She had to tell what she saw, no matter who got hurt. The truth must be voiced.

"Little Dove, Maria, I must tell you, Margo did something awful and said some terrible things. She was there on Lover's Lane that afternoon when the two ladies were killed. I don't see how I can tell what happened without telling everyone about the bad things she said and did. That would hurt you both and might destroy Brett. She was not nice! How can I destroy what little you have left of her?" Katie sobbed.

Maria and Little Dove wrapped their arms around her and pulled her close between them.

"Katie, we love you, and this is hard for a mother to digest, though I must. We all knew Margo. We knew what she was capable of. We couldn't cure her sick mind, and neither could a doctor. We accepted her for the way she was. Everyone knew she turned bad long before that day." Maria sobbed.

"You don't understand. Margo said some things that will hurt you for the rest of your lives. It will be hard for me to reveal what happened there that day! If there is a way I can tell the facts without destroying the ones I love, well, then I will do that. If I can't, then I may be unable to remember what happened." Katie cried.

Maria and Little Dove lowered their heads. Maria said, "Katie, you must tell what happened there, no matter who gets hurt. That's the law. The truth may hurt us, but we will survive."

Katie looked at what they believed in. Truth, no matter what happens, always tell the truth!

"I will think about this tomorrow," Katie answered.

"Mr. Talley, I would be pleased if you rode with me today. I need to ride fences and select where I want the cattle to graze this coming spring, as well as the growth of the winter rye. We often exchange grazing places with herds to preserve the grass. It would also be an opportunity for you to check out my ranch."

"That sounds good, Brett. I will get my coat and meet you at the tack room. Oh, by the way, call me Dom," He grinned.

"Alright, Dom, it is," Brett answered.

Dom said, "Tell me, Brett, are many wild animals here that kill your livestock?"

"We have a few Mountain lions, but they usually stay in the mountainous area away from the herds. I have one now and then to come down. I have it moved or sent to a zoo somewhere. I don't like to see any animal killed without it being used for food." Brett stated.

"I've lost a few to predators, but wild animals haven't given me much trouble. I let them roam at will if they don't mingle with the herd. I, too, hate to destroy an animal without cause," Dom said.

Brett looked at Dom and grinned. He appreciated a man who had respect for animals. "Dom, let me say, I always keep a dart gun handy just in case it becomes necessary to put one down. I raised a bear cub once, but he finally got so ornery I had to put him down. The village people used meat and pelt. Making use of it makes me feel a little better." Brett answered.

"Brett, why don't you come with us to Houston for a few weeks? I'm sure you could use some relaxation. We have plenty of room, and I could show you how we run our ranch." Dom suggested.

Brett replied. "I will take a rain check on that if I may. I've been away for some time and must get my ranch hands back on their schedule. I think your daughter needs her rest away from all of us for the time being. We will miss her, though. We have become quite accustomed to having her around. We all think a lot of that little lady."

"I understand. It's hard sometimes to leave a job you know must be attended. We'll make it another time, then?"

"Most definitely, I want to see your ranch. I will make plans to visit soon." Brett said.

When they returned to the house, Katie sat outside on the steps.

"Catherine, I must return home today and want you to accompany me. You can return here for the pre-trial, but I think you need the rest and comfort of home for now. I will make all the arrangements. My flight leaves today at three." Dom tried to grin, but the words came out demanding.

"I will take you up on that offer, Father." Katie said, "I do need to rest for a while and take time to think. I will be a nervous wreck when the pre-trial and trial starts."

Brett could see that Katie was stressed, but he didn't want her to leave. He thought they might share their lives, given time, and thought he might be in love with her. *The offer Dom made for me to visit his ranch in Texas sounds excellent. I will make plans to see him sooner than expected,* he thought, grinning.

"That is strictly up to you, Katie. You may go or stay here if you please. We have plenty of room, and the pre-trial will be quite swift. This community doesn't like crime, and everyone will want it finished as soon as possible so they don't have to worry about Benson Carver being around somewhere, waiting to harm another family. They are more than ready to put him behind bars where he belongs for a very long time. Benson Carver put a strain on the people of Spur Lacy." Brett looked at Katie with pleading eyes.

Katie looked into Brett's green eyes and almost agreed that she would stay by his side forever, but she heard herself say. "I must leave with my father, Brett. I must have time to gather my extremely scattered thoughts. I have been through a lot in the last five months. Benson Carver kidnapped me in August last year." Katie lowered her eyes, hoping Brett didn't see the tears building again.

"I will gather my things, Father; go ahead with the arrangements," Katie said, leaving the room.

Katie went to the room that had been hers the entire time she had been on Brett's Mountain.

She was crying so hard she could hardly see. She loved this Mountain and all the people she had met here. This house feels so much like home if only things could have been different.

She couldn't help but let her mind wander. What would have happened to her had Brett not found her that cold winter day? She, indeed, would have died. Now, she may obliterate his belief in women because she must tell all the bad things about Margo.

Katie walked to the big window. She could see the tack room from where she stood. She strained her eyes to bring into sight a small figure.

She recognized the little form holding Brett's big hand. It was Adsila. They looked like father and daughter. Katie couldn't help but picture Brett with their child! She shook her head. Silly woman, don't even think about something like that. That would never happen, not after her say in court.

Dominguez Talley and Katie caught the afternoon flight home. It was a comfortable flight, nice and smooth.

When they landed in Houston, Katie could see the familiar scenes she had left when she decided on a vacation, one so bad that she would never forget!

"The next time I want to go on vacation, you will be my escort, Dad," she grinned at her father. "You can bring your bodyguard so he can protect us both. The kidnapping was a horrible occurrence for me. I can't imagine Bennie doing such a thing. I thought he liked working for you."

"Bennie, well, he did like his job," Dom stated, changing the subject.

"I would still like to visit my mother's people as soon as the arrangements can be made. I will enjoy them much more now since I met Little Dove. She taught me a lot about my Indian side. I wish Mother had lived long enough for me to have met all her people."

Her father nodded.

"I understand, Catherine. Your mother has been gone a long time; you were only seven years old when she was thrown from her horse. I tried to tell her he was still too wild to ride, but she was like you, very hardheaded," he laughed. "I will go to the village with you before long. I haven't seen your grumpy old grandfather in many a moon. I liked him very much; that is one older man who will tell you like it is, whether you like it or not, and make you understand that he was right all along, and you are correct, we will take Horatio with us for protection. Now, I must get to the office for a little while. When I return, I want you to tell me exactly what happened to you and what that lousy man did. I could wring his neck with my bare hands." Dominguez hissed.

Katie enjoyed being home again with her father and all the familiar surroundings.

The days were going by so fast. Katie thought about Brett and missed him terribly. Her father couldn't fill that gap in her heart. Brett was the man of her dreams, her shining knight and armor. She couldn't keep him from her thoughts.

Katie picked up her cell and dialed Brett's number. "Brett here, what's up beautiful?" Brett asked, expecting something to be wrong again.

"Oh, I just called to say hello and see if you might possibly take my father up on the rain check he gave you to visit our ranch here. If you could come, I would love to show you our way of life too. I think you would be fascinated by what you see. I miss you," Katie crossed her fingers.

"Well, I suppose I could take off for a few days. Carl can take care of the grass sowing of the fields. He knows as much as I do about this ranch," he laughed. "Yes, I would like to visit your ranch very much. I will try to get a booking on the plane tomorrow. Tell your father I'm coming, so he will expect me, okay?"

When the plane landed at the Houston/Fort Worth airport, Katie waited beside the boarding area. She knew he would walk through there. She held an arrangement of yellow and red roses in her hand.

"Welcome, Mr. Canterfield!" When she handed him the flowers, she laughed. "They're not from my basement garden, but will do."

When Brett reached Katie, he hugged her lovingly and said, "I don't need flowers. I just need you, my lady."

He can always make me blush, she thought. *I wonder if I will do this forever when he gets near me. I can feel my freckles showing again.*

The limo pulled up in front of the mansion where Katie and her father resided. Brett could see the stables and the horses running in the fields. He was amazed at the size of their incredible home. He counted at least eighteen gables.

Katie was the first to depart from the limo. She turned and curtsied to Brett, saying, "Welcome to my humble home, sir."

"I had no idea the size of the estate where you lived," Brett whistled and continued to say, "I knew you were wealthy, but I didn't realize to what extent."

Katie giggled as she turned to Brett and said. "Well, it doesn't feel that huge to me. I guess it's just that growing up, I was taught that I'm no better than anyone else. It has never occurred to me that we were rich, just fortunate."

"It's my turn to be the host for a while. Now, sir, may I have one of the maids take your baggage to the room where you will be staying?" Katie laughed.

Brett was so amazed at what he was looking at that he just nodded. He was just too preoccupied with the incredible scenery. "Katie, this is magnificent. You could never have explained to me the way it looks." He exclaimed.

The maid took the baggage and went up the winding stairs as Katie slipped her small hand in Bretts and said, "Come on, I want to show you the stables."

Katie headed for the white picket fence that surrounded the yard. The gate led to the stables. Once inside the humongous barn, Katie walked Brett through the many stalls. The stable men looked up from their busy jobs long enough to say hello. A few men were shoeing horses, and another man was cleaning stalls. According to Brett's calculation, at least fourteen men, maybe even more, worked there.

"How many horses do you own, Katie?" Brett asked.

"Well, we own and train eighteen thoroughbreds. Then there are twelve Clydesdales, and they are for show-horses. I have no idea how many range horses there are; the last count was fifty Mustangs. We break them for saddle horses.

"How about cattle? Does your father raise them as well?"

"I will show you," Katie giggled.

"Rocco, would you please saddle my paint and the black? We want to ride for a while. When my father calls, tell him I have taken Brett around the ranch. We will be back in time for dinner."

Brett was mystified. The ranch was magnificent and well-groomed. There were more quality trees here than at his acreage. His ranch was beautiful, but this was completely different. *I knew Dominguez had money, but he might be wealthier than I,* he thought.

Rifles in scabbards were adhered on both horses. Katie watched Brett as he placed his hand on the gun. "It's just for protection," she grinned.

They rode from one valley to another. Brett noticed Katie was fidgety. She watched both sides as though she expected something to jump at her.

"What is wrong, Katie? Are you afraid of something? What are you afraid of?" Brett questioned.

"I'm not really afraid, just cautious. I heard one of the stable men tell about a wildcat coming down from the high country. Everyone is being careful not to be caught off guard. Mountain lions are quite dangerous. They only come down here when they are hungry or injured. That makes them dangerous."

They rode along the Brazos River, where the herd grazed. They dismounted and sat under a tree. The grass felt like carpet. The Texas Hardy Oak tree grew branches that spread far to shade the cattle from the summer heat.

"This place is so beautiful, Katie. If I lived here, I would never want to leave. Do you think you could be satisfied to live in another place?" Brett asked.

"Well, Brett, I have lived here all my life. I was on vacation visiting my mother's side of the family when I was kidnapped.

They are Seminole, but I have my father's white features too, don't you think?"

"Your skin has Indian tones. Your hair shines like an Indian maiden. You have the heart of a warrior when you feel threatened, but yes, I see some of Dominguez's features, too, such as kindness and thoughtfulness. Still, I see a woman, no matter her features, being the love of my life." Brett took Katie in his arms and gave her a long, meaningful kiss.

Shaking, Katie pulled away. "Brett, we need to head back. Dinner will be served with or without us," she said. She must distance herself from Brett Canterfield and do it quickly.

While riding back, Brett thought about their kiss. I could stand those kisses for a lifetime. I know I must wait to ask her to be my bride, and whatever she decides, I won't give up the fight for her, not ever!

"Brett, did you hear me? Brett!"

"I'm sorry, Katie," He grinned, looking a little shy. "I was deep in thought. What did you say?"

"My father should be home when we get there. He will want to speak with you about ranching. I'm sure he will fill you in about our ranch. He loves to brag. This ranch is his hobby." She laughed.

"Yes, we did speak of this ranch while he was there, but he didn't tell me the greatness or the magnitude of this incredible place. We must hurry back, I don't want to cross your father. I will speak with him at length about the beef cattle. He might want to know what I have been doing out here with his only daughter," Brett laughed.

After that remark, Katie kicked her horses' flanks and headed up the hill toward the riding stable. Brett was right on her heels. She needed to escape the proximity of her companion; she could hardly breathe from his last kiss, and she could feel her face redden again.

They dismounted and walked the two horses inside the stable. Brett picked up the water hose and washed the sweat from the horses while Katie rubbed them down. They worked together very well. Each one knew just what the other was going to do next.

It had been a beautiful day for horseback riding, and they had made a day of it.

"Tomorrow, I must return Spur Lacy. I wish you would accompany me. It's so lonely without you there.

Katie lowered her head; she wanted to look Brett in the eye and say yes. I will be there soon because Bennie's pre-trial will start, but instead, she heard herself say, "I need the security here at my father's home now."

"I understand. I will be there when you decide to come, maybe for a visit or some other reason." Brett said flatly, then turned so she wouldn't see his hurt. "I will wash up now, before dinner."

"Okay, Brett," Katie grinned. She realized that it made Bretts' heart flutter when she was this close.

It was later than anticipated when Dominguez Talley arrived home from his office. He wanted to chat with Brett before he left for Spur Lacy the next day. *Maybe I can still have a small conversation with him.* He thought as he drove into the curved driveway.

Dom parked his car near the wisteria, which climbed beautifully across the Trestle. Herman, his gardener, wiped it down and drove it into the garage for the night. The expression on Dom's face suggested he wouldn't be going out anymore tonight.

"Hello Catherine, how was your ride this afternoon?" Dom asked as he planted a kiss on Katie's forehead."

"It was great, Dad. We rode over most of the ranch. I took Brett down to the Brazos River. I believe he was impressed by the size and condition of the ranch." Katie grinned.

Just as Brett entered the foyer, Dominguez handed his jacket to Anetta, his maid. "Well, hello, Brett. What do you think of my ranch? Catherine said she took you over much of it. That is lots of riding."

"It was most impressive. It is quite different from my own, but a precisely well-managed ranch. The stable men were also quite inspiring. I watched how they cared for the stalls and shod the horses. They know quite well how to run a ranch. They are like the workers at my ranch. My hands take over anytime I'm away, as it should be." Brett answered.

They discussed the price of beef, Brett's real estate business, Dom's oil fields, and the private affairs they had that no one else knew of. They both had investments in the railways. It came as a shock that they had the same interest in their investment. They laughed heartedly.

Katie retired to the family room while Brett and her father talked. When she heard them laughing loudly, she was curious to learn what they had in common. "I want in on the joke," she grinned at her father as she entered the room. Katie knew she was never supposed to ask him anything on a personal scale. She expected to be told to return to her television program, but instead, Dom motioned her to come in and sit beside him.

"We have been talking, and you won't believe it, we have ventured into the same investments through the years. I am older than Brett, so I have been doing this for some time more than he, yet we both have done quite well." Dom grinned.

"Well, you both are intelligent men, so investing in the same commodities is fortunate," Katie laughed.

"Brett, will you come again when you have longer to stay? You haven't even begun to see many things around here." Dom asked. "I would like you to come back during the Mustang breaking season. It is pretty interesting; we will have a pig roasting on the spit that day, and then lunch will be served under that big tree in the backyard. All the ranchers come here and join us to dance and eat. It is a spectacular get-to-gather. The pool in the backyard will be filled with kids and grown-ups, as well.

We have a blast, and I would love it if you could bring Adsila if her mother approves." Katie grinned.

"That is very tempting and exciting, Katie. I will take you up on that. I will ask Adsila's mother, but she is very protective of the child. I don't know if she will allow it, but I will try. I didn't know you liked her that much. Call me about a week before the festival starts so I can make arrangements. The trip this time was too short to see all I would like to see of your ranch." Brett said, looking at Dom.

"I like the child very much." Katie reflected.

"Yes, Brett, you must come again," Dom stated. "The next time, I will make time to be home instead of being tied up at my office, even though I know you enjoyed the company of my daughter."

Dom looked at his Catherine, and she blushed again!

"Father!" Embarrassed, Katie turned her face away to keep from laughing out loud.

The following day, Brett was to catch his flight home. Katie went to the airport to see him off. "I hope you enjoyed your visit, Brett," she grinned at him with shining brown eyes.

"I have enjoyed it immensely," Brett replied. "Your father and I have a lot in common. We are both hard workers, love ranching, and love a cute little brown-eyed girl." He took his finger and flicked the end of her nose as he was about to board his plane. He bent down and kissed the top of her head. He couldn't afford to kiss her on the lips, or he would have asked to stay longer.

Katie had her chauffeur take her to her dad's office before she went home from the airport. When she arrived, she went straight to her father's desk. "Well, father, what did you think of Brett Canterfield?" She grinned, sitting on the edge of his desk.

"Well, now, my dear, I like the man, but it's more than me liking the man. What do you think about him? I think that should be the question. But that is only one man's opinion, of another. I think what needs to be asked is for you to tell me what he means to you.

Then I will say to you, use your best judgment," he grinned at his daughter.

"I really like him, Dad, but I want to wait until after--until after the trial before I say much. Dad, that will humiliate him when I tell him in court about Margo, and there is no way around it," she stated.

"But, Catherine, that may be for the best. From what I understand, he has been through a lot. He might need some space for a while until everything calms down." Dom answered.

She checked the mailbox on her way to the house.

The letter came. The one Katie dreaded so much to see. The hearing was to commence on the first Monday in June. The letter stated that she must return to Spur Lacy no later than the end of May.

Katie Returns To Spur Lacy

Katie kept in contact with Brett; he had visited Houston only once after she returned home. He was sad when he left for his Mountain, leaving her behind. He asked her to return with him, and although she had refused, now she must return because of the pending pre-trial to commence; this day will be dreadful for her.

It made her sad when she thought about herself and Brett's relationship and how it would soon be all over when she testified about what had happened on Lovers' Lane. Katie still couldn't bring herself to tell him about Margo, but now she had no choice. Time was running out. She wondered if maybe telling Brett first would be the best route.

The flight back to Spur Lacy was enjoyable. The sky was clear, no wind. Had it been under different circumstances, Katie would have loved the scenery. The trees were simply spectacular this time of year. The tops of the mountains were still snow-covered. The lakes are ready for fishermen to enjoy. The town of Spur Lacy sat in a valley surrounded by beauty. Yes, she loved it all! She also knew this would be her last time visiting this gorgeous place.

Brett met her at the airport; their hands touched as he reached for her luggage. He grabbed her, pulled her into his arms, and planted a well-planned kiss on her luscious mouth. "I must tell you, Katie, I love you very much. I want to ask you something."

Before he could finish, she pulled away and said, "Hold on, Brett. There may be obstacles that we cannot cross. We must wait until after the hearing. I have thought about what I would say should this happen. Well, this is what I have been considering. When the trial is over, and you have taken time to adapt to what I must reveal, we shall see where we go from there. Will you please trust me on this? It is very important." Katie couldn't look into the eyes of the man she wanted to spend her life with. She was afraid she couldn't be truthful in court; should she see the love he felt right now die right before her eyes, that would be most devastating.

Brett released her and backed away. "Don't make me beg, and don't make me wait too long for your answer. You are the one I want, but I can't wait forever. I'm not that young; after all, I am a man in love. Oh, and while I think of it, I have some things to tell you. Maria and Lattermar are getting married in September. They are going to Jamaica. That old geezer is loaded. They said they don't know how long they will be gone, probably a year. I suppose the women I hired from Spur Lacy will have to take over the kitchen work, such as the cooking and cleaning. Little Dove isn't able to do all that work. They are living at my house now, and it is permanent." Brett Grinned as though making small talk.

"Is Little Dove going to stay with you from now on? I know once upon a time, she wouldn't hear of it. She wanted to live on the reservation with her Indian relatives the rest of her life." Katie asked.

"I finally convinced her I needed her with me more than she's needed at the village. When you left, the only thing I could get her to talk about was you. She would grin and say, 'She will be back.' She loves you, Catherine Margaret Talley, and awaits your return." Brett said.

"I really like her too, Brett; I hope you didn't encourage her to think I might stay. I haven't decided on anything." Katie was dismayed at the suggestion that Little Dove had such hopes for her return.

Brett raised his eyebrows, looked Katie in the eye, and said, "Now, would I do that? Just because I want it to be so." He snickered.

Katie just grinned. She didn't answer, but she knew he would.

"I am glad the maids are living with you now. Your mother really needs help. I remember when Maria wouldn't hear of them doing all the cooking and cleaning as long as she could maneuver around the stove." Katie giggled.

"My, it's good to hear you laugh," he whispered in her ear. "I just want to get you alone and love you until you are senseless."

Katie blushed a rosy red and pushed away the charming Brett with her finger. "Behave yourself!" She exclaimed.

Brett thought Katie would go to the mountain with him, but she had other ideas. "Brett, take me to the hotel, please. I want to freshen up and rest before I go to the courthouse. I didn't sleep much last night and must be fresh when speaking to the prosecutor. I don't want to say anything out of context." She explained.

"I didn't ask you, but I just took for granted that you would come to the ranch with me. There is plenty of room, and you could rest there." Brett said with a shocked look on his face.

"Well, I know I'm welcome, but I don't want the town to think I'm some kind of loose woman trying to get your money," she giggled.

"Actually, I just need time alone and be closer to town," She said.

He dropped her off at the hotel. When he put her suitcases in the room, he turned to her and asked, "Will you dine with me tonight?" He was so persistent.

She faced him and said, "Brett, you must go now. I'm sorry, but I need to be alone."

Knowing she had crushed Bretts' ideal, but it was also for his best. Wait until I have to tell about Margo in court; He will hate me for destroying the memories he had of the woman he had loved for so long.

The following day, Katie went down to the prosecuting attorney's office; she knew she must talk with him before the pre-trial came about.

He grinned and asked her to come into his office. "Have a seat, my dear. Whatever you say here will be confidential. We must know what we are dealing with before we go into the courtroom with Benson Carver. I don't want something coming up that we're not expecting. I want the pre-trial to go smoothly and be finished as quickly as possible.

Most of the people in this town knew those two women on Lovers' Lane that Benson Carver killed that day." He said.

Katie shook her head. "No, that is not correct, Sir. He was not the one who murdered those women. As far as I know, Benson Carver never killed anyone. He is rotten; he is mean to the core. Bennie would rather hurt people for breakfast than have a steak for supper. Plus, he did kidnap Natasia and myself, but he's no killer. It wasn't he who killed those women that day. I can't stand the man, but I must tell the truth, no matter whom it concerns or hurts. I was knocked senseless that day by Bennie, but that was after the women were killed."

Katie mystified the prosecutor; he thought she had lost her senses. "Well then, who should be in jail, may I ask?" He became uncertain as the minutes went by. "I think you better start from the beginning, and lady, be careful you don't wind up in jail yourself."

"Oh, I'm not going to hide anything, and I know the truth will hurt people. I also understand the caution you spoke of about me going to jail. I must, at this time, request a lawyer before I say something that might incriminate myself because I believe you are trying to trick me; this doesn't sound the way it should. I don't think I can tell you the truth and be done with it; you have too much disbelief about the truth." Katie said, trembling.

"So you're saying you won't tell me what happened out there without a lawyer? Am I to believe that you are not somehow involved? It sounds like you are holding up for this Benson Carver character. Is that what you're doing, young woman?" His voice was getting nastier and nastier. She was at a loss for words, but she was her mother's daughter when push came to shove!

Katie stood enhanced, with her hands on her hips and eyebrows drawn together. She looked eye to eye with the prosecutor, and tilting her head in defiance, she turned away from him and said. "That's exactly what I am saying to you. I want a lawyer right now! I have nothing more to say. I will speak with you when my lawyer says it is appropriate. Good day, sir." With that said Katie retreated through the door.

The prosecutor was at a loss for words; with his mouth ajar, he nodded as she departed. He didn't expect her to be so sovereign.

Katie called Brett when she left the prosecutor's office. She was shaking from head to toe. *What have I gotten into,* she thought, as she phoned Brett's number.

"Brett, I need a good lawyer! Who do you recommend? You know most people here; asking about a good one might be wise." Katie asked.

"What's wrong? Are you in some trouble? I will be right there. I am at the hardware store as we speak." Brett reflected.

"No, I'm not in trouble, at least not yet. But if I don't get a creditable lawyer, I just might be." Katie answered with a quiver in her voice. She was at the point of hysteria. She thought about calling her father and asking him to fly up with the company lawyer, but she didn't want her father to know just how close she had come to death and now jail!

Brett passed Katie as she walked toward the hotel. He stopped and asked, "Would you like a lift, pretty lady?" Katie climbed into the Cadillac.

They sped away. Brett drove away from Spur Lacy a mile or so. He stopped and pulled off the road. "Now, my lady, let me hear it." He demanded.

"Brett, I can't go into that courtroom without a lawyer. The prosecutor may try to influence the court that I had something to do with the murders, but Brett, I am innocent of all crimes. I have to be careful, though. I don't want to say something that might incriminate myself. That's why I need professional advice." She answered, shaking and almost in tears.

"I will not ask you again about what happened that day, but I will recommend an outstanding lawyer."

"His name is Boris Wathen. He is a big-city criminal lawyer. I have had him several times, and he did a fantastic job for me. I will call him now, and I'm sure he will be here in the morning if that will be soon enough?" Brett said.

Katie felt a little calmer since Brett was there. She still had to keep him at arm's length, or he would forget that she had asked him to keep it on the back burner. He was already far too attached to her, and she knew one wrong word, and she would be fighting for her sanity. Katie laughed at her thoughts.

Katie had always held men at bay when it came to relationships. She blew out a breath to relax. Brett saw and asked with a grin, "Now what?"

She just shook her head. She definitely couldn't tell him what she was thinking. She just grinned and answered. "Right now, I was just thinking, I'm glad you are here. Tomorrow will be plenty of time for a lawyer. Brett, have you seen Markham around? I heard he had been reprimanded. I haven't seen him." Katie asked.

"Well, the last time I heard, he took his wife on a cruise. Why do you ask?" Brett was curious.

"I didn't know if he would be at the hearing. I wouldn't want him to miss it." She smirked at the name of Markham.

"Am I missing something here? Or did I hear a little sarcasm when you spoke the name Markham?"

"No, you didn't miss anything. I can't stand that man. I will explain it to you someday. Just be patient, okay?"

"Chief Davis, put Markham back on payroll so he could keep his pension. Markham has wanted to retire for a long time and has already applied for it. I hope he enjoys it and stays away on vacation permanently," Brett answered. He and Katie both laughed.

Brett didn't tell Katie that he had helped Markham to keep his job. He wasn't fond of the man, but he had worked hard in the force and deserved his retirement. He had given Brett a hard time before, but Brett always came out on top.

Brett drove Katie back into town. He did keep his distance, although he would have liked to grab her and give her a real long kiss. When they got back to town, Brett stopped at the steak house. He parked, opened the door for Katie, and said, "Lady, you have to eat, and I'm buying tonight." He held her hand as she stepped from the car. Linking her arm through his, they entered together.

He seemed to stare right through her during the meal. The steak was delicious, as he had said it would be. Katie thought, now he wants conversation, but I can't reveal what I'm thinking. I wish we were back at my father's ranch eating our Black Angus beef. It is much tastier than the one we have been served, but I would never say this to Brett. He has always been so kind.

"Why the stare Brett? Do I have something on my face? Or does my face look funny?" Katie snickered, making an ugly face at him.

"No, there's nothing wrong," Brett answered, "just a little embarrassed that you caught me staring at you again."

When Katie returned to her hotel room, there was a note to call her father. She picked up the phone and dialed his number. "Hello, Father, what's up?" Katie asked.

"Catherine, I have an eeriest feeling about you being there. I am worried. I have Horatio en route. He should be there by ten tonight. He is not to leave your sight. Get him a room adjoining yours, wherever you stay. I won't take a chance again with your safety." Her father said bluntly.

"Dad, don't worry. I will be okay here in Spur Lacy. Brett wouldn't let anything happen to me, I'm sure." She answered with confidence.

"Catherine Margaret, I won't hear any more about it; this is final." He stressed.

She had crossed her father a few times, but now, she pays attention when he calls her by both names. He was about to become enraged, and she didn't want him to be too upset, or he would be here himself, and she didn't want him at the hearing.

She loved her father dearly, and the things she had endured during her captivity would hurt him tremendously; no, she positively didn't want him here.

"I understand, Father. I will have a room ready when he lands tonight." She grinned. "I will feel safer with him around, just in case I need protection, and who knows, I might get in over my head."

When Horatio arrived at the hotel, Katie had prepared the room adjoining hers.

The Lawyer Arrives

Early the next morning, a knock awakened Katie; a note was slid under the door by a messenger boy; the note revealed that Boris Wathen had arrived and wished to meet with her in the hotel's dining room as soon as possible.

She knocked on the adjoining door. "Horatio, the lawyer is here. I will be in the lobby or dining area of the hotel."

Katie called Brett to say Mr. Wathen had arrived; he wanted to be present when she conferred with him.

"Hold on there, Miss Talley. I will walk you there. Don't open the door until I am with you, your father's orders." The bodyguard explained.

Katie impatiently paced the floor, waiting for Horatio to arrive. She was always in a hurry, not knowing why she had done this. A habit she wished she could break. Very annoying!

When Katie introduced herself to the lawyer, he asked that he speak with her in private. Then, if she wanted other people in the room, it would be okay.

Brett and Horatio went to the café next door for coffee. Katie explained what had happened in the prosecutor's office. Mr. Wathen advised her that she had done the right thing by leaving.

Katie told the lawyer everything that happened on Lovers' Lane. He was so overwhelmed by the incident that he just sat there for a while before advising her.

"Miss Talley, you have to tell all this in court. When is the court date to begin?" he had to get prepared. This little lady will need emotional support with the testimony she must tell the court to help her with the horrific things she endured. He shook his head. He thought, *how has she held up this long?*

Katie told him that the preliminary hearing would begin the next day. Mr. Wathen looked at her and said. "We need to see the prosecuting attorney today. Albert Jones must be served with papers before this can go any further."

Her body trembled so hard that she could hardly hold the cup of coffee. "Can't we just do it without Mr. Jones being present? That man scares me to the inners of my soul," Katie asked.

"No, it isn't handled like that; I'm sorry," The lawyer said.

"I wish Lieutenant Markham were here; it gives me comfort just knowing he is nearby. I don't really care for the man, but he is a good lieutenant. He was wrong going to Maria and Little Dove the way he did, but he was trying to see if Margo had anything to do with the murders. He just wanted to clear her name." Katie spoke softly.

"I heard talk in town that Markham had been seeing Margo the same time as Brett Canterfield. I think he was still in love with her." Mr. Wathen stated.

"Yes, so I have heard." Katie reflected.

"He is away right now. Brett said he's taken his wife on a vacation." Katie said, wishing that Markham had waited until another time to leave, but she understood why he needed to break the tension. *It had been hard on him. First, Margo died, and then when he tried to be a good cop, he couldn't stop Bennie in Chicago on a kidnapping charge. It was most upsetting for him, but he did his best.* She thought.

"We will present this to the prosecuting attorney and see what he wants to do first. I will pick you up in the morning, just before nine." Mr. Wathen stated.

"Okay, but make room for Horatio. He will surely be with me," she giggled. The lawyer gave her a half grin as to say I understand.

Brett walked Katie back to her hotel room, with Horatio following right on their heels. Brett wondered why Wathen gave him such a sad look, but sometimes a lawyer has his mind somewhere else, so he shrugged it off as unimportant.

The next day, as Wathen had said, he was there to pick up Katie for the court hearing at eight forty-five. "We must arrive early to speak with the judge in his chambers before court begins. I don't know what he will want to do with what you have told me about this case." He said.

When they entered the room, Mr. Wathen went to the podium and spoke to the judge. The judge had a surprised look on his face. He said very bluntly. "I will see both lawyers in my chambers before we proceed."

Brett sat in the courtroom to hear what was said. He looked at Katie and whispered. "I wonder what is up with that?"

Katie didn't answer. She sat still and faced the front. She just couldn't look at him. He was so innocent but was about to get the worst jolt of his life.

When the judge returned to the room, he said. "We shall continue. Miss Catherine Margaret Talley, please come forward."

Katie rose, walked to the front without looking at Brett, and sat straight in the chair beside the judge. She looked grimly at Benson Carver. She wanted to hurt him the way he had hurt her and Natasia. He had been so cruel to both. But then she knew she could never be revengeful. Her upbringing had been to forgive and not hold grudges, although she thought this might be an exception.

The stupid jerk sat there and grinned at her!

Katie's lawyer spoke kindly to her when he said. "Miss Talley, you must tell the court what you told me yesterday, word for word."

"Okay," Katie said. "Everyone must bear with me. Try to understand I have been through a horrifying ordeal. It will be very difficult for me to testify about what happened. I was kidnapped by Benson Carver and brought here in the first part of November last year. Bennie kept me tied and gagged most of the time. He always bound me to a chair or bed when he went out.

He said he wanted to get closer to his friends in Topeka, Kansas, just in case it got too hot for him in Oklahoma.

That was in case my father decided to report him. He didn't want to go there but said he would if he felt threatened by the people in Spur Lacy. He had passports made up, ready for us to enter Canada from the United States if things got too complicated. He made me have plastic surgery so I wouldn't be so recognizable. I don't look exactly the same as I did before.

The passport he had for me would have passed for me. The identification and passport were illegal, but he was perfect with this kind of makeover. He was trained to perfection when he was on the force in Houston. He is a magnificent make-up artist, and he knew how to put my picture on the front of the homemade passport to make it look authentic.

Bennie was tired of staying in the motel. He took me and drove down by the lake outside of town. He even bought us some fishing gear—Rod, reel, and bait. We didn't do any fishing; we just walked around the lake for a while, but it was too cold to stay outside long.

When Bennie decided it was time to return to the motel, the car wouldn't start. It was a stolen automobile, anyway. He said he would just leave it there. It couldn't be traced back to him. It was around eleven that morning, or maybe a little earlier. We had already gotten cold at the lake, so when we started walking back, he decided to walk through the woods. He said it was a shortcut. That's where you found the murdered people." Katie felt a floating sensation; the room began to spin, and the lawyer said, okay, continue, but Katie couldn't say a word. She could hear the women screaming for help in her mind. That was the last thing she remembered until she awoke from fainting in the outer room of the courthouse.

A doctor stood over Katie, asking if she could continue her testimony. She nodded her consent. She was still woozy but wanted to go ahead with the procedures.

The judge had called for a short recess due to the sudden occurrence. The lawyers were sipping coffee in an anteroom. Someone brought her a glass of cold water and asked if she needed anything.

Then, everyone was called back into the courtroom. The judge kindly asked, "Can you continue Miss Talley? If you feel you can't, we can postpone until tomorrow."

Katie looked at the judge and stated. "Yes, I can continue. I want this over with. It is hard, but yes, let's continue today."

"Now, Catherine, please try to remember what happened when you got to Lovers' Lane?" the prosecutor said. "That's where you left off, please continue."

"We went through some woods. Bennie said. 'I must leave you here until I return. I will tie you to a tree, and here you will stay.' I started screaming for him not to leave me there like that. That I would freeze to death; it was so cold.

Bennie slapped me so hard I thought he had broken my neck. He gagged me and said, 'I won't be gone very long. I know where there's a car garage, and someone should be coming out for lunch soon. I will just nab that person, then come back here, pick you up, and leave the car's owner afoot.' Then he laughed this weird laugh. I thought he meant he was going to kill the owner of the car.

After Bennie left, I heard voices. At first, I thought maybe someone was out there and would free me from the ropes. Then I saw a woman and a man. They were talking about some strange event. He was telling her she would be all right, that he would take her away from here, that he had always loved her and would never desert her. He would get her the help she needed to be well again. Even though he says, 'I don't think anything, what is wrong with you?' Then he says. 'You know we will need more money, so you must figure out how to kill your dear husband, and then we will have your money and his.' Tears fell from Katie's eyes.

The judge ordered a glass of water for Katie and asked if she was okay.

"Yes, Your Honor, I'm sorry, " Katie answered. "Just a moment, if you will."

The people in the courtroom were quiet as a church mouse. They were anxious to hear about what had happened on Lovers' Lane.

"Thank you, Your Honor. I can continue now. Then the man said, 'That would be enough money to care for us for the rest of our lives. I know you can't handle money, so we can have an accountant handle everything, but you must do it soon. We must be careful, or we both will be in prison for years to come. I love you so much; I can hardly live without you. I can't pretend much longer to my wife that I love her. You have to do something and stop putting it off.'

Katie knew Brett was listening, but she couldn't look at him. She took another sip of water and continued.

"Then the woman said, 'I love you too, but what about your wife? She won't just walk away; she will give you trouble. She will also want money from you. What will you do?' The woman then became angry. He says. 'We will have plenty of money. We will pay her off. That's all she wants anyway; she doesn't want me. There will be no problem with my wife. I have told you this so many times.'"

Katie scanned the courtroom, and there sat the wife of the man she was speaking about. The lady had no idea I was about to ruin her life by telling what I saw and heard. I had seen her before at the hardware store, where she was the proprietor for her husband. I overheard her say that he was away on business. *I'm so sad for her,* Katie thought.

"Miss Talley, please continue." The judge said. Katie was lost in thought about the man's wife.

"I am sorry, Your Honor, I will continue," Katie replied.

"Then the lady said. 'I kept that hunter in the cave. He is scared to death of me. I've held him there for some time. I don't know what to do about him. He saw us together that day at the lake. Should he ever leave, he would tell what he saw. A dead man can't talk,' she snickered. 'I may kill him too.'

"I was afraid to move. I had enough problems without getting into something else.

I saw them embrace, and then he told the lady, 'I will do whatever it takes to get you away from here. They won't miss you anyway. They aren't smart enough to understand that we have been together for most of the last ten years. We need to make our move soon.' The woman had a crossbow dangling from her hand. She dropped it to the ground while she and the man snuggled. Then she said. 'They think I am hunting again. I had a hard time escaping the Brave this time, but I ran fast; the young man couldn't catch me.' The giggle that escaped her was terrifying," Katie began to shake.

He swung her around like a rag-doll. It looked as though it fascinated her. I don't think she had a grip on reality, but that's just my opinion. Then, a car came up the lane. It was Bennie returning.

The man and woman hid when the car came into sight. Bennie was holding a gun on the driver. When he got out, I thought he would make the man get out of the car, but before he could do anything, this woman ran for the car, screaming like a panther. Her screams made my blood curdle. She then shot the man in the BMW with her crossbow. Bennie ran for the bushes while the lady was preoccupied with killing the man in the BMW. She didn't even notice Bennie's presence or concentrate on her surroundings.

I could see everything happening from where I was tied to the tree. The woman hissed at the driver." 'This is my car, you idiot. You can't have my BMW. My husband bought it for me. You can't be driving it, either. Where did you get my car?' The man with her tried to calm her down. She looked at the man in the BMW, and then she sliced the poor guy's face over and over. He screamed in horrific pain. He wasn't dead when she started cutting him. She had a big knife.

The man finally pulled her away and said, 'I told you I would buy you a BMW when we leave here; this one is not yours. You can't drive yet anyway; you don't have a license. Come on now, calm down. Your car will be green. Do you remember the one you looked at last night? It was your favorite color, the dark green BMW?'

I was afraid they would hear me breathing. I was tied and partially hidden behind a tree. I remained quiet. I knew I would be killed should they discover me."

Katie took a breath and sipped the water. "I need one moment, Your Honor; this part is hard to tell."

"Court will recess for one hour," the Judge slapped his gavel.

The courtroom was filled to capacity as the trial continued.

"Miss Talley, please continue," the judge said.

"Other women were jogging and laughing about something funny that happened at their office as they came up the path through the woods. One woman approached the BMW and began to scream. The man who was there previously went to her and said, 'Don't be afraid. I just found this man dead in his car. I will take care of it; you do know who I am, don't you?' He then put his arm around her, but when he did, the girl with the crossbow went into a rage; she screamed. 'Get your hands off her. She's nobody. Don't act so innocent. I know you want to sleep with her,' she tried to grab the woman's hair but missed.

The two women ran deep into the woods, trying to get away from her. I could hear them screaming as she chased them. I listened while the man pleaded to 'let them go,' but she screamed like a wildcat, slashing the women with a knife while they tried desperately to evade her; they screamed and pleaded, 'Please don't cut me anymore.' Finally, they became silent.

Then I heard the man yell. 'You probably killed them anyway when you hit them with that heavy piece of wood,' but she wasn't finished.

The woman hissed loudly. 'No, they're not dead. It's your turn; you take care of them,' You're going to shoot them, just like I did. You say you love me so much, well prove it. They will send us both to prison anyway, whether you kill them or not.

The man told her. 'Stop cutting them. I will do it. I will shoot them!' I suppose the man shot both women with the crossbow. I could hardly stand to witness what I saw and heard. It was so horrible."

I began struggling with the ropes, trying to get loose. I just wanted to run away. I couldn't stand the horror anymore. I didn't realize I was making a whining sound until Bennie hit me on the head with the butt of a gun. I guess he thought I was about to be detected. That's all I remembered until someone pulled me from that pit or a grave. I don't know who put me there, either. Benson Carver is the only one who can tell you what happened.

I will tell you this. Benson Carver may be the meanest man I have ever known. But he didn't kill those people on Lovers' Lane."

Bennie was sitting there with a grin, looking at Katie as if she had done him some big favor. He seemed to be gloating. Katie wanted nothing more than to slap that grin off his face with a blow that would turn his head around backward.

The prosecutor looked at Katie and said. "Miss. Talley, will you please tell the court who you saw kill the man in the BMW? and who made the sounds that you heard farther down the path? Can you tell the court who the voices belonged to that was attacking the women?"

Katie looked down at her lap; she couldn't bring herself to look at the on-seers.

"The two people there on Lovers' Lane were Margo Canterfield and Albert Jones from the hardware store. I know this to be the truth. I don't know anything else. I met Albert Jones previously at the hardware store. I never met Margo, but I saw her portrait above the mantle in Brett Canterfield's home.

I was knocked unconscious and lost my memory until the night of the Christmas Masquerade party. When I was abducted once again by Benson Carver, he used a cloth with ether, chloroform, or some other drug to knock me out. When I regained consciousness, I remembered everything that had previously happened to me."

The murmurs in the courtroom were that of unbelievable truth. The people from Spur Lacy were stunned at what had just been told. Albert Jones, they knew to be a little odd, but to be a murderer was just too much for this little town to accept. They knew the lady on the stand had been through so much that she could not have made up such a story.

When Katie finished testifying, she looked at Bennie Carver and gave him a gruesome look. "It's your turn, you slime bag. It's time you told the truth for once in your pitiful life. You can fill in the blanks that I missed."

When Katie began discussing the crossbow, she watched Brett leave the courtroom. She knew it had hurt him severely. *I know Brett started putting the murders together after I mentioned the crossbow. I'm thankful he left before I had to name the assailants in the murders,* She thought.

Katie noticed, too, that Albert Jones wasn't in the courtroom. *He should have been in there with handcuffs on. Why haven't they arrested him yet? I will try to find out when I return to my hotel room.* She thought.

The judge called for an adjournment for the day. She would have to face the people in the courtroom again tomorrow, but she had endured enough for today. Right now, Katie just wanted to escape from everyone she knew from the town of Spur Lacy.

Katie waited for Horatio to escort her back to her room. She asked him to walk beside her because she felt unsafe and needed to be near a bodyguard. Suddenly, something stung her arm, and blood streamed down to her hand.

Horatio grabbed Katie and shoved her into an alley beside a store. He drew his sidearm as he pinned her against a building wall behind his large body.

"What happened, Horatio? What was that?" Katie looked at the red stains escaping from her side and arm. She felt herself falling. Then she realized that she had been shot.

Horatio caught Katie, picking her up just before she hit the ground. "Hold on, little lady. I will take care of you." He rushed to the street and started yelling for someone to call an ambulance.

Katie awoke in a hospital room. It took her a while to understand why she was there. Then she remembered. She had been shot! "Horatio! Where are you?" she screamed.

The nurse came running to Katie's side. "Honey, he's right outside your door. He has been there all night with the policeman. They haven't left your door at all. He said he felt it was his fault. He should have been more attentive to the situation." The nurse grinned.

Horatio was inside the door before the nurse could even speak but remained quiet. Katie was shaking from fright.

"Who shot me? Do you know? I have never been shot before, and I will tell you right now. It hurts!" Katie cried.

Horatio held Katie's hand to comfort her. "You will be okay, little one. I am sorry this happened to you," He said.

The chief of police stuck his head in the door, asking. "May I come in? I need to ask you some questions, Miss. Talley."

"Yes, do come in. I want to know who shot me and why. I don't know anyone here that would shoot me except that man from the hardware store, Albert Jones, but you have him in custody, right?" Katie asked.

"I wish I could say we do, but to be frank with you, we haven't seen hide nor hair of him since the week before the trial started. He seems to have disappeared into thin air. We will find him. It's just a matter of time." He said.

"Well, it was probably him that shot me! I know now that I'm a sitting duck here in Spur Lacy. I want to go home to Houston. I will return when you need me. Right now, I need my father. You have contacted him, haven't you?" she inquired.

"Well, we haven't called him. We didn't know if you wanted that done or not. We can contact him today if you wish." He answered.

"What kind of Police Department do you run here? Of course, I want my father notified! He's my next of kin." She whimpered. She was agitated with the way the police handled things here. Albert Jones should have already been in custody.

"I will see that Jones is arrested, and I apologize for not contacting your father. I will see to that shortly, but first, can you positively identify Albert Jones as the assailant on Lovers' Lane? That was a question brought to my attention in the courtroom this afternoon. I don't want to arrest an innocent man. The judge said you would need to sign an affidavit to the effect that you saw him murder those people."

"Yes, I can positively identify him! I will do whatever is necessary; I will need an escort to the Police Station. I don't want to be a target again." She stammered.

"That will be arranged, Miss Talley. When you are released, someone will escort you to the Police Station so you can sign the papers. Is that agreeable?"

"Yes, that will be fine. Good day, Chief."

Chief Davis tipped his hat and left for the elevator.

Katie was so distraught that if she didn't hear from her father by six tonight, she would call him. She was hurting and scared Albert Jones might try to kill her right there in the hospital.

Katie heard a rap on the door. Thinking it was probably the Chief again, she frowned. "May I come in? I thought you might need cheering up a little. How's the pain?" Brett asked as he entered her room with a vase of beautiful yellow and red roses.

He had taken her by surprise again!

"Brett, I am so sorry." Katie began to cry. "I can't believe you're here after the things I had to say in the courtroom yesterday."

He lifted her head and wiped away her tears. "Pretty lady, I have known for a long time that Margo was unfaithful. She told me about herself and Markham. He was unaware that she could never keep a secret from me. We were also friends. Actually, we were more friends than man and wife. We told each other everything we did each day. Mostly, we just lived together for companionship. Yes, it hurts to know Margo faked most of her insanity, but she was very good at faking. She was extremely jealous of any woman she thought was close to her superior. She had to be the best in everything, to her standards." Brett had a sorrowful look on his face as he continued.

"After the twins died, she couldn't seem to live with herself. She said it was her fault for being so selfish. I think she was right about that part, but I never said it to her. I also never blamed her. I always told her that it was an accident. She said she had hurt me too much to be forgiven. She left after she tried to avenge me with Charlie. I think that's when she met Albert. The rest, you know already."

Tears of pain fell upon the floor. "Margo never told me about her new companion. That makes me realize now that she wanted to hurt me badly. Maybe she would have eventually killed me." Turning to Katie, he said. "I will go now. You get some rest. The trial has been postponed until next week. Can I get you anything before I leave?"

"Thank you, Brett, but I am fine. I am sorry," she answered solemnly.

"There is nothing for you to be sorry about. You were the victim here; you had to tell what happened. Don't ever be sorry for anything. Look toward the future." He grinned through tears as he walked out the door.

Katie spoke quietly to herself after Brett had gone. "The future. Yeah, right, what kind of future will I have? I found the man I love, and now he hates me. He can say it's not my fault, but how does he really feel? I know I'm not to blame, but I told on Margo, and after all, she was his wife. Maria will never like me again, and Little Dove will want me gone far from her son forever." After a long cry, she fell into a tormented sleep.

About an hour later, Katie is aroused by the telephone.

Dom Talley called his daughter that night, very distraught that a gunman had nearly killed her.

"What am I going to do with you? I better hire myself as your bodyguard; you would be safer." He laughed. "Really, Catherine, you must come home where I can protect you. You're a grown woman, but still my little girl."

The sedative the nurse gave her had begun to take effect. "I want to, but I can't right now, Father. I have to make sure that madman doesn't kill another person. I think he is the one that shot me, too. Dad, I must hang up now. They have given me something to make me rest, and it's working." Katie's voice slurred as she dropped the phone beside the pillow.

"I will call tomorrow," Dom stated.

The next day, Katie sat in the hospital room. She thought about what her father had said and decided maybe she should change her mind.

She asked to be released to catch the flight to Houston at three. Her father had already set up the reservations, and she would be on that plane. She had received all the pain and suffering she could handle for now, here in Spur Lacy.

The doctor brought good news to Katie.

"You are a fortunate lady. The bullet went near the heart but missed the vital organs. I don't see how either. I will let you go, but you must rest until your side heals. I will prescribe you a pain medicine, but remember, the main thing is rest."

"Thanks, doctor. I am catching a flight to Houston this afternoon. I will get plenty of rest there. My father dotes on me. I think a little too much." She giggled.

"It would be wise for you to stay here in Spur Lacy until that wound heals. Don't risk it getting infected or the stitches being torn loose. I can't make you stay, but it is advisable." He answered.

"I must go home, but I will be cautious. I will come back here for a check-up when I return next week if that's okay?"

"Okay, I will see you then but don't forget to come back. If it turns red or puffy, go to the nearest emergency room."

"I will, doctor, and thanks again for patching me up," Katie said, shaking the doctor's hand with appreciation.

It was a beautiful spring day. The birds were chirping, flying around, gathering twigs for their nests. It seemed so peaceful here in Spur Lacy.

Katie wished it were different. She wished she had been here visiting on vacation and met Brett Canterfield under other circumstances. He was a wonderful person. Well, there's no need to cry over spilled milk.

I can never look into his face again without feeling that I put a scar on his heart with what I revealed. I must remember, though, that I had no choice. The truth had to be told.

Now, if Bennie tells the truth about whatever else happened, he would spill his guts on the courtroom floor if he thought it would hurt Brett.

As Katie walked toward the desk in the airport, someone lightly touched her sleeve. She turned to see Brett standing tall next to her. She felt a sudden rush of blood come to her face. "What are you doing here? I thought you were at the ranch. I didn't expect you to come to the airport."

"Listen, lady. I've had about enough of you running off to Daddy every time something happens. When are you going to grow up and take care of yourself? There is a room and a bed at the ranch with your name on it. I have two women there to be at your beacon call. I will have someone watch after you, so you will never be harmed in any way. Now, what is the problem?"

"How can you even look at me after what I told in court? I am so sorry." Katie looked at Brett with enormous sadness in her eyes. She couldn't take advantage of his hospitality. The lady would like nothing better than to stay at Brett's ranch. She would love to see Brett daily, but she just needed space.

"I will be back next week. I need to spend some quality time with my father. He has been so worried about me. He's not a young man, you know."

"I understand, but when you return, you will stay at my ranch, correct? Not in Spur Lacy again to be a target. I hope I am making myself clear on this matter."

Brett walked with Katie to the seating area to wait. He felt like his heart would break if he watched her board the plane. When this court thing ends, I will make her understand how much I love and need her.

When Katie arrived at Houston/Fort Worth airport, Dom was there to meet her. He held her tightly and told her he had missed her terribly since she had been away. "Tell me what is going on, Catherine. I can't understand why these awful things are happening to you. I have always protected you, and now I can do nothing. Why is that?"

"I don't understand it either, Father. Benson Carver started all this trouble. Where did he come from? I know he was on the Police Force, but what caused him to go bad?"

"I suppose some people are born on the wrong side of the track. He became money-hungry, with the power that went with his job. It just happens. I have no explanation. Sometimes, I believe he thought he was above the law, and no one could touch him."

"Dad, I must return to Spur Lacy next week for the trial. I don't know what will happen then. I told all I knew at the pre-trial. I wish it were finished. I would like you to accompany me if you have the time and can be away from the office. I have never been afraid in any town, but there is so much going on there that I am petrified. It was such a quiet little place until Bennie hit town. These people were unaware of how dangerous he was. Benson Carver caused a multitude of pain and suffering. Father he has no remorse for the evils he has done while thriving on hurt and destruction. I fear he might slip through the judicial system and get out sometime. I don't think I would be safe should that happen."

"Catherine Margaret, he will never be on the streets again. The courts would never allow that to happen."

Robbie held the report in his hand as he hurried into Lieutenant Markham's office, which now belonged to Henry Paulsen. He couldn't believe the results. "Lieutenant, look at this. The ballistics show that Margo was in the BMW and the car at the lake. Her DNA is all over both."

"That doesn't surprise me, Rob. Remember all the talk in town? Well, when there's smoke, usually there's fire, and it will eventually surface."

"If we are lucky, that dim-witted Benson Carver will fill in all the details, and he may ask for a plea bargain before he testifies. Now, what would you say to that Paulsen?" Robbie asked, a little more than curious about the new lieutenant's answer.

"We don't want any plea bargain talk going around. Kidnapping is too serious of a charge for that, Robbie. Although, you know the judge as I do. He might do a little bargaining just to get him to talk. He will want Albert Jones arrested and his testimony. We need to find him, quick! I think he tried to kill that Katie woman when she was heading to her hotel room."

"Yeah, I heard she is back in Houston for Daddy to protect her." Robbie snickered. "I guess Mister Brett Canterfield couldn't protect her as well as her poppa."

Robbie thought it was funny that a wealthy woman like Catherine Talley ran home to Daddy. She could have hired herself as a bodyguard right here in spur Lacy. I would be her bodyguard if the price were right.

"Well, the trial will commence tomorrow, so maybe we can have some peace around here after this is all settled," Paulsen stated.

When the plane landed in Spur Lacy, Lieutenant Paulsen, and Robbie were there to meet it along with Brett Canterfield. When Katie exited the plane, she was escorted to the patrol car under Police Protection.

As she was about to enter the cruiser, she bent to remove a rock from her shoe. When she leaned forward, there was a pop near her head. Before she knew what had happened, Robbie threw her into the car.

"What was that?" she asked, with a quiver in her voice.

"It was a gunshot. It struck the front door. It would have hit you if you had not bent over when you did!" Robbie stated.

"Where did Brett go? He was here just a second ago. Did you see where he went, Lieutenant?" Katie cried.

The Lieutenant said. "No, I didn't see him leave. I thought he was already in the car. We can't wait; we must get you to the courtroom. The trial starts in less than an hour." He closed the door and sped away.

Brett raced toward the flash he spotted from across the tarmac. *What is going on?* He thought. *I will see if I can catch that gunman. The killings must stop. That shot was meant for Katie.*

When the trial convened, Katie sat in the second seat from the front. She didn't want to miss anything.

Benson Carver took the stand; they had his name and life history. The prosecuting attorney asked Bennie what he saw on Lovers' Lane.

A murmur erupted. Someone called Bennie a pig from behind where Katie sat while others pointed at him, calling him many different names, from a skunk to a lizard. The judge struck his gavel, calling for silence from the people so the trial could continue.

With animosity, Bennie snapped at the prosecutor. "What do I get out of this by telling you anything, huh? I haven't even said I was there yet."

The courtroom became silent. Everyone stared at Bennie as if he were an alien.

"I want something out of my testimony. I might even take a plea bargain. That is if you would consider it," Bennie leaned back in his chair as if he were king of the hill.

The lieutenant bent over the prosecutor's shoulder and whispered something in his ear. The prosecutor looked Bennie in his eyes and said. "No way. You have been accused of kidnapping with intent to kill or do bodily harm, extortion, and many other charges. There will be no plea bargain."

Bennie laughed and said, "Well, it was worth a try. What Katie said is true, every bit of it, but I saw it a little differently. I knocked Katie out, so hopefully, those two people wouldn't find her. I knew they would kill her, too. Then I wouldn't get any more money from her good old Daddy Dominguez Talley.

That woman heard Katie struggling with the ropes and ran back to check the noise. She must have thought Katie fainted. I returned to my hiding spot again before I was spotted. She yelled at the man named Albert to come running; that was right after he shot the other women with the crossbow, and then she said. 'I found another one; you have to kill her, too,' but the moment she cut the tape off Katie's hands, she looked like she had seen a ghost. Margo said. 'We can't kill her. She is one of my people.'

Albert says. 'Oh yes, we can,' and pointed the crossbow at Katie. That Margo person stepped between Katie and the arrow and screamed. 'No! I could never kill one of my people. That's why I could never kill Brett. He has Indian blood. Little Dove is my adopted mother, and she kept me safe.'

Then the man says, well, okay then, I will bury her alive. I won't kill her. The woman asked the man if he had the other graves dug yet. He told her he was working on it. She said, well, you better hurry before someone comes up and catches us.

They finished the grave for Katie first. Then, while the man was digging the hole for the other women, the Margo woman pulled Katie into the hole and partially covered her. That's when a little boy rode up on a bike.

The man came running back to the woman. He was going to kill the child too, but that Margo woman said, 'No, you're not killing a child.' The child didn't see anything. It scared the boy severely when he saw the man in the car. He got on his bike and peddled away.

Somehow, the blade on the crossbow had cut Margo's hand. The man says to her. 'We best get out of here.' They heard the siren from the police car blaring, 'That kid has the cops coming, and we don't have time to bury the women.' That's why they left, taking the same path we had walked up earlier from the lake.

There was no blood on the car at the lake when we left it. I don't know who or how the blood got there.

That is all I know about the murders."

About that time, the door opened to the courtroom, and Brett came in, dragging a protesting Albert Jones by the nape of his shirt. "I ask the court to please excuse me for the intrusion, but I think this jerk has something he wants to enlighten the court. He also needs to be charged with attempted murder."

The prosecuting attorney turned to face Albert Jones and said, "Arrest that man, the charge is murder."

He then turned to Albert Jones, who was now in handcuffs, and said, "How did the blood get in the car at the lake? Did you or Margo get into that car?"

Albert looked at Brett with a refusal on his face. Brett gave him a look that read; you best do as you're told or else.

"All right, I may as well tell you. It seems that everyone knows all about us anyway. Margo and I were leaving here to make a new life together. We were in love, but she wouldn't leave Brett because he was her best friend. I tried to get her to see things my way, but she wouldn't change her mind. He was always in our way. I told her to get rid of him, but she wouldn't listen to reason.

We stopped at the car to rest after we came down the hill. It was a long walk from Lovers' Lane. She got inside while I bandaged her cuts with my shirt. Then we left.

She went back to the cave. That is where she spent most of her time. I went there and stayed with her when I could get away from the witch I married. We had been staying at the lake a lot. After she kept that stranger in the cave, I stayed home. I didn't like that very much. I wanted to kill Brett Canterfield, but she wouldn't hear it. She would say that she and Brett had grown up together and didn't know if she could live without ever seeing him again. She left Brett right after that.

Then she said, 'I think he has a woman in our house. I believe I saw her through the window, but it may have been Little Dove. It was an Indian. If I find out he has another woman, then I will kill him.' Then she said she saw her in the sunroom, and it wasn't Little Dove. She said, 'I tried to get to her and end her life. One night, I almost did, but Brett came to her rescue. I couldn't get near her after that.'

We had been trying to scare Maria and Brett into leaving. I went into their house while they were sleeping and destroyed the garden. We thought after that they had been scared enough to leave. While doing all this, I saw that Brett Canterfield has all kinds of bravery and special force medals for different things. I knew then he wouldn't scare off easily. Brett wasn't even afraid of the screams she portrayed as a cougar.

She wanted the house and all the land to sell. I didn't know what she was thinking half the time. I told her the land wouldn't be hers as long as Brett was alive.

While I would be inside doing the dirty work, she would stay outside and scream like a banshee. Sometimes, she would come inside the house. She always cried when she did, though. She would scratch like an animal on doors or scrape her nails on the windows.

I could never understand why the brave Brett Canterfield didn't catch us. I thought him to be a courageous man."

Albert showed all the signs of a mentally disturbed person right there in the courtroom.

He turned to Brett and asked, "Why didn't you catch us."

Brett couldn't take anymore. He looked at the man and told him, "I could have, but then I would have had to kill you, and I didn't want to kill Margo."

"I went back after Margo died and destroyed the garden you loved so much. How'd you like that?" Albert snarled at Brett.

The wife of Albert Jones sat quietly with lips drawn tight as she had to endure the painful hurt from her husband of forty-five years. She left the courtroom just as the jury was told to go into the ante-chamber to discuss the case and hand down the verdict.

"The judge said with intensity, get these characters out of here. Lock them up." The court was dismissed until the continuance of the next day.

The next day, court resumed on time. The judge called the court to order. The jury was called in. The bailiff asked for the verdict. The jurors handed the court's deputy the verdict. "On the charge of the "1st count of murder in the first degree, we, the jury, find Albert Jones guilty as charged." The sentencing will commence on the 1st—Monday in August.

"The hearing in the kidnapping case against Benson Carver will commence two weeks from today." The judge stated then called out, "Court adjourned." The slap of the gavel made it official.

Nobody knew when Mrs. Jones entered the courtroom with the pistol hidden in her purse, but there she was! She stood up, pointed the revolver at Albert Jones, and fired. Albert Jones lay dead on the floor. The sheriff and deputy drew their side arms, but not in time to stop Mrs. Jones from taking her own life.

"I have made sure he never hurts anyone again." These were her dying words. "Never again."

The people in the courtroom were shocked at the horror they had just witnessed. Mrs. Jones had always been a quiet woman. She stayed home and raised their children in church, teaching them to be good, upstanding citizens. No one would have guessed she had the nerve to do what she had just done!

When they left the courtroom, Brett took Katie by the elbow. As they walked, Brett held her close to his side. As they approached the church, he turned to her and said.

"Catherine Margaret, you see that church? You and I will stand before Father Ryan in six months or less and exchange our wedding vows." He bent and gave her a tiny peck of a kiss on her cheek.

"That is if you will have me. I am so in love with you. I will stand by your side forever, and if I raise another bear cub, I promise I won't let him eat you." He grinned at Katie with love. He was so afraid she would say no that his heart was pounding like a drum.

"Brett, I will give you my answer in two weeks. Is my room still available at the ranch? Or, have you given it to some lost soul in the woods?"

Pulling her into his arms, Brett said. "There is this dark-haired lady that stole my heart. She will always occupy that room of which you inquire. There shall be no other." He then kissed the lips he desired for so many months.

When they reached Bretts' ranch, Katie went to her room to freshen up. It had been a long day, and she wanted to sit outside in the shade of that big oak tree beside the gate. The wrought iron benches and the sculptured chairs made the scenery the most gorgeous spot to sit in the afternoon.

Her father sat at the kitchen island, reading the stock market from the paper. It had been a long day for him, too. He sat there in that courtroom, with his nerves on edge, listening to all the bad things that had involved his daughter.

The maids were preparing dinner in the kitchen, and Brett was nowhere to be seen.

A carriage with two white horses appeared as Katie walked outside and headed towards the tree.

"My lady, may I interest you in a picnic and with an afternoon swim? I know of a quiet place, and I think you might enjoy the relaxation."

The carriage was new and beautiful. The horses were magnificent. They were dressed like they were trying out for first prize at the county fair, tassels and all.

"What have I done for you to treat me like a queen," she grinned as he picked her up and seated her opposite the driver.

"I will always treat you as my queen because you shall be. I will return in a moment with the best picnic basket that can be made." With that, he rushed inside.

The horses began to twitch and stomp. Katie knew the horses were getting upset. She picked up the reins and said easy, boy. She talked to them, as she had done many times to the mares in her father's stable, but they still stomped.

Then suddenly, they reared and ran, with Katie hanging on for dear life. They ran fast down the mountain. Katie realized that should the rig flip, and she would pick gravel from her rump for a month.

Down the steep grade they ran. Katie kept her foot on the brake rod, but they weren't slowing down.

She remembered seeing a hornet flying around the horse's head. *I bet it stung one of them,* she thought.

"Oh my God, Katie screamed. Whoa! Whoa! You crazy horses, Whoa!" Just up ahead, Katie saw a waterfall and, under it, a pool of water that looked like a lake. They were headed right for it!

KERSPLASH!!! - In she went rig and all!

"What is wrong with you crazy horses!?" she screamed at the team. Both white horses were up to their shoulders. One horse turned and whinnied at her.

I guess the hornet did get one of them.

Katie was wet from head to toe. She began laughing.

Her dress had just been tailored to fit, and now the skirt floated above her head. "I could drown," she said, laughing loud.

The beautiful carriage was entirely under the water, except for the top. Katie was laughing so hard she could barely stand up.

Finally, she took the reins and led the horses around so they could pull the carriage from the water.

Katie led the horses to the grove, a short distance from the water. She tied the reins to a tree limb and then sat under the tree to wait for Brett. It was so funny that she never thought about the beautiful dress she had just ruined.

While sitting under the tree waiting, Katie thought about what a sight it would have been should someone have seen what the horses did to her or the predicament she had been in.

She had no idea how far they had come, and she knew it would take Brett some time to get there.

She looked at the filthy garment and grinned. "The heck with it. I'm going swimming." She said aloud

Removing the soaked dress, she headed for the pool of water under the waterfall.

The water was so refreshing to the skin; she wondered why Brett or Maria hadn't mentioned it before.

Katie swam under the waterfall and felt the splatters on her face. *Fantastic*, she thought.

This lake is the most beautiful place I have ever seen, with unique quietness.

She was so lost in the magnificence of the summer afternoon swim that she nearly forgot where she was.

Katie heard a noise, which made her aware she wasn't alone. She turned around, and Brett sat on a rock beside the pool. *He is so handsome,* she thought.

"Hey, come on in. It's wonderful. I couldn't wait any longer, so I decided to go for a swim," Katie laughed.

Brett laughed. "Did you, now?"

"Who got here first, you or the horses?" he was really laughing now.

"They beat me by a head," she called to him from under the falls.

When she flipped her hair back to dry some of the water from her eyes, she bumped into someone.

Astonished, she opened her eyes just in time to be kissed by Brett.

She hadn't seen him enter the water, but there he was. He held her close and asked. "How do you like our natural water source?"

"Very exceptional indeed," she grinned.

"How did you get the horses out? I usually have a hard time once they get in."

"Oh, it was easy. I just buzzed like the hornet that stung them," Katie laughed.

They swam a while longer, then returned to the bank to rest.

She was so embarrassed when she looked down and realized she only had a petticoat and knee-length leggings to cover her body.

"Surprise, I brought you a change of clothes. I knew where they would go when they ran away, so I asked the new maid to find me one of your outfits. I hope she did okay."

"These will be fine," Katie answered. Her face reddened from being almost nude. She looked at him, realizing he had brought dry clothes for himself, too.

"Did you put the horses up to this? Or do they always run into the lake, like wild stallions?"

"I must admit, they did great," Brett laughed, "but I had nothing to do with the wild ride you just endured."

She grinned. "I bet you watched from somewhere."

"I assure you, my dear, I would have liked to very much." He roared with laughter.

After they dressed and relaxed on the carpet of green grass, Brett suggested breaking open the picnic lunch he brought.

He spread the plastic cloth on the ground, and she watched while he talentedly handled the basket. He had red wine to compliment home-fried chicken, potato salad, coleslaw with homemade bread, and two pieces of pecan pie. "Fit for a king," she stated.

Then, there was a yellow rose wrapped in a paper towel. He put the rose in a small vase and handed Katie a tall-steemed glass of red wine.

"You came well prepared, huh?"

"Always," he stated.

"Now, I have a question. Will you become my wife, to love and let me love you forever?" he solemnly asked as he knelt before her.

"Yes, Brett, I will marry you. I do love you."

Their kiss was deep and meaningful. They both knew this would last forever.

The next day, the plans for a wedding began. Little Dove was the first one they decided to tell. She was very thrilled by their decision.

Dominguez Talley was the next to ask his approval for their marriage, which he gave willingly.

As for Benson Carver—Well, he wouldn't be out for years!

"**I** know, I have been told your name, but I will always know you by Little Dove Two. Now though, I shall call you my daughter," Little Dove grinned. "I must say I am so happy my son has chosen you."

In the days that followed, Benson Carver was convicted and sentenced to thirty years on two kidnapping charges to run concurrent and thirty years on the conspiracy charge. He apologized to Dom Talley and the girls for being so hard on them. They all three forgave him, but not Mr. Mason. He said he wanted to avenge him until the day he died. Natasia thought her father was cruel and unforgiving, but Mr. Mason said. "No, I'm not being vindictive. He should have been put to death for what he did. I had already lost my wife and nearly my daughter; no, it's not cruel."

Dom Talley and Catherine Talley walked away with their thoughts about the situation. Neither believed in capital punishment; they felt that was God's decision.

As Brett and his new wife left the church, they were handed a note from Bennie. When they opened it, it read, "Congratulations, may you both be happy always." Signed: Bennie

They turned to each other and grinned, knowing that he had actually brought them together.

Ten years have passed since the awful days there in Spur Lacy.

As Brett and Katie walk together near the waterfall, Brett looks back at their two daughters, walking hand in hand. Then there was little Adsila, well, not so little anymore, playing with their baby boy, who had Brett's green eyes and Katie's skin tone and dark hair.

Brett and Katie love their three children dearly, and yes, they have little Adsila with them most of the time. She is more like their daughter, too.

____ What a happy family____

___May God grant to you___
For every storm, a rainbow
For every tear, a smile
For every care, a promise
And a blessing in each trial
For every problem life sends
A faithful friend to share
For every sign, a sweet song
And an answer for each prayer
May there be peace with you always

Author: Sandra K Lee

For permissions requests, contact:

Writersway Solutions, LLC

4833 Glendale Avenue

Glendale, CA 91204

www.writerswaysolutions.com

1-888-666-4258

Due to the constantly evolving nature of the Internet, any web addresses or links mentioned in this book might have changed since it was published and may no longer be functional. The opinions expressed in the work belong only to the author and may not represent the publisher's opinions. The publisher takes no responsibility for them.

The individuals shown in Shutterstock's stock imagery are models, and these images are used for illustrative purposes.

ISBN (Paperback): 978-1-96273-319-9

ISBN (Ebook): 978-1-96273-320-5

Printed in the United States of America